Shining a Light on the Truth

Based on a True Story

Ramona Jenkins

Table of Contents

Dedication

This book is dedicated to my three children. Who walked with me through a most unpleasant journey. In appreciation for all their patience, love, and support. To my seven grandchildren for their love and encouragement to complete this book. To my wonderful husband, Steve, for his encouragement and motivation.

Acknowledgments

I want to thank my children. They stood beside me on days that I wanted to scream. They never asked questions when I sat there, my face swollen with tears. They tolerated my actions when I confused them while searching for the truth. They continued to love me, respect me, and support me even today.

My parents gave me support and love throughout my life. Thanks to my mom, who was a strength for me through all these years of confusion and pain. My pastor, like me, didn't believe in divorce but supported me as my husband walked away. My Sunday school teacher was devoted to getting me through this ordeal as a strong, successful person. I am so grateful for my neighbors who supported me throughout the years. They listened to me, babysat my children, and motivated me to continue standing tall. I am grateful to my sister, who read the manuscript and encouraged me to publish it. I want to thank my sister-in-law, who read the manuscript and encouraged me to burn it and said I should have killed him. Absolute honesty is a treasure.

I want to thank the man in my life today, my wonderful, kind, loving, and understanding husband. We only met three years ago. I had started this book so many years earlier. He has encouraged me to finish it. He listened to me as I read it aloud and reacted with love and strength, the love and the strength I needed to complete it. He reminded me how inspiring the story was and how important it was to publish it so it could help others.

Thankful to my publisher, project manager, editor, and designer for their hard work.

Grateful for Dona Rutowicz, LCSW & Relationship Coach – Founder and CEO of Divorcing Gracefully and Beyond. Not only did she teach me I had worth and purpose, but she also showed me how to move forward with dignity and grace. Without her, I don't think I would have ever been ready for a relationship when I met my wonderful husband. And without him, the motivation to complete this book.

About the Author

Ramona Dee Jenkins is a resilient entrepreneur who has not only built a successful business but also raised three children single-handedly. From a young age, her passion for writing sparked, leading her to embark on a journey of self-expression and discovery. In her novel, "Shining a Light on the Truth," Ramona draws upon her feminine instincts and diligent research to uncover profound truths. Together with her husband and family, she calls Middle Tennessee home.

A woman of unwavering strength and determination, Ramona credits her resilience to her deep faith in God. Throughout her life's ups and downs, He has been her constant source of support and guidance. From working diverse jobs, such as a secretary, private investigator, and car salesperson, to eventually owning her own business, Ramona's tenacity has propelled her forward. However, her most cherished role surpasses any title or position she holds—being a loving mother to her three successful children.

In addition to being a devoted mother, wife, and grandmother, Ramona embraces her identity as an entrepreneur and writer. With her heartfelt storytelling and unwavering commitment, Ramona captivates readers, inviting them to embark on a transformative literary journey.

Chapter 1

Where does love go wrong when the man of your dreams, your childhood love, your loving Christian husband, and the father of your children leaves you and deceives you as to why he is leaving?

Does he do it just to break you?

Does he think he can get by with it?

Will you lay down and let him take your life away from you and leave you broke and broken? Or do you dig your heels in and try to figure it out? For me, it was digging my heels in and try to figure it out.

My life had never been easy. Why would I think this would be any different? Growing up with an alcoholic father, I constantly tried to pretend to the world my life was just as good as theirs. Hiding the truth from the world because the truth hurt too much. Protecting my family then, and now I will have to protect my husband from himself.

I must do that to protect myself and the kids. They are my life, and I will go to the ends of the earth to protect them and give them a good life.

My life growing up has just made me stronger to face today's challenges, and I knew God was always with me then and will be with me now. I know this isn't going to be easy. Just like when I was younger, I know God will be beside me through each step. How did my life get to this? I don't know. Where will I go from here, I don't know that either, but I must search out the truth. Just like in my younger days, the truth hurt. I am afraid this truth will hurt too. But in the end, the truth shall set you free.

When I met Ronald at a theater in downtown Nashville, I was a junior in high school. I went into town to see a movie. I was not doing well in American History. I was doing horrible; I was going to fail. There were four of my friends in the same situation. Our history teacher, Mrs. Warren, told us we would need to do some extra work to graduate. There was a movie playing downtown titled, The Heroes of Telemark.

The extra work would be to go see the movie and write a book report about it. She would then pass us with a D-. That would be enough to graduate. We all thought that would be a great idea. We wanted to graduate for sure.

I got up early on a cold Saturday morning in February. When my feet hit the floor, I was always hungry and ready to eat. Dad would get up early every morning and cook breakfast. It would be ready when I got up. Dad had been in the army during WWII. Maybe that is where he learned to cook so good. He would cook eggs and the best-fried potatoes ever. He could slice them so thin you could see through them. I always thought breakfast was the best part of the day.

After breakfast, I went into my room and got dressed. It seemed cold that day, but it was in the 60's. Miniskirts and go-go boots were the style. There I was in my purple and white mini dress and my white go-go boots.

I often wondered why we named our boots. We were silly teenagers. After getting dressed, I told my parents I was leaving and would see them this afternoon.

I walked outside, where I met one of my best friends, Ann. She lived in the house next door. We walked down the street to catch the city bus. We were all 16 years old. They all had cars, but we decided today we would ride the bus. That way we wouldn't have to worry about parking.

Wendy was already on the bus when Ann and I got on at our stop. The next stop is where Diane and Lisa would get on the bus. We always had so much fun together. We knew this was a necessary trip to graduate. We also thought it would probably be a boring movie, but we would still make it a fun day.

When the bus arrived in Nashville, we got off and began looking for Church Street, where the theater was showing the movie. We found it and got our tickets. There weren't too many people there. We decided to take up two rows in the middle of the theater. Ann, Diane, and I sat in one row, Wendy and Lisa sat behind us.

For me, the movie was no more interesting than our history class. I needed a break from the movie, and my contacts were bothering me. I decided it was a good time to slip out and clean the lenses. As I was getting up, I noticed a few people down by Ann and only one guy on the left of me. I thought I would just go out that way to the restroom. As I was going out, I noticed that guy was cute too. I went to the restroom and fixed my contacts. When I returned, I came in the same way, right where the cute guy was sitting.

As I entered the aisle, I said, "Excuse me." He said, "Sure, why don't you sit here?" I thought seriously, did he just ask me to sit beside him? I wanted to so badly, but my friends were sitting on the other end. I said, "I am here with my friends. Would you like to sit down here with us?" He said, "Sure." He grabbed his jacket and followed me where I had been sitting. I was so excited, and the girls must have thought, what is this? You go out to the bathroom and come back with a guy? We talked, watched the movie, and talked some more.

I knew I had to focus on this movie if I wanted to graduate. It was hard to focus when I just met this guy, and I wanted to talk to him and get to know who he was. During the conversation, I found out his name was Ronald and where he went to high school. Would you believe my friend, Wendy, that was sitting behind us, was dating a guy from the same school as Ronald? I asked, "Ronald, do you know Tim Carver?" He did. They were in the same class. This must be fate. What were the odds of that happening in this big town? I introduced Ronald to Wendy and told him she was dating Tim. Boy, when I did, she was quick. She says, "We could double date sometime." I wanted to slide under the seat. Here, I had just met Ronald and Wendy had us dating. Ronald may not even like me. What was she thinking?

When the movie was over, we all got up to leave. He turned and said, "It was nice meeting you. Could I have your phone number and call you sometime?" I thought, sure. I felt some comfort that he wasn't a real stranger. After all, he knew Tim.

Wendy could ask Tim about him. I thought if I gave him my number and found out he was a snake, I would just never talk to him or see him again. I gave him my number and said, "It was nice to meet you." Then we both turned and left.

The girls were asking, "What the heck was that? Did you know him?" It was fun explaining that no, I didn't know him. He was sitting at the end of the aisle; he asked me to sit beside him when I came back in. Instead, he came and sat here beside me. I was so glad I was the one that had met him. I had my suspicions if I would ever hear from him again. I knew I couldn't get my hopes up. If I did, I could be disappointed. However, it was a challenge for me to stay calm about it.

I sat in the kitchen that night working on my history book report, or so my parents thought. I was really sitting in there, so if the phone rang, I could jump up and be the first to answer it. The phone never rang that night. I thought, maybe I just thought he liked me. He did seem like he did. I guess I will find out sooner or later. If he never calls, then I was wrong.

The next day as my family and I were coming in from church service, the phone rang. I ran and answered it. I caught my breath and said calmly, "Hello." It was Ronald. We talked for hours, with my family coming in and out of the room. I had very little privacy. Mom was in the kitchen cooking lunch, and my sisters kept coming in and out, asking "Mom, who is she talking to?" Mom just shrugged her shoulders, she said, "It must be someone special for her to be talking that long!" My younger brother was pestering the daylights out of me the whole time.

I had not told anyone in my family about meeting Ronald at the movies yesterday. I knew once I hung up the phone, my family would start asking me questions about who I had been talking to. They would think I was crazy for giving a strange guy my phone number. My parents would probably be really upset with me.

They had always preached don't give strangers your phone number. I would explain to them how he knew Wendy's boyfriend, and that he even went to school with him. Hopefully, that would help them understand why I gave him the phone number and keep me out of trouble.

In the following days, Ronald continued to call. He played the guitar. When he would call me, he would play and sing to me. It was so romantic! I loved guitar music and singing. My dad, uncles, and cousins all played the guitar. It wasn't unusual for some family members to come over and play their guitars way into the night. I knew Dad would love the fact that Ronald played the guitar too. He would fit right into our family. I was acting like I was in a committed relationship, but he had not even asked me on a date.

He continued calling, and our conversations lasted for hours. It wasn't long until he asked if he could come over. It was something like a date, but I knew it wasn't going to be like other dates I had had. Ronald didn't have a car of his own. He would have to ride the bus to see me or borrow his dad's car. We didn't have a car in our family at all. Since Daddy drank, he said he would never drive. He said, "I will never take the chance to be drinking and driving and someone get injured." At least his thought process was responsible, even if his drinking wasn't.

No one else in my family had a driver's license, so there wasn't a need for a car. We would always live close to the city bus line. We would ride the bus everywhere we had to go, except for school and church, we would walk. If the weather was bad, our dear neighbor, Mrs. Brown, would come by and give us a ride to church.

I was so excited that Ronald wanted to come see me. Riding the bus will take him a long time to get to my house. He would get the bus where he lived and then go into Nashville and wait for the bus to my house. It was a lot of effort and time on his part. I was very glad he was willing to do it. Although we lived far apart, at least we both lived close to the bus line. When he would come over, we would walk down the street to the lake, sit and talk. We would then walk back to my house, go into my bedroom, and listen to music, of course, with the door open. Mom wanted to be sure that there were no shenanigans going on. I bet my older sisters got into trouble with the guys. That is probably why Mom was cautious with me. Being the youngest daughter has its advantages but also disadvantages.

As time passed, Ronald's dad finally agreed to let Ronald borrow the family car. It was a Chevrolet convertible. Ronald was going to drive over to go to church with me. This was our first date. His dad's car was a beauty. It was a beautiful blue with a white top. Since my family didn't own a car, this was luxury for me. Ronald drove us to our church. After church, we came back to my house for lunch. His dad said he had to be home before dark, so I knew he couldn't stay too long.

Ronald was so grateful he finally got to borrow the car; he wasn't about to get home late. If he had gotten home late, his dad would probably put a stop to him borrowing it again.

After he had been home for a while, Ronald called, as always, we had a great long conversation. He told me his dad was asking him 100 questions.

His dad just couldn't understand of all the girls in his school, why in the world he had to find a girl across town to date. His dad seemed like a grump to me. I knew one day, if we kept dating, I would have to meet him. I sure was dreading it. Although my dad drank and drank too much, he was kind. He would listen to me and let me talk when I didn't understand why he would tell me no about something. I could ask why questions and Dad would calmly explain. Ronald would tell me his dad was the type of parent that would say, "Because I said so" and "that he didn't want to hear another word about it, parent."

I felt his dad should have been very proud of his son. Ronald was going to high school and working at the same time. He worked at a gas station on Nolensville Rd. He would ride the bus to and from work until he got a car. He worked hard there and long hours. When a car came to the gas station, Ronald would fill the car with gas, wash the windshield, and check the oil in the car. As it got closer to closing time, he would clean up the station and balance the money in the cash register. After he locked up at the station, he would wait for the city bus to ride home. Fortunately, it was only about a 10-minute ride for him and then a short walk from the bus line to his house.

He was eager to get a car. It would make his life much easier. I knew how hard he was trying to save his money. I tried to be a thoughtful girlfriend. I would suggest that we could save money if we had picnic lunches and go to places and do things that wouldn't cost anything. I would like to think I helped a little. He worked hard and did without a lot to save his money. It wasn't long until he had saved enough to buy his first car.

It was an older car that needed a few repairs. He knew he could work on the repairs as time and money permitted. The worst thing about the car was the front seat. Every time he would stop at a traffic light or stop sign, the seat would slide forward. Then, when he took off, back we went. It was funny. He was so thrilled to have his own car, even with the seat challenge. At least, now we could date without waiting for his dad's car to be available.

10

We started dating more and double dating with friends. We double-dated with Wendy and Tim, and another good friend, Mary, and her boyfriend, Bob. Our relationship was strong, and we were having so much fun. Two of our favorite things were going to the movies and the park.

There was a huge pond at the park with walking available all around it. People would go there to fly kites. Baseball teams would go there for their games. You would always know there would be something to do there, and it would be free.

We spent a lot of time together and got to know one another very well. I needed to know how he felt about God. Had he ever accepted Christ as his Savior? He had been going to church with me. We never read the bible together or prayed together. Was it because I didn't initiate it first, was it because he didn't do it when he was alone, or that he just didn't initiate it either?

Was Christ as important to him as Christ was to me? I had been raised that it was very important for a couple to have the same beliefs. That way, they would attend church together and pray through their problems. Should they end up getting married and having children, the children would be raised with the same beliefs.

We were having a revival at our church the next week. I asked him, "Ronald, would you like to come Friday night to our church revival service?" He said, "I would love to. Who will the minister be?" "It will be Clyde Chiles." He drove over, and we went to church. It was a wonderful service. Brother Chiles preached about salvation and the meaning of baptism.

After church, I asked, "Ronald, have you ever accepted Christ as your Savior and been baptized?" He hesitated and said, "No." I should have discussed the plan of salvation with him then, but I didn't. I'm not sure why. I just accepted his answer and didn't follow up.

Ronald came back to our revival the next night. That night, after the service, he went and talked with the pastor. They prayed and Ronald accepted Christ as his Savior. The following Sunday, he was baptized. I felt our life could now go forward if that is what we decided. I knew with God; we could survive anything that came our way. We would need to talk to one another and ask God to help us work through any problems.

However, that is not what happened later in our life after we were married. He decided to leave without any explanation. It was as if he had made his decision, and talking to God or to me was not something he was going to do.

But why? Why would he not talk to me? He knew we could talk and pray about anything together. I will spend the following months searching for the answer. I would soon realize he was deceiving me and lying to me. But why? How will I find out the truth? If only I could have seen into the future. I don't know if I would have continued dating him. I don't know.

We have been dating for two months now. We were having the best time. I felt I was getting to know him so well. I knew I could trust him. I needed to; after all, it is a must for a good relationship.

But something happened that made me doubt a little. One night, he was driving me home. We stopped at the traffic light, of course, the seat flew forward, and so did a pack of cigarettes. He had told me he had quit smoking. I asked him, "Are you smoking again?" He said, "No, why?" I told him I was wondering because these flew out from under the seat. I showed him the pack of cigarettes. He looked shocked and said, "Oh, they must be Dads; Dad was test-driving the car and checking the brakes this week. He must have placed them under the seat." I accepted his explanation. My dad smoked four packs of cigarettes a day. If Ronald smoked, I didn't care, it was his choice. I just felt like he wasn't telling me the truth. It seemed unlikely to me that his dad would have put them under the seat to just test drive the car. I need Ronald to know he can tell me the truth, whatever the truth is. We must be honest with one another.

Chapter 2

Our dating continued every weekend for the next year. Then, he popped the question. He came over, I was so excited to see him. That night, we drove to the drive-in theater. As we were watching the movie, he said, "Babe, open the glove box, I have some candy in there." "Sure, I am always up for any kind of candy." I opened the glove box and saw an oil rag. Of course, there would be an oil rag there, he worked at a gas station. I probably had a strange look on my face. I got the oil rag out, and I quickly saw it wasn't candy that was inside. It was a jewelry box.

My mouth flew open, and he asked me to open the box. I did. There was a beautiful solitaire diamond engagement ring inside. I was very surprised. I couldn't help but think, how could he afford this? I guess that should not have mattered to me. But I did think about it. After all, we were only 17, and he was working for minimum wage. Buying a diamond ring must have been very expensive. After I quit kissing him, I said, "But how did you?" He interrupted me and said, "Remember the car wreck I had?" "Yes, of course." He said, "I got the insurance settlement last week and bought you this ring." Then he popped the question, "Will you marry me?" "Yes, I shouted, Yes! Yes! Yes!"

We were so excited to share the news with everyone. We started with Mom and Dad. When we got to the house, he came inside with me. It was then he asked them if he could marry me. He probably should have done that before he gave me the ring. Oh well, they seemed to love him and were excited. They said, "Yes, we would love for you to be our son-in-law." My sisters had all gotten married. This would be their 4th son-in-law.

Mom was so funny. My sisters would say things to Mom about what their husbands had said or done. I would hear Mom say to Dad, "If they can stand those guys all the time, surely, what little time I am around them, I can tolerate them." I don't think she felt that way about Ronald. I think she truly liked him, probably even loved him. With their blessing, we could go forward, but we had to get his parents blessings too. That might not be so easy. His grumpy dad was a bit controlling, and I was sure he probably wouldn't like the idea.

Ronald left and drove home to talk to his parents. Ronald called me after he talked to them. I was right. They weren't as agreeable to the idea as my parents had been. "Can we have your blessings?" He asked them. "Absolutely not," his dad said. "I will not sign for you to get married. Boy, you are only 17 years old. There is no way in hell you can get married and support a wife. Heaven help y'all if she got pregnant." His dad had no idea that my dream was to have twelve children. Yep, twelve children. I loved kids and thought it would be great to have six sets of twins. We decided that was some information his dad didn't need to know.

We checked into the marriage laws in TN. You could get married at seventeen if your parents signed for you. If not, you would have to wait until you were eighteen. We won't have to wait too long! This was April. We will graduate in June. Ronald will turn eighteen in late August, and we would get married in September. Bingo, no one could stop us now. My parents were cool about it. Although I would still be seventeen, my parents would sign for me. So now it was planning time.

Our first and probably biggest obstacle was money for the wedding. I would be responsible for most of it. I was working part-time. It was time to manage money, just like my mom had taught me. I would start with my dress. Our prom was around the corner, and I thought perhaps I could convert my prom dress into my wedding dress if I could find the right one for my prom.

I went shopping with my friends. After a few days of shopping, I found the perfect prom dress. It was a long white sleeveless dress with an empire waist. I thought with Mom's sewing ability, she could easily convert this dress. Now, I just had to find a picture to show her what I wanted it to look like.

I worked at the drug store down the street from where I attended high school. I loved working there. I got out of school early to go to work. I would only have a block to walk to get there. After school was out, this would be the corner spot for all the kids to hang out. I worked behind the counter, making milkshakes for everyone. It was fun.

At work, during the slow times, I would look at the bridal magazines and all the styles. I wanted to be in style, but at the same time, style usually meant money. While I was looking at a magazine one afternoon, I found a dress that looked almost just like my prom dress. The only difference was the one in the magazine had lace sleeves and a long train.

I thought Mom could make a pattern with this picture as her guide. Then she could use the pattern to convert my prom dress. I got off work, grabbed the magazine, and rushed home to show her. She was in her sewing room. "Mom, look what I found. What do you think?" She looked at it, smiled, and said, "We just need a little satin and some lace." "I knew you could do it, Mom. You are the best!" With Mom on board, all I needed to do was to shop for the satin and lace.

I had three older sisters that had already gotten married. The oldest had eloped. Mom helped my other sisters plan their weddings. She would be my wedding planner too. She gave me a list of the people I needed to call for the music and people's names and numbers to call for the other details of the wedding. I needed to check to see if the church and the pastor were available. We needed to select our bridesmaids, groomsmen and decide on their apparel. Then, I would check on the flowers, cake, and food for the reception. Ronald's parents would take care of the rehearsal dinner.

I am not sure where Mom had gotten her strength or her knowledge. She was only fourteen when she married Dad, he was twenty-one. Not a lot of education, just a lot of street smarts. But smart she was! She tried to teach each of us everything she knew. I remember one thing she would always say, "Some women can take more out the back door than the man can bring in the front door." She would then say, "Don't be that woman, your husbands will be working hard for the money, and you girls need to work just as hard to save and manage it." Good advice my mom always gave.

I started making my phone calls from the list Mom gave me. I called the church office, the pastor, pianist, bridesmaids, florist, photographer, and bakery and started planning a reception. It all seemed easy enough. But on my budget, I was not sure. Perhaps my oldest sister, Diane, had the best idea, elope. I really wanted a church wedding. I was determined to make it work.

I was hoping I had made the right decision when I said yes to Ronald. I was only seventeen and loved him. I wanted to be his wife. I wanted a family with him. Doubts were entering my mind, or was it just cold feet? I have learned when I have those doubts, it's possibly my feminine instincts giving me warnings. I often wondered if he had lied to me about the cigarettes that one day. The day when they slid out from under his car seat. I saw him smoking another time when I stopped by the gas station with some of my friends, but I never asked him about it. I can't have a marriage without trust. I must decide to trust him. I must believe him. I must relax, our wedding was in a couple of weeks.

The night before the wedding, we had a beautiful rehearsal and rehearsal dinner at our church. At the rehearsal, while Dad and I practiced walking down the aisle, I noticed how much peace it gave me with Dad by my side. He was so tall and stood so straight. I could almost feel the strength in his arm when I was holding it as he escorted me down the aisle. I think standing tall and straight is something he learned in the military. I was so proud to have Dad with me. I knew with his kindness and reassurance; he would calm my nerves. Although he was an alcoholic, and there were days I hated him, I really loved him with all my heart and was so proud of him. After all, I was his baby girl, and we did have a close relationship.

The ladies of the church had made the rehearsal dinner and had the banquet hall looking so pretty. White tablecloths, candles, and flowers were on the table. They were so supportive. Everything was perfect.

Ronald and I were excited and ready to start our life together. We were young, but we were both very responsible and hard workers. We both had full-time jobs. I was working at City Bank as a secretary in the finance department. Ronald was working at the factory for the Cola company. We had found an apartment in East Nashville. It was in the same area of town where the park was that we loved to visit. The apartment was furnished and within our budget. The ladies in the church had given me a wonderful bridal shower. We had gotten all the kitchen items, linens, and accessories we needed.

After the rehearsal, Ronald and I went for a drive and talked about how wonderful the rehearsal and dinner had been. We talked about the wedding and about our life together. Ronald would kiss me, hug me, and tell me how happy he was. Then he said, "We are getting married tomorrow. We could get started with our honeymoon tonight." That shocked me; he had always been so patient. Perhaps all guys get impatient. I guess we girls need to always have the strength to say, "No!" I told him, "We can't begin the honeymoon tonight. What if you get killed tonight going home? I would not be a virgin for someone later in life should I decide to marry later. I am going to wait for marriage." He knew I was not going to change my mind. We kissed and he said, "Okay, I will take you home. Our wedding day is tomorrow and then we will begin our life together."

When we got to my house, we talked for a while. I said, "You know it is bad luck to see your bride on the day of the wedding. The next time I see you is when Dad is walking me down the aisle." He hugged me so tight and said, "I love you." I said, "I love you too, and I will see you tomorrow." With a good night kiss, he walked off the porch to his car and drove home.

I went inside, Mom was still up. We talked for just a bit, and then she said, "Tomorrow is a big day, you better get to sleep." She was right, as usual. I went to bed, but it was hard to get to sleep. My mind was just spinning with thoughts of our wedding day and thoughts of what our future would look like. All I ever wanted was to be a wife and a mom. Now, it is coming true. Well, at least the wife part. Becoming a mom would be later. I didn't want to wait too long though. After all, if we were going to have 12 children, hopefully six sets of twins, we couldn't put it off too long.

I knew tomorrow would be a busy day. We had to decorate the church early in the morning. I would then need to go to the beauty shop to get my hair done. Come home, do my nails, and get dressed.

Chapter 3

My sisters and I, along with our mom, went to the church and arranged the greenery at the front of the church. We pulled out the candelabras and placed the candles. The church had a few flowers that were left from the Sunday service and a white runner for the bride and her dad to walk down on. We placed the runner in the center aisle. We were blessed our church had all these things for their members to use. That left us paying for the cake, punch, and of course, a few more flowers. It is amazing how you can bring things together when you learn to manage with what money you have. It was a good thing I had a smart mom, and I listened to her instructions on money management.

After the church was ready, I went for my hair appointment. Our pastor's daughter was styling my hair for my wedding gift. That was a blessing; she was a great stylist. I would polish my nails. Marjorie did a beautiful job on my hair. I loved it. I was so excited about our day. Everything was almost ready. I only had a few last-minute details to be ready before the wedding.

When I got home, I could tell Dad was there. His paint ladders were out in the front yard, although, I didn't see him anywhere.

I finally asked Mom, "Where is Dad?" Mom said, "Honey, I am so sorry, he is in bed." "Is he sick?" "No, honey, he isn't sick." My stomach was in knots; I knew what she meant. I could not believe it. He had to be drinking. Some people can't just have one or two; some have addictions. For Dad, it was an addiction or medication for him from what he saw in the war.

Once he started drinking, he couldn't stop, it always went to "falling down drunk." He would fall, sometimes hitting the bed, and sleep for hours. Sometimes, falling on the floor or in a ditch beside the road, and a local sheriff would bring him home. Dad didn't set out his life to be this way. He had goals and ambitions like everyone else. His one drink just could never be enough. That was why he always would tell all of us kids, "Never take that first drink, you never know if you will be the one with the addiction."

He had been at the rehearsal the night before. Everything had been perfect. I was so excited to have his arm to hold on to walking down the aisle. I just knew my wedding would be perfect. But now? What would I do? Who, who would give me away? Would I be walking alone? How did this happen? I had so many questions and no answers. I knew he would not be able to walk with me down the aisle and give me away. He wouldn't even be able to come to the wedding.

I had so many decisions to make now at the last minute. I was so upset; I could barely think. Where was my mom's brother, Uncle Bill? He came to my sister's weddings. If Dad wasn't available to walk them down the aisle, then Uncle Bill would do it. My sisters never needed Uncle Bill; Dad was available and sober to walk down the aisle with them. Why not me? I felt so unloved. Wasn't I just as special as they were? Here I needed Uncle Bill, and this time, he was sick and couldn't be there. Why did Dad do this to me? Why? I was broken-hearted, scared, upset, angry, and confused.

Mom saw how upset I was, how confused and heartbroken I was. I knew this was upsetting her too. I tried to calm down. I wanted to get my head out of this spin cycle it was in. I just couldn't seem to stop it. Mom had an idea, a Valium! I was a 115 lb. 17 yr. old that had never taken anything to relax me. Fortunately, she only gave me a very small part of it. It knocked me out for the rest of the afternoon. If she had given me all of one, I guess I would have missed the wedding too. Perhaps, if I had known then what I found out in my investigation later, that might have been the best, if I had just missed the wedding.

When I woke up, I wished I had been dreaming, but no, it was my reality. The one day, my wedding day that I really needed Dad to be sober for me, and he was anything but sober. I was getting married within two hours, and I had no one to walk me down the aisle. I had to figure all this out. Who could I get to stand in for Dad, or would I be walking alone? The only person I could think of would be my oldest brother-in-law, Glen.

I asked my sister, Diane, what she thought, "Do you think Glen will do it? Would he walk me down the aisle?" I was only five years old when they got married, and I knew he loved me almost as if I had been his own child. They would come over when they first got married for dinner. I would cry to go home with them. They would always take me. Glen would sit for hours playing his guitar and singing to me. One favorite song he would sing was "Pop and a bubble gum." He would sing it like Donald Duck. Diane told me she was sure he would be honored to walk me down the aisle. I called and nervously asked him. She was right. He was thrilled. He said, "Ramona Dee, you are like my little girl. It would be an honor. Thank you for allowing me to do this for you." He always called me by my first and middle name. He loved me, and his willingness and joy in doing it made me very happy. At the last minute, I had a stand-in for Dad.

I just had to pull myself together and make the best of things. After all, I was marrying a man who loved me, and my focus had to be on him and our wedding.

I had not talked to or seen Ronald all day. So, until I walked down the aisle, he didn't know my dad was not there. He knew Dad had been there for the rehearsal. I had no idea what Ronald and his family would think. Well, I guess it didn't matter what Dad did or didn't do or what anyone thought, we got married just the same. In between the wedding and the reception, I told Ronald the horrible truth. I said, "Dad got drunk and is at home passed out." As far as anyone else, it was none of their business. I was embarrassed and upset enough. I was not going to explain this to anyone else.

The reception was beautiful. There wasn't an elaborate reception, no dinner, no dance. No dinner, I didn't want to put a burden on my family. The reception was enough and was beautiful. No dancing because at our church, Brother Adams preached against dancing. And absolutely no liquor because of Brother Adams and my dad. Even if Brother Adams allowed it, we would not have had the temptation there for Dad. As if that ended up being an issue since he was already at home, passed out.

The cake was three tiers with the traditional wedding icing that I love. There was a figurine on top of the cake of a bride and groom. Ronald and I cut the cake and served it to one another carefully. Ronald knew how upset I had been with my dad's absence; he wasn't about to smash a cake in my face at that point. We had green ice cream punch that we used for a toast. After we cut the cake and toasted with the punch, it was tradition for the bride to throw her bridal bouquet to a crowd of single women. I turned with my back to the group and tossed it. My maid of honor, Jenny, caught it. It worked; she got married the following summer.

Tradition was also for the husband to remove the garter from the leg of the bride and toss it to a group of single men. It was time to remove the garter, and I was shy. Pulling my dress up and showing my leg for him to remove the garter in front of God and everyone was embarrassing for me. Slowly and nervously, I pulled my dress just above my knee. He gently and respectfully removed the garter. He turned with his back to the guys and tossed it. His best friend, Tony, caught it.

We then went upstairs to the sanctuary to have our pictures taken. It was heartbreaking to have my wedding pictures taken without my dad. I really hated he had missed the wedding, and now I won't have any pictures with him on my wedding day. I guess we should have taken pictures at the rehearsal.

After we finished upstairs taking pictures, we went downstairs and visited with our guests. As we were visiting with them, my younger brother Frank, and his friends went outside and decorated our car. I guess that is how you end your wedding. Walking out to your car while the guests throw bird seed or rice at you. Then riding off with the horn honking in a decorated car and a sign saying, "Just married." Who came up with all those rituals? I don't know, but it was a fun part of the evening. As we drove off, everyone was watching and cheering.

We had planned a honeymoon in Gatlinburg. It was 4 hours away. We knew it would be late by the time we left the church, and we wouldn't want to drive to Gatlinburg. Ronald had reserved a hotel room for us about 20 minutes away. I was incredibly nervous about our honeymoon night. I knew how much Ronald loved me and what a gentleman he would be. We talked for a while, then I went into the bathroom, got dressed, and came out to greet my husband. He was so kind, gentle, and affectionate. I was right. He was so patient with me and gave me as much time as I needed to calm my nerves. He was a perfect gentleman, the perfect husband. If only he had stayed the perfect husband later in our marriage. How could I make the right choice at seventeen and see a different man at thirty-four?

Chapter 4

Our trip was wonderful. We hated we had to end the honeymoon and return home to the reality of work and responsibility. The weekend was over, and it was time to begin our life as Mr. and Mrs. When we got home, the first thing I wanted to do was to talk to my dad. I called first to be sure it was a good time. Mom answered and said, "Yes, your dad is here, he is sitting and watching TV." For some men, they wouldn't want to be interrupted while watching their show. Dad was understanding, and I knew he would turn it off, and we could talk. I drove over by myself. Yep, I can drive now. Thankfully, Ronald had taught me, and he had driven me to get my driver's license before we got married. I drove over to Mom and Dad's while he was doing things around our apartment.

When I got to there, I opened the door and went in. Without a word, Dad got up and gave me a big hug. That hug was all it took to bring all the emotions back. It brought back all the pain of not having him with me as I walked down the aisle. He just held me and said, "Baby girl, it is okay to cry." He understood why I had the tears, and he immediately apologized. "I do love you, and I am so sorry." I just stood there in his arms, crying on his shoulder for what seemed an hour. Finally, I got control, and he walked with me over to the couch, and we sat down. He asked me, "Can I explain?"

"Of course, yes, I want to understand." I just sat there waiting for his explanation.

He said, "Sweetheart, you are my baby girl. I know you would think since you are so special to me, there is no way I could let you down. I never intended to disappoint you. I couldn't bear the fact that you were leaving. To give you away just felt like my baby girl would never be back. I was selfish, very selfish. I thought I could take one drink, and everything would be okay. You know what that is like for me. I can't stop at one drink. I should have never taken that first one. One led to two, two to three, and before long, I passed out. I disappointed you. I stressed you. I put you in a position of confusion, and, worst of all, I made you feel you weren't loved. I am so sorry. You are very loved. Can you please forgive me?"

How could a Christian daughter say no? God forgives us. I am not God, but I am to live as close to his example as possible. So, of course, I said, "I forgive you." Dad hugged me, and now he was crying. He stopped crying long enough to say, "I am going to make you a promise. I have never been to the hospital when your sisters had their children. I make you this promise today. When you have your children, I will be there for you. Please remember I love you; you are my baby girl." As we both hugged and cried, I knew God was in the room that day to heal me through my pain and support

30

him through his pain. Although I did forgive Dad, the pain of rejection never left.

Rejection in any form is a challenge. Unfortunately, when you start your young life with rejection, it seems that sometimes you are being rejected, but you really aren't. Rejection tends to create a feeling of unworthiness. It takes a lot of strength to realize you are important. You must pull from deep down to get through some days. Remember, life isn't always about you, and what you feel as rejection really isn't an attack against you at all. It could be a weakness from the other person. Just like Dad not being at my wedding, had nothing to do with him rejecting me. It was his weakness.

Chapter 5

Life with Ronald was great. We worked hard and played harder. We stayed active in our church. We stayed close to our family and friends. We were busy building our life together. God had blessed us with two precious, healthy children, Rachel and Reid.

During the years, there were a couple of strange incidents that came up that shouldn't have happened. They made me wonder about Ronald's honesty. My trust did waiver. I just had to put the incidents out of my head if I wanted a happy marriage. That is exactly what I wanted: a happy marriage. I ignored my instincts, and the facts, and believed what he told me.

Ronald was working at a Ford dealership and was the used truck manager. This dealership wasn't too far from his parents. One morning, after he left for work, our home phone rang; it was his mom. She asked, "Is Ronald there?" I said, "No ma'am, he just left for work. Is everything okay?" "No, honey, it isn't. I need you to find Ronald and have him come pick me up and take me to the hospital. His dad has been in a terrible car accident and has been airlifted and is in ICU." "Oh my gosh, I will call his office right now and have them get him to leave and come to you the minute he gets to work."

Rachel was five and Reid was two, I felt I needed to be at the hospital with Ronald and his parents. I called Mom and told her what had happened. She came right over. It didn't take Ronald long to pick up his mom, nor my mom long to arrive at our home to keep the kids. I rushed downtown to the hospital.

His whole family was there, and his dad in the ICU at death's door. I found out that Mr. Jenkins had been on his way to work when someone hit him and left the scene of the accident. It was a while before anyone found him, and he had not only lost a lot of blood but oxygen to his brain. It was a touch-and-go for him all day.

At about 10 P.M., Ronald said, "Why don't you go home and get the kids to bed?" I asked him if I should take his younger sister home with me, she was only 11. I knew she must be tired too. I told Mrs. Jenkins I was leaving to go home to be with the kids. I asked her, "What if I take Tammy with me?" She hugged me and said, "Yes, that would be great. Tammy needs some rest. Please drive carefully." I assured her I would.

When I got home, my sweet Mom had already put the kids to bed, and they were fast asleep. We talked about Mr. Jenkins's condition briefly, and then she left to go home. I got Tammy settled in; it didn't take her long to fall asleep.

I started getting ready for bed when my phone rang. I answered it; it was our pastor, Brother Adams. He asked, "Honey, how are you?" I told him, "I am okay." He asked me, "Are you alone?" "No," I said, "The kids and Ronald's younger sister is here." "Is there a neighbor close by if you need them?" I said, "Yes, but I will be fine." Then he continued to tell me, "Honey, I have some bad news for you." I said, "What?" All this time, I thought he was calling about me and checking on the condition of Ronald's dad, but that was not the reason for his phone call at all.

With empathy and love, he told me, "Honey, when your mom got home, she found your dad had died." "What? NO!!!! Ronald's dad was supposed to die. I spent all day at the hospital with Ronald and his dad because his dad was dying, No! Brother Adams, No! It can't be my dad who died.

Do you mean I had my mom here with our kids when my daddy was taking his last breath? He needed Mom. He needed to go to the hospital. This is all my fault! I shouldn't have asked Mom to keep the kids for me to go to the hospital to be with Ronald. Why did I even ask Mom to come over today?"

Brother Adams attempted to calm me down. He told me, "It is not your fault! I don't think your mom could have done anything, and possibly the Lord didn't want your mom there in your dad's last moments. Honey, let's have a word of

34

prayer." He prayed with me, and then he talked to me some more. I finally calmed down a little. I thanked him and told him that I will be okay. But I wasn't. I was anything but okay.

Why didn't I just let Ronald go to the hospital to be with his dad? Why didn't I just stay home and take care of my own kids? Why did I ask Mom to come over? Here I was, crying and thinking about me, then I suddenly realized what about my mom. I have got to go and see Mom. Then I remembered, I can't go there; I am here alone with all the kids. Somehow, I had to figure out a way to go see her.

I called my neighbor, Norma. I told her about Mr. Jenkins and dad dying. I explained I needed someone to stay with the children for me to go see my mom. Without any hesitation, she immediately came over. I was so glad we had bought this home in this neighborhood with some great people. Norma hugged me and said, "I am so sorry. I will stay here all night with the kids. Don't worry about anything here. Take care of your sweet mom, and please tell her how sorry I am." I left for my mom's, crying all the way.

When I got there, it was after midnight. All the lights were on, and cars were everywhere. I knew I must have been the last to arrive. I wanted to be alone with Mom and tell her how sorry I was. How sorry I was for her being with our kids and not home with Dad.

I wanted her to know I knew Dad's death was my fault, and it was okay for her to agree with me. It was easy to forgive Dad for not being at my wedding. But how could I ever forgive myself for having Mom at my house when Dad needed her? She could have taken him to a hospital if she had been home, and he wouldn't be dead now. I was going to have to live with this truth and guilt for the rest of my life. Why, why did I call Mom? And why is Ronald's dad alive? He was the one that was supposed to die. Not my dad! Why, dear God?

I stayed at Mom's until morning and slept on the couch. Or should I say, I tried to sleep. I couldn't stop my brain from thinking about all the what if's. The next morning, once again, I was hoping that this was all a bad dream. It just seems they are never bad dreams. They are always real. It was reality, my dad was dead, and I had been the cause of my dad's death. Now we had a funeral to plan. A funeral for my fifty-six-year-old dad, that would be alive had it not been for me. I was only trying to do the right thing by being with my husband while his dad was dying. But here I was with my grieving mom and me without my dad. How is this fair?

After my sisters came back the following morning to be with Mom, I left to go home to be with the kids, and Norma could go home to her family. I got home before anyone woke up. I called the waiting room at the hospital to tell Ronald this horrible, devastating news. The news that my dad died while I was with him at the hospital, waiting for his dad to die.

He came home immediately and tried to console me. It was impossible. I was dealing with the loss, the guilt, and the pain all at once. While at the same time, he was receiving phone calls from his older sister saying, "Ronald, you need to come back to the hospital, we are losing dad."

Here I was, that sweet, loving Christian who tried to live right. When at that moment, I didn't care if his dad died. Mine had died because I was there at the hospital with his dad. I told Ronald, this isn't right; your dad was supposed to die, not mine. I was just so hurt. All I could think of was all the pain I had caused by leaving my mom with our kids yesterday. If only I could reverse the clock. But I couldn't. I cross-stitched a pillow for Mom once with a poem; no one knows when the hand will strike. It is so true.

I had to compose myself so I could tell our kids that their Grandad had died. I had to be there for them, I had to be there for Mom, and I had to be there for Ronald; what if his dad died today? I was so pulled; he was so pulled. Here we were, going from the funeral home to the intensive care at the hospital, back and forth. Thank God for Carl Dotson. He was a deacon at our church. He wouldn't let us drive. He would drive us from the funeral home to the hospital, wait and pray with us, then drive us back to the funeral home. Who kept the kids? I don't even know. It is still a blur. I have no idea how we survived during this time.

Somehow, we did, and somehow, throughout all the loss, stress, and heartache, I apparently had gotten pregnant. I had always heard you couldn't get pregnant when you were stressed. Well, that is a myth, evidently. I was pregnant with our 3rd child. I felt this was God giving me a blessing since I just lost my dad. I could now focus on our baby, not my guilt so much. God is so good. God has always been a step ahead of me. He has always shown me a solution to any pain.

I had gone to the doctor and found out the baby was due July 2nd. I thought no, not July 2nd, that is Mr. Jenkins's birthday. At this point, I think I hated that man. And you know what? That man loved me. We would go visit him, and he wouldn't want his wife, his daughters, or his son to feed him. He wanted me to feed him. If he only knew in my poor guilt-stricken mind how I felt about him. It was so hard to accept he was alive, and my dad was not.

Mr. Jenkins was in the hospital, in the intensive care department for months. It seemed like the staff were ready to let him die. The doctors were at a loss as to what to do to help him. The insurance money was running out. He was a veteran. He was in the Navy in WW II. We knew he would have veteran benefits at the Veteran Hospital. After prayer and discussions, the decision was made to transfer him. Hopefully, with new doctors, new nurses, and different eyes, they could find a way to help him. We all felt this would be the last hope for him to recover.

He was transferred to the local Veterans Hospital the following day. In a few days, he made a turn and got better, it wasn't long before he was home. He had to retire with a disability, but he was alive. I wish I could say that about my dad. I miss my dad every day. I even miss the bad times with him. The good times I cherish in my heart and my memories.

I delivered our 3rd child, Ryder, on July 4th. He was our little firecracker. I wanted to name him after my dad. I was not too fond of Dad's first name, Kenneth. I thought about my maiden name, Thomas. However, my sister had named her son, Thomas. That left Dad's middle name, Axel. That was perfect, Ryder Axel, and we would call him Ryder. That sounded like a strong, tough name for this July 4th firecracker.

It was time to go home and introduce Ryder to his sister and brother. When we got home, the kids were so excited. I think Rachel thought I had bought her another baby doll. I had to be sure she was incredibly careful around him. I found her putting her baby doll pacifier in his bed. She would try to feed him her baby doll's bottle. She was being a little mommy. While Reid, I think he just thought, well it was a baby at least at that time. Once Ryder got older, Reid was very excited he had a little brother to play with and take care of.

We haven't gotten our 12 children yet. But we were on our way with our 3rd healthy child.

Chapter 6

With our family growing, we decided it was time for a larger home and a bigger yard. We looked and soon found the perfect lot. It was an acre and down the street from the lake. We fell in love with the neighborhood. Funny, when Ronald and I started dating, we would ride in this neighborhood. He would say, "Someday we will live here." I thought, sure, some day we will live in this neighborhood in a big home with a beautiful yard. This was something I couldn't even imagine. Fortunately for us, Ronald could. He reached that goal.

We bought the lot, looked at house plans, and before long, we were building a beautiful home. This was a larger home, two stories, 5 bedrooms, and 3 ½ baths. Rachel would have her own bedroom and private bath; the boys would also have their own bedroom and share a bath that was in between their bedrooms. Wow, and to think when I grew up, I had to share a bath with 6 others. I never had my own bedroom until I was 16. Ronald provided not only shelter but gave us so much love. Life seemed to be getting better each day.

It took a while to build our home, but it was so much fun. We would go over to check it out at least twice a week. The builder had mounted a huge amount of dirt in the backyard that the kids loved to run and play on. We planted trees in the backyard that would be home plate, first, second and third bases. There were tons of boys that lived close by in the neighborhood. Sweet Rachel would have a challenge finding little girls there. But she was a little social butterfly. We knew it was only time until she knew where all the girls lived. Here we were, so young, no college and building in this exclusive neighborhood. We were so blessed.

Our life had been very happy, especially after we moved into this new home. Our life from 1976 to 1983 would be a storybook with all good stories. Opryland Park had opened, and we had yearly passes. We would go to church every Sunday, go home, eat lunch, change clothes, and load up in the car and drive to Opryland Park.

We traveled a lot. One trip we took, Ronald had taken 14 days off from work for us to drive to Los Angeles and up to San Francisco. We saw almost every site on that trip, including Disneyland, the Red Rocks, and the Grand Canyon. We even saw Roy Roger's Museum. We would take trips to Disneyworld and Long Boat Key in Florida. We even went on a trip to Michigan with our neighbors, Doctor and Mrs. Cothern. Their older sons were about Reid's age, and their younger son was a couple of years younger than Ryder. We had a wonderful time staying at their cabin on Lake Michigan. It just seemed living around so many successful people motivated all of us to do our best in life.

Ronald was still in the car business, and I was now a stay-at-home mom. I loved every minute of being a wife and a mom. That is all I ever wanted. At our church, Ronald and I both taught Sunday School classes. We were active in the children's school. The school was close to our home, only a mile down the road. We decided to keep them in the public school for now. They loved it. The children could ride their bikes to school. They preferred riding their bikes on the pretty days. On the other days, I would drive them to school.

Ronald wanted to leave the dealership where he was working and open a used car lot. My uncle worked for the company that owned the land that Ronald wanted to lease. It worked out once Uncle Bob stepped up and got the lease contract for us. It was only a short time until Ronald had his business up and running. He was living his dream.

With the kids all in school, even Ryder was in kindergarten by now. This gave me the privilege to work with Ronald at the business. He would buy and sell the cars. I did the bookkeeping and registration of the vehicles. It was great. We were having so much fun working together. It seemed everything we did, we enjoyed doing it together.

I adored Ronald. I would just sit and watch him shave in the mornings. I loved picking up the clothes he dropped on the floor and washing them. I loved sitting on the sofa at night and holding his hand while we watched TV. I loved cuddling and being close to him. Even in our king-size bed, I wanted to be close to him. We only needed a twin bed; it would be enough.

Our life was so beautiful. Ronald surprised me with this beautiful poem, expressing his love for me and showing me, in writing, how happy he was.

This poem will not come easy for me. A poet, I AM NOT.

A poem written by a novelist.

I will give it my very best shot.

This poem is for someone very dear,

Who is always loving and fair,

A someone who is always near

To show me she really cares.

Her smile is as bright as sunshine.

And she wears it for all to see.

She only deserves the best in life.

Which is more than she receives.

She has never had the better things.

Aigner, Goochie, or Mink,

But she never complained a single time.

At least none that I can think.

She has always settled for second best.

From Penney's or Castner Knott,

She saves us money from A to Z

And of that, I have not forgot.

So, on this Christmas morning.

The best will be hers to know.

Aigner this year, then Mink comes next.

Because I love you so,

Your husband Ronald, 1981

That Christmas, he gave me an Aigner purse. Also, that same year, he called a family meeting and asked us to decide if we would want a boat or a swimming pool. The vote was for a pool. In the spring, he had a 16 x 40 Lazy L inground pool installed in our yard. He built a huge deck around it. The following Christmas, he gave me not one fur coat but two fur coats. They were both blue fox fur; one was a full-length coat, and the other a shorter coat.

Our life kept getting better and better. We loved each other so very much. The gifts were nice, but it wasn't the most important thing. I knew nothing was more important than love, time, and just being together.

We were together most of the time when he wasn't working. We were still active in church. We had transferred all three children to a local private school, where we served on the Parent-Teacher board. We were still members of the Country Club. We loved taking the children there and watching them swim and play tennis. Ronald would play golf there, and I would socialize with the ladies. Life was good.

Ronald had gotten a call from the owner of another car dealership. He offered him a great job. Ronald decided to take it and sell his used car lot. Changing to a different position, I felt he needed nicer clothes. I went shopping and got him all decked out. The secretary at the dealership, Martha, was an older lady. One day, she told me, "You sure keep him looking sharp for other women." I thought that sounded strange, but then I just forgot about it. I did love him. I did want him to look the best he could as the manager. He was highly respected in that position.

He was doing great, but it just happened to be the time of year when commissions weren't the best. Since the kids were in a private school now and things were tight, we decided it would be a good time for me to return to work. I didn't mind. I had done this throughout our marriage. Then things would get better, and I would quit again.

I went to work at the local hospital in the emergency room. My shift would be from 11:00 P.M. to 7:00 A.M. It seemed perfect. I would be home until Ronald and the kids went to bed, and then I would go to work. I would get off by 7:00 A.M. and be home in time to get the children to school. Besides, I only worked two nights a week. This would be perfect for all of us.

I enjoyed the work. I really enjoyed the feeling of helping people in need as they came into the emergency room. I thought Ronald liked the idea of me working as well. It seemed that everything was working out with the hours, and the children's school schedule.

Chapter 7

His management expertise had gotten around in the car business. It was only a short time until he received another company's offer. They wanted him to be the General Manager. That would mean even more money. We would both receive company cars. It was an excellent promotion for him. He would be given a guaranteed salary plus a bonus. We talked about it and prayed about it. He felt this would be a great career move. He accepted the position.

After he got that promotion, he asked me to quit my job at the hospital. He said, "I can sleep better at night if you are at home with me." I thought that was so sweet. I knew he loved me, but it surprised me that he missed me that much. I was raised to be a submissive wife. Although I enjoyed getting out of the house and I really enjoyed my job, I felt I should do as Ronald asked.

Did I want to quit? The answer was no, but I loved my husband, and he wanted me to quit. I went to work the following night and gave my two weeks' notice. They asked me, "Why?" I explained, "My husband has asked that I not work anymore and that I stay at home." My manager said, "We will miss you, but I understand."

Ronald drove home his new car, his company car. He asked me, "What do you want for a company car?" I said, "I want the red Toyota Supra." "Ramona, you know that is the car the owner drives. You know you cannot have it. I think sometimes you think you can have whatever you want." "No, I just think maybe Mr. Dennis might be tired of it. We won't know until we ask." Ronald loved me so much and always wanted me to be happy. He agreed to ask Mr. Dennis the next day and find out if I could get the car that I wanted, the red Toyota Supra. It was beautiful and so sporty.

Guess what? Mr. Dennis said, "Sure, she can have it." Mr. Dennis told him he was ready for a change. Ronald had the service department assistant manager clean my beautiful car. He wanted to bring it home to me that night and surprise me. Boy, did he ever; I thought if I do get it, it will probably be a week or so. But no, that night, he drove my sporty car home to me.

He came in, and I was inside cooking dinner. "Hey, sweetie, how was your day?" I turned and gave him a big hug. "It has been a great day." "Well, it might be getting a little better." I was surprised and thought, how could it get any better? "Let's walk outside." I turned down the stove and walked outside with him. There was my beautiful red Toyota Supra. I reached up and hugged him so tight it was a wonder his head didn't fall off his shoulders. I thanked and thanked him. I took nothing for granted.

When he had worked at the Ford dealership years earlier, he brought an order form home. We sat down, and he explained this is how they ordered cars. He said, "I am going to get you a new car, and you can pick out any options you want, and we will order it special for you." I got to pick out the interior and exterior color, and the extras for the car. I decided on a blue/white Ford Thunderbird. Having grown up without a car in my family, this was unbelievable.

Our life was filled with God, good health, good friends, good family, and an abundance of happiness. Here it is six years later, my Thunderbird is paid for, and now he just brought home a Toyota Supra for me to drive. It wasn't one he purchased for me. I knew the company cars would come and go. I knew we would get different cars when those were sold.

The Thunderbird was totally mine and going nowhere, I thought. I had the Toyota Supra for only a few weeks when Ronald told me, "Darling, you have a brand-new car, and I have a new car. I think it is time to sell the Thunderbird." I loved that car, and it was paid for. I wanted to think realistically.

Do we need it? The answer was no. Did it cost us each month for insurance and service, and did it take up room in the driveway? That answer was yes. He was right. I guess we didn't need it. I just liked it and hated letting it go. It was the first car in my life that was mine, and I had gotten to special order it. I finally agreed and said, "Okay, you are right." The next day, he drove it to his work, and I never saw it again. It was okay; it was just a car. I had the red Toyota Supra that I had wanted, and we were happy. That was all that was important.

Ronald was so romantic and sentimental. It was April 22; we went on a movie date. We had a sitter for the kids. It was a fantastic, beautiful night, just like April 22; the day we had gotten engaged years earlier. On that day, we also went to the movies. It was a drive-in movie in Madison. During the movie, he said, "Open the glove box, I put our candy in there." I opened it, there was an oil rag, and inside the oil rag was a jewelry box with my diamond engagement ring.

Once again, it is April 22, and he does the same thing. He asked me, "Open the glove box, I have some candy inside." I opened it, and again, just like years before, I saw an oil rag. Again, little did I know inside the oil rag was a gift for me. There was a jewelry box inside the oil rag, just like before. This time, the jewelry box contained a pair of 1-carat diamond earrings.

I was blown away. I was not expecting this. The earrings were so beautiful and sparkled so brightly. I was so blessed to have the man of my dreams and for him to always be so loving and caring. Our life was only getting better.

Chapter 8

But just in a few days, my life would change forever. It was May 2; that is just one date I will never erase from my mind. I went out to get into the Toyota Supra, the company car, to drive the kids to school. We were running late; it had been a hectic morning. I started the car, put it in reverse, backed up, and then I heard a loud "boom." I had hit Ronald's company car. There I had damaged both cars. Evidently, I didn't look behind me.

We had a large turnaround driveway. Ronald always parked beside me. I just assumed nothing was behind me. That was a huge mistake. Now I would surely be late getting the kids to school. Plus, now I have got to go and tell Ronald what just happened.

I went inside and said, "Ronald, honey, I was backing out of the driveway and didn't see your car. I …." Before I could finish, he started screaming at me. His screaming scared me more than the accident. Ronald was always so kind and easy-going. I have never seen him this mad. He screamed, "Are you kidding me? What were you thinking? Did you even look behind you?" I couldn't get a word in, and he just kept asking questions, "How much damage is there? How am I supposed to get both cars into the shop? Looks like now we won't have a car at all." I kept trying to say, I am sorry. But he wouldn't let me. Seeing him so angry,

I quickly turned and said, "I am sorry!" as I left the room. I decided that I just needed to leave and let him calm down and drive the kids to school.

On the way home from their school, I stopped by the grocery store and picked up a few things. I would need to make a good supper for Ronald. I was in hopes that would help smooth over his anger at me. And, of course, I would make his favorite dessert, German Chocolate cake. I knew that would be a good idea too. I checked out with all the items I needed. I was going to try to make tonight a little better.

On the way home, I recall thinking, things cannot get worse! When I got home, Ronald had already left for work. I cleaned the house, did some laundry, and waited for him to call me. I had just finished lunch when the phone rang. I wanted it to be Ronald, and him telling me everything would be okay, but I was unsure who it could be. If it was Ronald, I didn't know how the conversation would go. It sure didn't end well earlier this morning.

Thankfully, it was Ronald. I could tell by his voice he had calmed down, and once again, he sounded like the guy I was so in love with. The first thing he said was, "Honey, I am sorry I overreacted. I didn't even ask. Are you okay?" "Yes, I am fine. I feel horrible for causing damage to the cars." He said, "The damage isn't so bad. The guys in the body shop can fix the cars without much effort." I thought, thank goodness. Thank goodness we don't have to pay for the damage I caused.

Then he scolded me like a child. I deserved it. He reminded me to look where I am going in the future. He reminded me to look behind me before I backed up. I listened and said, "Yes, honey, I am sorry and will pay more attention." After all, he was the one that had taught me how to drive. I knew he was right. I guess I needed a refresher course and a reminder not to rush. I was grateful that he worked at a car dealership and the body shop could fix the cars, and we wouldn't be out of pocket for the expenses.

I was so grateful he had calmed down, and things did not escalate, at least not that day. What was going to happen in a few weeks made me realize never to say, things cannot get worse! They can! I was about to find out how bad things can get.

The next three weeks would be a series of events I would have never predicted, not in my wildest dreams. I thought we were both happy. Everyone else thought so too. Guess everyone but Ronald. He apparently had an insight that I didn't have.

Ronald began telling me that the car dealership where he worked was having some break-ins. For some reason, he thought it was his responsibility to protect the dealership, perhaps because he was the General Manager. Ronald told me, "I will need to stay at the dealership at night for a while. If someone breaks in, I will be there to scare them off and call the police before they can steal any cars or totally vandalize the place."

I thought and said, "Seriously, the owner, Mr. Dennis, does not expect that of you. I don't think he would expect his General Manager to spend the night at the dealership and oversee the place. He knows theft and vandalism is a job for the police." Ronald kept insisting it was his responsibility. I did not understand this, and I sure did not think it was his responsibility at all.

I finally decided I might as well agree. He was not changing his mind about it. For a few nights, he would come home for dinner, leave about 10 P.M., and return to the dealership. He would sleep in the break room, come home at about 6 A.M., and get ready for work. This continued for about a week.

Ronald said, "Mr. Dennis has installed a security system, and everything should be okay now." I was so glad. Now he can be home. Not only did I miss him, but I was worried he would get shot or worse, killed. People who break into car dealerships, I would think, come prepared for anything going wrong and would have a weapon with them.

That weekend was wonderful. After all the security stress at the dealership, Ronald was back home. Now we would have some family time. We went to church on Sunday. After church, we came home, changed clothes, grabbed a sandwich, and went to Opryland Park for a day of fun and rides.

When we got home from Opryland that night, I got some hamburger meat from the refrigerator and patted it out for Ronald to cook on the grill. It was a beautiful night sitting outside, grilling, and enjoying the evening. The kids put on their swimsuits for a night of swimming and splashing while we got supper ready. Now life can get back to normal, or so I thought.

That Monday morning, Ronald left for work; I drove the kids to school. When I returned, I got busy cleaning the house and doing laundry. I was going through his suit coat pockets to take the suits to the cleaners when I found a ladies' watch in his coat pocket. I was having a "DeJa'Vu" moment.

About six years earlier, when I was doing this same thing, cleaning out his suit coat pockets for the cleaners, I found condoms. I had already had my hysterectomy, so he did not need condoms, but there they were. I remember that day thinking the worst. He is having an affair. I didn't want to believe that. I had not noticed any other signs.

That day, when I found the condoms, I said to Ronald, "Look what I found in your coat pocket." He dismissed it as a practical joke, saying, "The guys at work were playing a trick on me. I always have my suit coat hanging on the coat rack just inside the dealership door. Those guys are constantly trying to find some way to get me in trouble." I told him, "They need to stop the practical jokes that could interfere with your home life." I then let it go.

Now, here I am finding a lady's watch. How will he dismiss this? That night, when he came home, I said, "Look what I found in your coat pocket!" Then, I showed him the watch. He says so innocently, "There it is." I said, "What do you mean, there it is?" "Oh, this girl came into the dealership to buy a car and didn't have any money with her. She wanted me to hold the car for her until she came back with the money in a couple of days. I told her I couldn't, and then she offered to leave her watch. She is coming back tomorrow, so I am glad you found it."

Boy, either he is a smooth, convincing liar, or I am naïve. I loved him so much, and when you love like that, you want to believe, and you know you must trust. So, once again, I let it go.

Chapter 9

The following week Ronald told me he needed to get away to think. He said his work was driving him crazy and that he was so disappointed he couldn't get his novel published. He had written a novel about Big Foot, Sasquatch, in the East Tennessee mountains. He had sent it to a publisher but had gotten a rejection letter. He sent it to another publisher and got another rejection letter. He sent it to another and again, the same thing, a rejection letter. He had even sent it to a Hollywood movie producer. The producer did call him one evening. But nothing came from the phone call. He never could get it published.

He said, "I am so stressed from the break-ins at work and my book not getting published, I need a break." I know you never know how someone feels until you walk in their shoes. I knew I didn't understand exactly what he was going through.

I had helped him with the book every night, and I was frustrated nothing came from it. He would write it, and I would proofread it and then type it. I didn't feel like I needed a break, though. I wanted to help him to accept it hadn't gotten published and encourage him to continue writing and to keep trying to find a publisher. I wanted us to do whatever we needed for him to feel better.

I was not the General Manager. He was, and with the break-ins happening there, he probably was stressed. I tried to be sympathetic and understanding. I said, "Honey, that sounds good, a vacation would be good for us. Where would you like to go?" He said, "Not a vacation. I can't take that much time off. I just need a couple of days." I said, "Sure, just a couple of days would be a good getaway for us." He was getting frustrated, "Ramona, you are not getting it. I need to get away alone." Alone, what did he mean? We had never spent a few days apart. Why now does he need time alone? What is he thinking? I just couldn't figure out why he needed time without me and the kids. Why would he need time alone?

I said, "Ronald, I don't understand. Why don't you want us to all go together like we always do?" I was just trying to understand. He said, "I need some total relaxation, no talking, no laughing, no kids, just total peace and silence."

I told him he did not have to leave to think that I would drive to Knoxville with the kids, and visit our friends, Carol, Gary, and their son, Chip. We can stay there for a few days so you can have some quiet time at home to think. He agreed to that. I called Carol, and she was excited for us to come to their home.

Carol and Gary had been our neighbors when Ryder was born. Gary had taken a job transfer to Knoxville, TN. They were great people and had been great neighbors. They also attended our church. They only had one son, Chip, he was the same age as Reid. I knew the kids would have a great time, and I would enjoy their company.

The kids came in from school, and I enthusiastically or at least attempted to be as enthusiastic as possible. I said, "Guys, there is no school Monday and Tuesday, I think it will be a great time to get away. What do y'all think about going to visit Chip and his mom and dad in Knoxville for a few days?"

They were excited. I told them, "Pack up a few things for a couple of days, and we will head out tonight." They went upstairs, and each one packed a bag. When they came downstairs, I heard Rachel say, "Mom, Dad, we are ready." I said, "Great, let's go." We headed for the car, and then Rachel asked, "Where is Dad?" I had to tell her and the boys that their dad couldn't go on this trip, he had some work to do. They accepted that story as it seemed normal for him to be working. They had grown accustomed to his long hours, just like I had. Although, we had never taken a trip without him.

We got in the car and set out for our 3-hour road trip. The kids laughing and enjoying the ride, and me; I was still thinking about why this trip is happening without their dad.

From the time we arrived at Carol and Gary's house until the time we left; the kids were outside playing every day. They spent their nights playing games and having the best time. I was so glad they were enjoying themselves.

Carol and I would be busy, either shopping or in the kitchen cooking and catching up on our lives. She was great to talk to, and I knew anything discussed would be confidential. We hadn't seen one another in about five years, but it was like we had been seeing one another every day. We all were having such a great time. I was hoping Ronald was relaxing, doing some soul searching, and thinking like he said he needed.

After a few days in Knoxville, I got this gut feeling that we needed to come home. I woke the kids up in the middle of the night and left Carol and Gary a note. I thanked them for their hospitality and explained I felt I needed to return home. We left and started our drive. When we got home, it was about 5 A.M., we all climbed into bed with Ronald.

About 6 A.M., the phone rang. Ronald was in the bathroom. I answered it and they hung up. I thought, what is really going on here? Why would someone call at 6 A.M.? Better yet, why would they hang up when I answered?

I immediately had flashbacks. Cigarettes coming from under the seat, condoms Ronald told me the guys at work left in his coat pocket, ladies watch he said was given to him for a down payment to hold a car, now this. Have they all been lies? Can I trust him? Ronald came out of the bathroom and asked, "Who was that?" I said, "I don't know. They hung up when I answered." All he said was, "Oh." He turned and went back into the bathroom.

He continued to get dressed. I went into the kitchen to cook his breakfast. I was looking forward to talking to him to see if he had rested and had time to think while we were gone. But it didn't turn out that way.

Chapter 10

That morning, before Ronald left for work, he told me, "Ramona, you did not stick to the agreement, so I will have to leave." I asked him, "What do you mean?" He said, "You were going to be gone until Monday evening to give me time to think. Here it is Monday morning, and you are back." I said, "Honey, I woke up in the middle of the night, and I got this feeling something was wrong. I didn't want to call and wake you, in case, everything was okay. I had to come home to see you. Besides Ronald, it is just a few hours earlier."

Angrily, he told me, "If something was wrong, I would have called you. Monday night is not Monday morning at 5 A.M. Now, I am more stressed than ever. When I get home tonight, I am going to get my clothes and leave." "Leaving? How much time do you need?" "You don't understand Ramona. I am leaving!"

What is he talking about? Leaving? Leaving because I didn't give him a few more hours to think and relax. He was working on Monday anyway. What was the big deal? I waited until lunch and called him. He was so hateful. He answered, "What do you want?" I said, "I would like to talk if you have a few minutes." He was not going to talk to me; except to say, there was nothing to talk about. I didn't know what was going on. I told him, "I gave you all weekend to think, and we only returned home only a few hours early. We never even had a chance to talk about your weekend. How was it?" "It was great." I said, "Then that is great, and everything is good. We missed you; do you really need more time to get away so you can think?" He said, "No."

I felt relief. I knew now he wasn't leaving like he said this morning. Until he said, "I made up my mind. I am getting my clothes tonight and leaving." "But you just said you didn't need any more time." He so adamantly said, "I don't need any more time. I have decided I am moving out! This time is forever!"

"What? What do you mean, forever? Isn't this something we need to talk about?" "No, he yelled. My mind is made up." Then he hung up on me. Stunned, I couldn't believe what I had just heard. I couldn't believe he hung up on me. What is wrong with him? What is he talking about?

I just couldn't understand. He just had me quit my job, sold my car, and now he was leaving me? He said, forever, but he wouldn't do that. Or was that his plan? Did he want me to be left stranded with no car and broke? And why? Why would he want to do this? Why was he leaving me, or did he mean he would be leaving for a few nights to think? Was he thinking since he was the General Manager, he would have to leave to protect the dealership again? I was so very confused. Surely, he was not leaving me. Why would he ask me to quit my job? Why would he sell my car that was paid for? He had to know if he left me, the company would take the car they lent me away. He had to know I would need to work.

What is he really thinking? What has happened so suddenly that would make him talk like this? To have this attitude with me? It had to be just talk. He wouldn't leave me, leave the kids, leave his home, his dog. That is all I could think about. I spent the afternoon looking at our pictures. You can see the love we shared. I thought I would post them on the bedroom mirror; just maybe he needs a reminder of our love.

That night when Ronald came home, it was a beautiful night. The kids and I were playing badminton in the backyard. It was about 6:30 P.M. when Ronald pulled into the driveway. The normal time for Ronald to come home. Today was not much different except this morning, he had told me he was going to leave tonight, leaving tonight forever!

I could not believe it. How could he? He had it all, a beautiful family, a home, and a cute little white poodle, Beau, Beau Pierre Jenkins. He had a wonderful job. How could he? Why would he? What could he ever find better than what he had? Almost 16 years of what I thought was a perfect marriage, and he was going to leave? He could not do this! He just couldn't!

Rachel says, "Dad, do you want to play some badminton?" He said, "Sure, who is ahead?" Like a cutie, I said, "Now, who do you think? If you play, you will have some real tough competition." "You know I can handle it," he said with a smirk. He picked up the racket and said, "How about I play a short game with your mom?" Sounded good to me. It reminded me of when we dated and would play croquet together. "Get it, Daddy, get it!" Ryder yelled. "Yeah! Dad is winning." "What is the score," I asked? Reid standing on the sideline said, "I don't know, Mom, but Dad is sure outsmarting you." Ronald replied, "Yeah, I sure am!"

Little did I know then, his remarks, "Play a short game with your mom" and "I sure am outsmarting you," would have hidden meanings. Little did I know from this point on, I would have to take what he said and twist it around to figure out what he meant.

About that time, Ronald turned and said, "Kids, let's go inside. I want to talk to you." Would he tell them he was leaving? Was this it? Or was he just trying to scare me? If he was thinking about leaving, one look at our pictures I placed on the mirror would change his mind. Who wouldn't? We always had so much fun and so many wonderful times.

If he said he was leaving, the tears from the kids would be too much. He would change his mind. I sat outside on the deck, looking at the beautiful pool he had installed just last summer. I sat there reflecting on our life. I just couldn't think of anything that had happened to make him think that he needed to leave. We could talk and pray about anything and everything.

About fifteen minutes went by, one by one, the kids began to come outside where I was sitting. There were tears, tears, and more tears. Reid, my eleven-year-old, came out first. "Mom, I cannot believe it, Dad is leaving. This is not supposed to happen to us. This happens to other people, not to us. I cannot live without Dad." I was speechless. What could I say? As he was running out to the yard, I went to hug him, but he ran by me.

Then Ryder, my eight-year-old, came outside. This took a real toll on him. Crying and crying, "Mom, Mom, Dad is leaving us. He said it would be better. He said he would see us more now than ever. He said we would get more because you both would buy for us. I don't care about that, Mom, I just want Dad! I am going to let the air out of his tires!" I said, "Ryder," about that time, he just ran past me too. As he passed me, he just said, "Mom, he can't leave us, he can't."

Finally, Rachel, my fourteen-year-old and daddy's little girl, came outside. Her heart was broken. She asked about me, "Mom, are you okay?" Before I could even answer, she asked, "Where are Reid and Ryder?" By now, Reid had found a secluded spot in the corner of the backyard. We looked up, and Ryder was in the other corner on the swing set. Rachel started walking toward the backyard.

I was broken hearted and so confused. I just sat crying, hurting for myself, and I was hurting for the kids. He couldn't! He couldn't! He just couldn't hurt these kids this way! For what? Why?

At that moment, Ronald came outside and said, "What a lousy way to do this. You must upset the kids more than ever by all this crying and carrying on. Thanks a lot!" Devastated, I just looked and asked, "Please, do not go? We love you, and we need you. Please, do not go?" He just looked at me and so coldly said, "Goodbye!" and he walked away. I adored him. I loved him, and I knew he loved me. He would soon realize it.

The boys sat outside for a while. Rachel went up to the back of the yard to talk with them. I gave them some time, the time I felt they might need. I couldn't imagine what they must be thinking now. They couldn't understand. I couldn't understand! How could anyone?

I sat on the deck, thinking about what was happening and how I could console the kids. I had no way. I had no thoughts. I was at a total loss. All I knew for sure was that I loved them, and although their dad just left, I knew he loved them too. That's all I could tell them. Is this going to be enough? I didn't know, but I knew I had to be and do everything they needed to get them through this.

Chapter 11

I knew the next few days would be long and hard, but it would be worth the wait when he returned. I felt sure he would return. How long would it take for Ronald to realize what a wonderful family he had left? A family that loved him, with all our hearts. I decided not to contact him. I would show some tough love. I would just wait until he came back home. I asked God, "God, what is your will for my life?"

I turned to God's word and was led to 1 Thessalonians 5:18. "In all things give thanks for this is the will of the Lord for you." But God, "How do I say thank you, when my husband is walking away?" I hung onto that verse. I prayed to the Lord to please help me to understand, and trust in Him. I have got to trust that someday; I will understand all of this. For now, I only have God's scripture, to give thanks!

It had been almost a week since the kids had seen their dad. He called on Saturday and talked to Rachel. He said, "I will come over after y'all when you get out of church, about 1 o'clock, and I will take y'all to lunch." What Ronald didn't know was that none of us had the energy to get up and go to church without him. We had always gone as a family. None of this seemed right. Sundays had always been our church day, lunch day, and family day.

I wouldn't get to be with Ronald, but that was okay. The phone call to Rachel, I knew, was just for the kids to have lunch with him. I was just happy to see him briefly as he picked up the kids. Seeing the kids happy to be with their dad was enough for me for now.

I had bought him a shirt while we were in Knoxville. I hadn't even had a chance to give it to him. I thought when he came over, I would give it to him. I also baked some chocolate chip cookies for him. I stood in the living room; I could hardly wait to see him. I looked out the side window, watching and waiting.

About that time, I saw a sporty convertible pull into our driveway. It was Ronald, he honked. I really thought he would come inside, but he didn't. He honked again. I told the kids, "Your dad is here. I am going out to give him the cookies. Y'all hurry up, so you won't keep Dad waiting. I am sure he is excited to see you guys."

I went outside. Ronald seemed different. He was wearing a gold chain necklace, and his shirt was unbuttoned. I tried to ignore this and said, "I thought you might like some chocolate chip cookies." "Yeah, that sounds great." Then I told him, "I got you this shirt when the kids and I were in Knoxville." He said, "Okay." He took it, and then he lowered the boom on me. I guess he wasn't expecting me to come outside. It made him angry, not too angry, for the cookies

71

and the shirt. But after he got them, I was told exactly where to go, what I could do with myself, and to send the kids out. By now, the kids were coming outside. I just turned toward the house. Once again, I was so shocked as to the way Ronald was acting and talking.

I tried to hide my feelings from the kids as I hugged each one and said, "I love you. Have a good day with Dad. I will see you later." Ryder said, "Mom, aren't you coming with us?" It was all I could do to hold back tears. I said, "Sweetie, Mommy can't come today." "But Mommy," Ryder said. I hugged him with all my might and said, "Sweetie, I will be here waiting for you when you get home. I know you are going to have a fun day with Dad."

He was so sad that I wasn't going with them. I was too, but there wasn't anything I could do about it. Ronald had left me, and he wasn't about to let me be a part of their day. I had to stay at home and know that, for now, the kids are with their dad. I wouldn't have kept the kids from their dad for anything. They needed to spend as much time as possible with him. Their little hearts had been broken and confused enough. They needed their dad's time, his hugs, and love.

I didn't want Ryder or any of the kids to think I wasn't going with them because I didn't want to be with them. It is such a fine line to walk. How do I say I can't go because your dad won't let me? I can't say that. So, they just had to think, Mom was the bad guy here.

His anger and hostility toward me were so surprising. Four weeks ago, we were celebrating our original engagement when he gave me the diamond earrings. This was the same man, hugging me and saying, "I love you." This was the same man that had been teaching with me the youth group at our local church. This is the same man who had been leading the family prayers at the table. How could someone change so drastically, and why? I just could not understand. I just sat at home crying and trying to understand, trying to rationalize everything while the kids were with their dad.

It was 5:30 P.M., and Ronald brought the children home. He pulled into the driveway and let the kids out. I thought, really, at the very least he could have walked his kids to the door. He didn't even wait until they got in the house before he was gone. What if I hadn't been home? Then they would be home alone. He knew I was a great mom. He knew I would be here waiting for them.

The kids came in, and they seemed to be in mixed moods. They were confused, but they were happy to have seen their dad, and to spend some time with him. I asked them, "How was lunch?" Reid said, "We just went to

Grandma's for lunch. We stayed there and talked to them until we came home."

I just wondered; how much fun that was for the kids. I knew it had to be anything but fun. They haven't seen their dad in a week, and he takes them straight to his moms for lunch and to visit. It was a beautiful day. They could have gone out to eat at a Dairy Queen and gone to the park. They could have flown some kites. But just to sit at his mother's house. I loved her, and she was a great grandmother. But how much fun could that have been for the kids?

The following day, I called Ronald. I simply said, "I do not understand." Once again, he was so rude and abrupt. "What is there to understand?" I said, "What do you mean, look at our life, I don't" Ronald interrupted me and said, "There is nothing to understand. I don't live there anymore, and this is the way it is going to be."

I was almost speechless. I finally said, "What can I do to change your mind?" He said, "Only one thing, leave me alone. If you leave me alone for two weeks, that is your only chance. For two weeks, I don't want to talk to you. I don't want to hear your voice. I don't want to see you. If you do this, then we will talk." I said, "Okay." We hung up.

For the next two weeks, if the phone rang, I would not answer it. If the kids were not home to answer it, it would just go unanswered. I wouldn't call. When he came to see the kids, I wouldn't see him. I would do as he asked. I didn't understand, but I would do it. I would have done anything just to get a chance to talk. To find out what had happened and what was going on. If he would just talk to me, we could work this out.

The kids would call him at his mother's house, their grandmother, where Ronald was living. He was never there when they called. Today was Memorial Day, a holiday. We would always spend a holiday together as a family. But here it is, Memorial Day, he is off from work. The kids call, and he wasn't at his mom's. We had no idea where he was. They just moped around like their best friend had died. I guess it had seemed that way to them. I know it did to me.

They stood around looking out the window. They would see other families outside. Those families were together having fun in their pools. They were so puzzled and confused. There was nothing I could do but say, your dad loves you, and dad is only confused. I would never say, Dad will be home again, and things will be okay. I didn't know that. I couldn't take a chance on them getting disappointed again. I had no idea how our life was going to play out. I thought it would be okay, I hoped it would be okay, but I didn't know for sure. I didn't know about anything for sure right now.

I told the kids, "I need you to promise me that regardless of what I am doing or who I am talking to, if you need to talk to me or need anything, let me know right then. Always talk to me, don't hold tears back, and with God's help, we will be okay." They did! They were super good kids. They knew I meant every word.

Later that night, Reid came into the kitchen where I was cooking and said, "Mom, I don't want to go to football camp." "But Reid, you always have so much fun there, and this would be a great time to go and get away for a few days. Most of your friends are going." "Mom, please don't make me. Mom, I don't want to go."

I didn't know what to do. He was just like Rachel and Ryder; they were so upset about everything that had happened. I didn't want him to go and be worried about what was happening here while he was gone. I finally told him, "Reid, I will not make you go. But before we make the final decision, let's think about it." He said, "Mom, no, I don't want to go." I didn't want to push him. I said, "Okay, you don't have to go."

We all began to sleep downstairs. The kids were having a hard time getting to sleep upstairs. The house now seemed too big. We didn't even need or want the upstairs. We would talk, laugh, cry, and pray together. We would get through this one day at a time.

Their dad would return their calls the following morning, after they had called him the day before. He would talk briefly just to answer their questions. After days of begging, he finally agreed to come over to fix their bicycles, only if I promised him that I would stay inside so he wouldn't see me. I agreed.

We were still in the two-week period when I promised, he wouldn't hear my voice or see me. I needed to honor this, so, we could talk and discuss what was going on in his head.

He pulls into the driveway, and they meet him outside. I watched out the window as they hugged him with all their might. To see just a glimpse of him from the window would satisfy me for now. At least he was alive, and I could see him. That was better than nothing.

They all went into the garage for him to work on their bikes. He had been here about ten minutes when I heard Ryder come running inside hollering, "Mommy, mommy Rachel needs you." At the same time, I heard tires squealing out of the driveway. My heart almost stopped! What had happened?

I ran out to the garage, and Rachel was sitting on the lawn mower. She was screaming and crying, "Dad doesn't love me. He wouldn't even hug me. Mom, it is my fault." After several minutes, I had calmed her down, at least enough to find out what had happened.

What had occurred between the children and their dad during the ten minutes? I soon found out. The boys had asked him, why did he leave? He told them it had nothing to do with them. It was because of their mom. Ryder said, "But dad, you left us too. You never call us. You rarely see us. You promised it would be better." Rachel had started crying and begging him to stay. She said, "Dad, I love you and need you." Before long, an argument broke out, he left, and the children suffered an unneeded rejection again!

There I was with three crying children that I was so worried about. I was also concerned for Ronald. What must he be going through? If there had been a way, I would have gone after him. I knew I would take care of the kids, but who would take care of Ronald? His pain? His hurts? He was not acting like himself. Ronald was a man that was always full of love and happiness, a great dad, and a great husband. Now he is filled with hate and sadness! What is wrong? How is this happening?

Chapter 12

All I could think of was him saying, "Just give me two weeks." Two weeks seemed like months. But finally, he called and told Rachel, "Give your mom a message. Tell your mom to meet me Wednesday, June 15, at 7 P.M. at Tempo's Restaurant for dinner." Excited wasn't the word I felt. Everything would be okay now. We could talk everything out and resolve any issues he was having. Tempo's Restaurant is where I had been wanting to go for months, and he said we didn't have the money to eat there. But now, we were going to have dinner there and talk. This must be a good sign.

I went to the shopping mall and bought me a new sexy black jumpsuit. I did think I looked good. I worked on my hair, my make-up, and my nails. I got dressed! Excited but nervous, I drove to Tempo's. Finally, the two weeks were up. It was a tortuous two weeks, but I did just like he had asked. Now we can talk. Now this can all be resolved.

We got there about the same time. We were cracking jokes as usual. He even slipped and called me, "Honey," a couple of times. He held the restaurant door open for me, and everything seemed to be life as normal. Until, after he ordered, he sat across the table and calmly said, "I have filed for divorce!" As we sat there, I felt I was in another world.

Divorce? I didn't just hear that, I thought. No, this night was for us to talk about any issues and resolve them. I just sat there stunned.

He couldn't mean it. "Why?" I asked him. All he said was, "We just have to for now." "But I don't understand. We just have to for now, what do you mean?" He wouldn't explain. "What does just have to for now, even mean?" He finally said, "I have already seen an attorney. If you go along with everything in the divorce papers, until the divorce, we will do everything as a family. When I come to get the kids, and we go out to eat, you can come with us. If we go to a movie, you can come with us. And who knows, after the divorce, maybe we can date, and maybe even get married again."

"Get married again? If we are going to get married again, why are we getting a divorce?" He said, "We just have to do it this way!" This was all just too mind-boggling. First, I kept thinking about him saying, I don't want to see you for two weeks, and then we will talk. This talk has turned to no conversation, just him saying, he had filed for divorce! Now I am thinking about him saying, if I go along with everything that is in the divorce papers, maybe we can date and maybe get married again. What will that look like? If it's anything like the two weeks were supposed to be, this too, will be just another disaster. Am I just letting him walk all over me? Do

I just love him that much? Or is it, that I have no control over this situation? He apparently has made up his mind for whatever reason, and I am part of this whole terrible ordeal! He reminded me if I don't go along with everything, then things will get dirty. I thought, is he trying to threaten me? Why is he talking like this?

All I could think about was loving the man I married. I asked him, "Can we wait for a few months? Why are we rushing with this decision? This decision affects not only us but our children for the rest of our life. Let's just wait for a while and think this through and be sure." He said, "No, because then it would be Christmas." I said, "Fine, after Christmas, then we can decide." He insisted, "No, it had to be done before December." I just kept thinking, why does it have to be before December? Why rush this and ruin Christmas when we can wait, take our time, and think about it? If we waited until after Christmas, it could make a horrible Christmas, at least a bearable Christmas.

Our food came, and we got off the divorce subject. I was grateful for that. That was one conversation I had all I could take for one night. We started talking about our recent vacation to Long Boat Key, Florida, and how nice everything was. The hotel was Holiday Inn, and he said that was his favorite chain hotel. I said, "Yeah, we have always had good times. You know there is a Holiday Inn just down the street. Why don't we go there after dinner, and we can talk some more?" He informed me his attorney had advised him not to be seen with any women, so he couldn't. I said, "The attorney wouldn't mind if it's me. I am your wife. Let's call and see. Besides, you are being seen with me here." Nothing I said was convincing. He just kept saying, "No, we can't do that."

We joked for a while. I tried to get him to see the funny side of me. Maybe he would remember all the fun days we used to share. The night was ending. I used all the time as best I could to convince him what we had was worth saving. I tried to get him to postpone everything, but nothing I said or anything I did, would change his mind.

As we were leaving, he told me he was going to the car dealership to move some cars for a car show. I offered to help; he wouldn't let me. I was so disappointed. I had always helped him with business adventures. Now I couldn't help him. At least he walked me to my car, no kiss, no hug, he just said, "Good night; think about what I said." I assured him I would.

I left and went home to our three beautiful kids, that had built their hopes up that their dad had met me to tell me he was coming home. I never should have let them think anything, at least not that. But I just knew in my heart, that was what was happening. I was so happy when I left the house to go meet their dad. They could see my happiness. This was going to be hard to confront these excited children. I was going to bust their bubble and their hopes.

When I got home, I knew I had to look into their eyes and once again break their hearts and say, Dad is not coming home. When I got home, I opened the door, and there they were, sitting on the couch, waiting for me. Rachel said, "Is Dad with you?" I said, "No honey, he had to go move some cars for a car show." "Is he coming home later?" I said, "Let's go into the living room where it is quiet, and we can talk."

We all went into the living room. I said, "Guys, you know how much I love you and how much I love your dad. I would do anything for any of you. I would do anything to make our family a complete family again. But sometimes, we do not get what we want. Sometimes people make decisions that we don't like. We need to accept that is their decision, although we don't understand why they are deciding that. It may not be the best decision for anyone, but it is their decision to make."

"What are you trying to say?" Rachel asked me. I said, "Sweetheart, your dad has, for whatever reason, decided he is not coming home." "No, momma you must make him come home." "Rachel, this is what I am talking about. He has his decisions to make, decisions I do not understand, nor do I like. But a decision we all must accept. All we can do now is pray for your dad. We know that God will help us all get through this. We have one another. We are strong. We can do this!"

I had to be honest with them. I knew facing facts, as bad as they were, had to be much better than constantly broken hopes. I said, "Daddy is not coming home, but Daddy said that the next visits y'all had together with him that I could come too. So, when he comes over, and you go somewhere, we will all go. It might be out to eat or to go to a movie, wherever it is, we would all go together.

You know every time we have had a challenge, we talk about it, pray about it, and God hears our prayers. It isn't always answered the way we want him to answer it, but God will be our strength every day with every trial. God is with us now, and he will not let us down."

Chapter 13

I do not know if I will ever understand why he left. I was raised until death do you part. It was scriptural. I had been a virgin when I married him. Now here I am, thirty-four years old, with three kids and my husband of my youth saying he wanted a divorce. He was blocking me totally out of his life. It couldn't be. It just couldn't be.

I told Ronald I would agree to his plans. I would accept his divorce as he had asked, if; he would keep to his agreement and allow me to be part of his life when he is seeing the children. I am not sure why I accepted it, not seeing the documentation of what he wanted, except for once again, I trusted him to be fair. Also, I only told him that for two reasons. One, I could be with him, and we could be a complete family. Secondly, praying that, hopefully this family time would make him see the wonderful life we had. Hopefully, he would realize he didn't want to walk away from it.

He stuck to what he said he would do and included me in the visitations. The next visits Ronald would have with the kids were wonderful. Ronald would come over to see the kids, and I would fix supper. We would go to the movies or to Opryland Park or go play miniature golf. We would laugh and have a wonderful time. Everything was beautiful until, it was time to go to bed. At night he would leave and go back to his parents' house.

I felt confident that things would work out. All we needed was just a little time. I loved him, and I would give him time to see and feel that love. I was going to agree to everything in hopes of getting things to work out later. After all, what other option did I have?

But as time went by, I thought this charade was just confusing the children and me. Although it made me happy, and they were happy. I began to feel that me agreeing with Ronald, to be with him and kids, was just giving all of us false hope. The kids would tell me how wonderful it was doing everything as a family. Should I continue this charade? Is it going to help anything? I didn't know what to do.

I just needed to try to find out what was really going on. Knowing the truth is the only way I can have any sanity. But how could I get to the truth? He won't tell me. I am going to have to be very observant, and pay close attention, and see if there are any clues to all his insanity.

Chapter 14

Ronald called and said, "I am going to get an apartment. Living with my parents is just too hard for everyone." I said, "Why don't you live here? You have already filed for divorce. This way, while the divorce is going through, you would be here with the kids. It would save you a lot of money." He was quick to say, "The whole reason I left, to begin with, was to be alone." I said, "Ronald, I know you had to leave to think and make decisions. You have already made your decision; you filed for divorce." He reminded me, "Ramona I know, but just remember, maybe after the divorce, we can date and possibly even get married again."

Once again, I thought this is crazy, but I just needed to let it go. I need to keep being the wife he knew. I would dream that it could happen. I would pray, wish, and dream that he would come back, and our family would once again be together, and this whole crazy ordeal would be behind us. But I couldn't help wondering what the reality would be. I wish I knew the truth as to why he left to begin with, perhaps, this would somehow make sense to me.

He asked for some furniture for his apartment and gave me a letter with a list of things he needed.

Ramona,

Here is a list of the things I'll need to get from the house. It's either this or I'll have to buy things without any money.

Stereo, 9" color tv and stand, Grandfather clock, a dresser or chest of drawers, my recliner, video camera, pictures in the foyer, some dishes, glasses, knives, forks, spoons, pots, pan, skillet, a pair of sheets, pillowcases, (2) pillows, end and coffee table in the dark room, some towels and wash clothes.

If any of these items contradict your thinking, you can call me on Wednesday between 9 o'clock and 10 o'clock in the morning. If I don't hear from you, then I will assume all is approved. By the way, I will be moving on Wednesday night between about 6:45 and 8:30. I would think it better if you AND the children were not present. Again, if this represents a problem, call me between the previously mentioned hours on Wednesday morning.

Ronald

P.S. You're really doing a terrible job of getting the kids through this. You should have insisted Reid go to his camp, but it doesn't matter - I'm getting all tensed up just thinking about having to come over there tonight and Wednesday night. So, I guess I've said enough - better close before I say more than would be advantageous for me to say.

I was so surprised when I got this letter from him. It seemed so cold, so formal, and so nasty. Here, I thought we were getting along well. He, on the other hand, from the sound of this, did not think the same way. But why? I couldn't figure out anything. I don't know why he left, why he wanted a divorce, or why he was acting so hateful. Or what was he talking about, I was doing a terrible job getting the kids through this. I didn't even know him anymore. What was making him change from the man I had known?

For now, I guess I would need to keep on trying to figure him and our situation out. I would keep on thanking God in all things and trusting God to help me through this mystery. For now, I will get out the things on his list. After all, all of this is his too. We had worked for 15 years and had accumulated it all. Of course, I would share it. I began to get out towels, silverware, pots and pans, a shower curtain and I had to include a toilet brush. That one gave me a thrill. I thought, sure, let him clean the commode a few times. Let's see just how long he will stay away. I gave him the coffee pot and the coffee. I was being the sweet little housewife to show him how much I loved him, and how agreeable I was. He was going to come over Wednesday to pick up these things.

I called Mom and asked if she could keep the kids Wednesday night. I told her that Ronald was coming over to get some things, and I really didn't want the kids here when he came. It would just be too hard for them. She was shocked things had progressed to this stage. She was just like I was; she was hoping and praying that Ronald would come home. She could always see, just like I could and everyone else could, how happy we were. Why couldn't he see it?

She said, "Of course, bring them before supper and you and the kids can eat here. Then they can stay the night." She was always very supportive and always there for me when I needed her. Especially now, while I was going through this situation. I was more grateful now than ever for her.

Wednesday, the kids and I drove over to Mom's and had supper. I left after supper and came home. I decided I would park my car at one of our neighbors' so Ronald wouldn't know I was home. I just had to be there and see who he would bring to the house. What would they say? Was it going to be a woman with him? I was so confused. I felt the only way I was going to find out anything was to do this. He could have saved me from all this insanity and curiosity. Why wouldn't he just talk to me and tell why he was leaving? Why couldn't he tell me so I could understand?

I hid upstairs in Rachel's bathroom in her bathtub. I was afraid he would know I was home. Our dog, Beau, followed me upstairs, I panicked. Oh No, I am going to get busted. Beau always followed me everywhere I went. If he didn't see Beau, and looked for him, he would find me. Fortunately, he didn't look for Beau. I guess he was so focused on getting whatever he had come for that Beau never entered his mind.

He came with a male friend. I was upstairs, and it was hard to hear any conversation. I heard another voice, it was a guy's voice too, one I didn't recognize. He quickly got the furniture and left. I waited for a few minutes to be sure the door I thought shut was indeed him leaving. I also wanted to be sure he wasn't coming back in for something else before I left the bathroom. Finally, it had been quiet for a few minutes. I went downstairs to see what he had taken.

He had taken the boxes of personal and kitchen stuff I had boxed. I didn't see any furniture gone, not even the grandfather clock. Then I went upstairs to the bonus room. When I got there, it looked like he had cleared out "all" the furniture. He got the couch, game table and chairs, and the dining room buffet. I had no idea at the time he was getting that furniture.

I sat there holding Beau and talking to myself and to Beau. I just kept repeating; I just cannot believe this. What will I ever do without Ronald? Without his love, his strength, and his ability to solve decisions that we always had to make. Just how can I?

The next morning, I found myself at the same spot I sat crying the night before. I had to get up, shower, go to Mom's, and get the kids. I got up and thought, how will I tell them about the furniture being gone? I had to find a way. I couldn't let them just go into the house and go upstairs and see the almost empty room.

When I went to Mom's, I tried to have a cheerful face. I asked the kids, "Are you ready to go home?" They loved going to Mom's, where they were totally spoiled, with love, fudge, cookies, and everything all kids love. But they were ready to come home. They said, "Yes." They hugged Mom bye, and we all walked outside. Mom hugged me and asked, "Are you okay?" I lied and said, "Yes, I will call you later." I hugged and thanked her for keeping the kids, and we left.

I had no idea how the kids would feel when they saw the furniture gone from the bonus room. I knew they would be upset. I just didn't know what they would think or how it would affect them. While we were in the car, I explained to the kids what had happened the night before. I explained that their dad needed some furniture and some items for his apartment. I explained that we had purchased them together and he had the right to some furniture. I explained once again everything would be okay.

Reid says, "Mom, I understand, but what will my friends think? What will I tell them? How will I explain to them our furniture is gone? My friends will think that we have been robbed." They understood he had to have some furniture and wasn't upset about him taking it. They were afraid their friends would see the furniture gone and ask questions. They were embarrassed. Just another issue the kids had to deal with due to their dad's decisions.

Chapter 15

Ronald had told me that a sheriff would come to the house and serve me with divorce papers. I had no idea how a divorce event happened. My sister had gotten divorced, but I never talked to her about the legal aspects. I guess I just thought I would get something in the mail about a court date. But not that simple; it had to be a sheriff coming to the door. This just could not be happening. How could I stop this? Can I delay this? I need to find a way to give Ronald time to come to his senses. I know he loves me and the kids. What is wrong with him?

I kept anticipating the sheriff coming to the door with the divorce papers, but it never happened. Each time Ronald came over, he included me in the visit, and he would stay at the house longer. We would have a wonderful time. Could it be he was just testing me for some reason, and he hadn't even filed? Maybe he just wanted to know what my reaction would be if he did file. I wouldn't dare ask him. I decided to call the courthouse. I called the Stanson County Courthouse divorce court to see if the papers had been filed. Every day I called, and every day, the answer was no. There were no papers on file. Then July 1, when I called, I was told, "Yes ma'am, we have the papers here. Judge Wiser will be the judge." It was true; he had filed. This couldn't happen, but it was happening.

When would the sheriff arrive? Would I say anything to Ronald about me calling the courthouse? I just couldn't, and I wouldn't. I was too afraid that would make him mad, and then he would stop coming to the house.

Ryder turned nine on July 4th in just a few days. I didn't want any issues to come up to mess up his birthday. Ronald had said he would come over. I was in hopes this would be a fun-filled day. Hopefully, Ronald would see our happy family. He would see the fun he was walking away from. I knew he would eventually cancel all the paperwork. I kept thinking how wonderful this day was going to be. We would swim in the pool, grill out, go to Opryland Park, and see the fireworks. We would be a wonderful, happy family.

July the 4th, finally, was here. Ronald pulled into the driveway, and I yelled upstairs, "Ryder, your daddy is here." He came running down the stairs, and as always, he ran and jumped into his dad's arms. "Daddy, come look at the cake Mama made me. She made me a Dukes of Hazard cake." Ronald and Ryder came into the kitchen to see Ryder's birthday cake. Ronald seemed impressed, "Ryder, that is cool. I love the car your mom put on top." I told Ronald that Ryder wanted mountains on each side of the valley and the car jumping over the valley; that's how I made it.

"Ronald, Ryder wants to grill out, is that okay with you?" Ronald said, "Sure, let's start up the grill." Everything was going great. I wasn't about to say a word about calling the courthouse. I just did my best to put it all out of my mind. I stayed in the kitchen as he went out to start the grill. I patted the meat and got out all the food we needed. By now, all the kids and their dad were in the pool. Swimming and splashing like everything was perfect. It did seem perfect today. We grilled out and finished eating.

I went into the bedroom to put on my swimsuit. I heard someone behind me. I turned around to see who it was; it was Ronald. Our eyes caught just at the right time. I reached up and kissed him, and he kissed me back. We walked into the bathroom. When we did, he turned and locked the door behind us. He hugged me, and we stood there caressing one another. I unbuttoned his shirt and slid it off. Then, as abruptly as it began, he said, "Wait! This isn't right. We can't do this." I said, "Do what, Ronald? We are married." He said, "Estranged!" Then he walked out of the room, putting his shirt back on.

Why couldn't he realize what we felt was right? Was good? This was our normal response. We were always so passionate and affectionate with one another. It seemed for a moment; we both had forgotten what we had been going through. For a moment; he had forgotten that he had moved out and that he had told me he had filed for a divorce. Worse yet, I knew from my call to the courthouse yesterday, it was true. He had filed, and it was already recorded and being processed.

I got dressed, wiped away my tears, took a deep breath, and went on outside. It was a beautiful day; it was about 89 degrees and sunny. We sat on the deck and watched the kids swimming in the pool.

I got to thinking. He had the pool put in the yard and he built the deck all in the spring of 1982. We were so happy. He evidently had no plans on leaving when he had all that work done here.

So, what happened from summer to May that I had not noticed? We sat and watched the kids swim, dive off the diving board, and play. Everyone was having a wonderful time. Ronald said, "Hey kids, are we going to Opryland?" "Yes," they all responded at about the same time with so much excitement, "Yes." He said, "Then let's get going. Ryder, you can ride with me." I asked, "What do you mean?" He coldly said, "I am not going to come back to the house after the fireworks, so we need to take two cars."

Why couldn't he, just this one day, give 100%? Why couldn't his family be first? At least, this one day? I don't understand. I tried to explain, "Ronald, Ryder really wanted you to shoot fireworks with him off the deck, like we have always done." Ronald agreed but wanted to do it before we left for the park. I wanted to say, forget it, it is daylight; how much fun will that be? I wouldn't do that to Ryder. Ronald might walk away, and Ryder would be upset. Who knows, maybe after we get to Opryland Park and are having such a wonderful time, he will decide to come back over. All I could do at this point would be to hope that would happen.

I went out into the garage to get the fireworks and the lighter. Ryder loved this part of his birthday each year, and I tried to get his favorite sparklers and fireworks that he loved. These last few weeks have been so horrible. I wanted to try my best to make Ryder's birthday one he would remember and remember with happiness. We shot the fireworks off the deck, and then we left for Opryland. Just like Ronald wanted, we went in 2 cars. The kids all wanted to ride with their dad. I drove my car and followed them to the park.

It was so crowded at the park, and very late by the time we got there. I didn't know how much we could even do. We did get to ride some rides. The kids were so cute. They made sure that their dad and I were together on the log ride. All three jumped in the front, leaving nowhere but the back for Ronald and me to sit. It was wonderful laying back on his chest, the warmth of his body close to mine. We were so wet when we got off the log ride, we decided this would be a great time to ride the grizzle water ride. This ride was the same way. The kids sat together, leaving their dad and me, side by side. This ride swaying over the rapids, Ronald and

I were constantly falling into one another. Of course, I didn't mind one bit. We left there and went to get a good place to see the fireworks.

The fireworks at Opryland Park were always unbelievable. The officials in charge weren't worried about the cost at all. They wanted the fireworks to be the best in the nation. They were always beautiful. We were walking across the bridge to go see the fireworks; I stopped, turned, and said to Ronald, "Thank you for this time. I will never forget this night."

I haven't. It was a clear night, full of stars, a slight breeze blowing, and I was with the only man I had ever loved. It was the perfect romantic setting. But the night ended just as he said it would. The fireworks ended. The park closed. We took the tram to our cars. When the tram stopped, we all got off. He said, "Good night." He hugged each of the kids. Then he said, "Love you." Of course, the "Love you" was not for me. He then got in his car. He went his way, and the three kids and I got in the car and came home. I was emotionally drained. I just knew or hoped so badly that he would change his mind and come home with us. But that didn't happen.

The kids were tired. It had been a long day. They all fell asleep in the car. That was really a good thing. That way, they couldn't think about what didn't happen today. We got home, and the kids hugged me and went upstairs to get ready for bed. In just a few moments, I went up and said prayers with them, hugged each one, and told them sweet dreams, I love you, and I will see you in the morning. Then I went downstairs to another night of being alone. I sat in the kitchen. I just sat there once again, thinking, and trying to understand. I couldn't. I couldn't understand and I couldn't understand why he wouldn't talk to me about it. I was tired. It was getting very late, and I needed some sleep. I hoped maybe tomorrow things will make sense.

Chapter 16

I went to bed. I laid there and tried to go to sleep. I had so much on my mind. It was midnight, and the phone rang, it was Ronald. He was screaming at me; "You ----- you took my favorite towel." "What are you talking about?" "The big rust-colored towel, you took it." I told him, "There were two. Yes, I used one. I...." He hung up before I could say another word. I thought that was so weird. It is midnight; what is the deal with the towel? We had two rust-colored towels in the linen closet. When he came over, he got them out, I thought, for us to use at our pool. So, I used one and I left the other on the bench at the deck for him to use. I never thought another thing about it until he called. His phone call made me wonder if he got the two towels out and had planned on taking them both with him. When he left, he must have grabbed the towel, thinking he had two, but he only had one. What was the deal? Why was he so upset about a towel? Now, my mind was really going crazy while I was trying to go to sleep. It took me forever that night to finally doze off.

The kids woke me early. They were hungry. When I woke up, I was hungry too. It had been a long time since hamburgers by the pool. I got up and made the best pancakes. The kids were still excited from the night before. They wanted to go to their friends and tell them about their day at Opryland and Ryder's birthday celebration. They wanted to tell their friends about doing things with their mom and dad as a family. I wondered if they did this, if they thought no one would suspect their dad had moved out. If everything was normal, then there would be no questions to answer. They were happy this morning, and I wanted them to stay that way as long as possible. I told them, "Sure, you can go to your friends. Have fun."

They left. I cleaned up the kitchen and started on the laundry. As I was doing the laundry, I began thinking about that strange phone call last night and that dang rust-colored towel. The way he called me "-----." That was the first time he had ever done that. I was thinking about the wonderful day before and the last few weeks. I was thinking about the night with Ronald when we met for dinner at Tempos Restaurant. Remembering how wonderful our time together was until he told me he had filed for divorce. Then told me that a sheriff would come to the house with divorce papers.

I could not believe any of this. My mind was such a puzzle. This just could not be happening. I just kept thinking like I had the last few months. How could I stop this? Why is he doing this? I must delay the divorce and give him time to come to his senses. But how do I do that? I know he loves me and the kids. What is wrong with him? He is making drastic changes without even realizing what he is doing. It seems like he is in a trance or something.

We had such a wonderful day on July 4th. The kids and I spent the next few days doing normal things. The kids were playing, and I was cleaning the house. In between chores, I kept thinking about the clerk at the courthouse saying, "Yes, the divorce records are recorded." I kept thinking about what Ronald had said, "A sheriff would come to the house and serve me divorce papers." I was getting so anxious about the next steps and when everything would take place.

It didn't take long. The following Wednesday, just like Ronald said, the sheriff came to the house. The doorbell rang; I went to the door. The guy at the door asked, "Are you Ramona Jenkins?" I said, "Yes." Then, just as I feared, he said, "Mrs. Jenkins, I have some papers for you." I immediately started crying, I couldn't control the tears. He apologized and said, "I am sorry, but I must do this." I said, "No, you don't. Can't you say I wasn't home?" He was very compassionate. He said, "Honey, I wish I could, but I can't do that." "Yes, you can. What will it hurt?" He then asked, "Do you have an attorney?" I told him, "No." He said, "I will give you some names of some good ones, and you need to select one and contact them." I told him I would and then I asked if we could go outside to the back deck. He agreed. We walked outside onto the deck, and I wrote down the attorney's names. I poured out my heart to him and just kept crying. He apologized again as he handed me the papers. He again said, "I am so sorry." I told him, "I understand, it's your job. Thank you for listening and for the list of attorney's names." He then left.

Thank goodness, the kids were all at the neighbor's playing while waiting for their dad to come pick them up for the afternoon. I stayed outside on the deck and kept crying. It seemed like hours. I heard the doorbell ring again. I cleaned up my face and answered the door. It was the same sheriff that had served me papers. He said, "Mrs. Jenkins, do you have the papers handy?" "Yes sir, they are right here." He said, "Give them back to me, and I will hide them behind the file, and say you weren't home." I hugged him and thanked him. I told him how much I appreciated it. He said, "I don't know how much more time it will give you, but maybe some time for you to prepare yourself for what is ahead." Then he turned and left. He got into his car and pulled out of the driveway. As the sheriff was leaving, I saw Ronald pulling into the driveway. I knew Ronald wouldn't know it was the sheriff since the sheriff was in an unmarked car.

Ronald walked up to the door. I was standing in the foyer. He came inside and said, "Who was that?" I couldn't say, oh, it was the sheriff coming back to get the divorce papers to hide them for me. I said, "Just a salesman!" Yeah, I did lie at this point, but I was in survival mode. He acted like he knew I was lying. At least he didn't ask any more questions. Besides, why did he care anyway? Unless I had told him the truth, then he would have cared. He would have been on the phone calling his attorney before I could have turned around. I really and truly was only trying to delay this divorce for all of us.

By now, the kids had seen their dad had driven into the driveway and they had came home. They went upstairs and got their things to leave with their dad. They gave me a hug and a kiss and said, "Bye, Mom, we will see you later." This time I stayed home.

As always, they were so excited to see their dad. Ronald had told them that the divorce would mean that he would see them more. That their life would be better. They wanted to believe him and hoped it was true.

They left, and I sat there thinking about what the sheriff had said. I sat there looking at divorce attorney names while, at the same time, hoping I would not need an attorney. I did not need an attorney for now. The sheriff took the papers and was going to put them in the back of the file. How much time would that give me? I had no idea, but for now, I would focus on my love for Ronald. I wouldn't even think about divorcing him. I would continue to pray that God's will be done in our life. I would lean on the verse I was led to back in May when I hit Ronald's car. "In all things, give thanks, for this is the will of the Lord for you." I would focus on God's word and our wonderful family.

I did exactly that. I stopped and prayed. After I prayed, I called my friend, Sybil. I talked to her about the sheriff and the list of attorney names he gave me. I thought maybe she might have known one of them. She had been divorced a long time ago. But she didn't recognize any of the names.

When I told her about the sheriff coming back to get the papers, she was totally shocked. She said, "That is God working for you. That guy jeopardized his job by doing that. Maybe this is your answer to prayer. If everything does proceed, at least this will give you some time to understand, some time to maybe find out why he wants this divorce in the first place." She was right. I needed time to understand.

Sybil suggested that I return to the hospital to see if I could get my job back. She reminded me, "Ramona, he has filed for divorce, gotten an apartment, and you have been served the divorce papers." I said, "Yes, Sybil, but the sheriff came and got them, so technically, I haven't been served yet." "Ramona, it is just a matter of time until the sheriff is back at your door. It is time to pull yourself out of this shock and plan for your future. It is time to face reality." I didn't like hearing this, but I knew it was true.

I enjoyed my job. I was a good employee, and hopefully, they would hire me back. If they gave me the same part-time job, 11 P.M.-7 A.M., Tuesday and Wednesday, then I would still be with kids in the waking hours. Rachel is 14. Our neighbors live close by, and if there was an immediate emergency, they would be here instantly. Well, if they knew the situation. I guess it is time to talk to them about what is going on before I pursue my old job position at the hospital.

While the kids are with Ronald, this is a good time to call a couple of neighbors. I would only talk to the neighbors that I knew would keep this confidential. The neighbors that I knew would listen, and not judge. First, I called Marilyn. She had been keeping the kids a lot and probably wondered why suddenly, I needed some help with the kids. I called her and asked her if she had some time to talk. She said, "Sure, the kids are gone. Stan and I are here and not doing anything. Why don't you walk on over?" I told her, "Thank you, I will be right over." I was emotional, but time to let someone that lived close by know that the kids and I were living alone.

I got there and knocked on the door. She answered it and immediately gave me a big hug. She said, "Ramona, honey, we know." I was so shocked. I just sighed and said, "How do you know?" She said, "Come on in, and I will get you a glass of iced tea. Stan is in the den." I walked into the kitchen with her as she got my tea. Then we walked into the den. Stan got up and gave me a big hug, and asked, "Are you okay?" I began tearing up but tried hard to hold back as much as I could. I said, "I am trying to be okay." I understand he said, "We are here for you." I thanked him. Marilyn said, "I didn't want to call you and let you know we knew. I knew you would talk to us when you were ready." I asked, "How do you know?"

We were out walking the night Ronald came and got some furniture. Of course, we had no idea what was going on. We had never heard of any problems, and you guys always seemed so happy. We just thought y'all were getting rid of some furniture and getting some new. We didn't think anything about it. We saw Ronald in the driveway. We just walked up and said, "Did you get new furniture?" He told us, "No getting a divorce." Honey, we were flabbergasted. Not only of the news but how outspoken and cold he was about it. Marilyn turned to Stan at that point and said, "Tell Ramona what you told me when we left their house."

Stan looked at me with empathy and kindness. "Ramona, I have no idea for sure what is going on. But in the past, when I have seen men suddenly do this and be so cold and determined like he sounded; I don't want to upset you, but my thoughts are he is having an affair." I just sat there listening. I was thinking no, that is crazy. Ronald wouldn't do that. The only thing I could say was, "I really don't think so. Ronald had told me that he had been really stressed due to work and not getting his book published. I think he just needs a little time, and then everything will be okay." He said, "I sure hope so. But during this time, we are here for you. Day or night, just call, and we will be there whatever you need." Marilyn chimed in, "Yes, day or night."

I said, "Thank you so much. You guys have always been great neighbors and friends. It means the world to me that I know you are close by and here for me. It is scary. I don't have any idea what my future looks like. I must trust God and live day by day. All I can do is try my best to keep it together for the kids right now."

Marilyn said, "You are doing a great job." "Well, speaking of jobs. That is one reason, besides telling you that he had left, I wanted to come over and talk to you. I need to go back to work. I think right now, is time for me to see if the hospital will hire me back on my previous 11 P.M.-7 A.M. shift on Tuesday and Wednesday nights. I think Rachel is old enough to take care of the boys. After all, I would get them to bed before I left and be home before they woke up. I just needed to ask if Rachel could call you guys if they needed anything during the night, until I could get home." Without hesitation, they said, "Absolutely! Anything you need."

That was such a relief. I knew they would be understanding. I just didn't know they already knew that Ronald had moved out. That sure made our visit much easier.

I didn't have to go into any detail. I would get through this! I was seeing as time went by, that people were supporting me emotionally. I think they all thought what I didn't want to accept. That he probably was having an affair, and our family was probably ending forever. Perhaps it is time that I pursue what the truth really is and try to go forward.

The kids still weren't home. I was walking across the yard, and I saw my neighbors that lived beside us out in the yard. They were great neighbors. I thought it is time to talk to them about my situation too. I thought with them being outside, they would probably think I was stopping by to say, hi. If I didn't feel good talking about it, I wouldn't. If I did, I hoped they would be as kind, and understanding as Stan and Marilyn had been.

As I approached, Al hollered, "Hi, their neighbor, we haven't seen you in a while." "I know I have been busy. What have y'all been up to?" Al started telling me of his mother moving into their home and of the preparations they had made for her. She was a lady I had met before and was a very sweet, kind woman. I let him tell me about it. Then I said, "That's strange." He said, "What is strange?" "Some neighbors are moving in, and some neighbors are moving out." He asked, "Are you moving?" "No, not me. Ronald has decided he needs a break for a while." He was stunned. I said it so passively; I think he was confused. I didn't want them to think it was a big deal. I just wanted them to know I was alone with the kids.

I told them that Ronald told me he was stressed with work, and he needed some time alone. I think it will all be okay. I am going to reapply and try to get my job back at the hospital, working part-time at night. Is it okay if I give the kids y'all's number in case they need anything? Anita spoke up then, "Of course, Ramona, for sure, and tell them to call anytime. We will keep a watch out for them. Is there anything else you need?" "How about a prayer or two?" She hugged me and said, "Of course, we are here for you." Al chimed in, "Absolutely, and please do not hesitate to call anytime." I said, "Thanks." I walked back home before Ronald got back with the kids.

The kids were never gone with their dad for a long time. Each time he would pick them up for a visit, he would only have a few hours at a time for them. They would leave with such joy and come home with so much sadness. It broke my heart to see my children hurt. It was the hardest part of all of this. Seeing their pain was worse than any pain I was enduring or could ever endure.

The kids came home at about 5 P.M. That was the usual time Ronald would bring them home. Once again, they came home sad. I asked, "What is wrong?" Rachel said, "Mom, Dad just seems so different. All he ever wants to do is to go to grandma's and sit and talk at her house. We are bored there. We want to be with Dad and do fun things with him." I just listened. What else could I do? His time with them is his time. I have zero control over how they spend it. I suggested, "Let's go see a movie tonight. That will be fun." That cheered them up, at least for the night. One day at a time is all I could do-just one day at a time.

Chapter 17

A few days passed, and we had not heard from their dad. The kids would call him at his work, the only phone number they had to reach him. He wouldn't be at work. They would leave a message. It would be two days before he called them back. Nothing seemed to ever change. When he did call back, they would ask to see him. He would usually say he couldn't. He always had an excuse. He was tired. He was busy. He was sick. He would tell them, "I will see you every two weeks. That is what the attorney said I should do. I should pick you up every two weeks." Like the kids could understand attorney language. I doubt she even said that.

The kids were beginning to be so upset with all his excuses. They just could not understand. How could they? I couldn't. This was the dad they loved with all their heart. This was the dad that was always there for them. This was the dad who coached the little league and football when the boys played. The same dad that took them to amusement parks and vacations. This is the same dad who went to all of Rachel's cheering events. He prayed with them, went to church with them, and suddenly, not only had he moved out, but now had no time for them. Gradually, the rejection the kids felt was overwhelming. They were all confused.

It seemed Rachel was having a harder time now with her dad's rejections. She was a 14-yr-old, a teenager who had wrapped her entire world around being daddy's little girl. Now, suddenly, he wouldn't or couldn't have time for her. It seemed he just didn't understand what he was doing to them. I had to convince him, somehow, how important it is to give them some time.

I called him at his work and begged him to see them. I told him, "You can see them anytime, not just every two weeks. You can see them whenever you want. They need to spend some time with you." Once again, he used the excuse, I am sick, and I am going home. I begged again, "If only for a few minutes, Ronald, you don't realize what these kids have been going through. Can't you just meet them at the corner grocery and buy them ice cream or something? Just spend a few minutes with the kids." "No," he shouted, "I am going home." Slam went the phone. Sure, seemed like he was getting good at hanging up on me to end our conversations.

What was wrong with him? What had happened so drastically to cause this wonderful man to turn on me and our children? I don't understand. How could I explain this to them? I covered for him and told the kids he was sick. Although, I didn't believe it for one minute. They were too smart, and they didn't buy it either.

"Sure, Mom," they said. I just kept comforting them and telling them your dad loves you. He does love you! The more

I said it, the more frustrated they seemed to get. Reid said, "Mom, if he loved us, he would be with us." Sometimes, kids can see things that we don't want to see. As an adult, I guess I was really living in a dreamland! It was I just knew Ronald, and I knew something had to be terribly wrong to make him act this way. I had to figure out what, and I knew we could fix it.

I stayed up most of the night so confused and upset. I cried for me, for him, and for our children. I decided the next morning I would go over to his apartment. I would ask if he would please try to understand what we were going through. Ask him to see the kids for a while, if just for a little time.

It was his day off. I knew he had a golf game, and there was no way he would have time except before or after the game. I thought just maybe he would change his mind and decide to give the kids some time before his golf game. I thought surely, if he realized how important it was, he would. Or at least the man I married would give the kids time. This guy, I wasn't sure who he was, what he was thinking, or what he would do.

I got up early, at 5 A.M. I wanted to be there by 6 A.M. That way, I would see him before he left for the golf game. I didn't want to miss him. When I got there, I looked in the parking lot to find his car. I drove around until I found it. I knew his apartment number from the divorce papers. His apartment was on the 3rd floor, right beside the stairs. I walked up the 3 flights. I thought if I woke him up, the answer would be no. He would be mad at me. I knew I had to wait until I knew he was up and awake. I went to knock on the door. Before I knocked, I listened for a television, radio, or something to know he was up. There was silence. I had seen his car there; he had to be home. I decided to sit on the steps and wait until I heard some noise. Then I would knock. I wanted to give him time to get up, get his morning coffee, and get dressed.

I just sat down outside his apartment door on the steps and waited. It was now 6:30 A.M. or so. Finally, about 7 A.M., I heard some conversation and knew he had gotten up and turned on the television. I got up to knock. About that time, I heard laughter, a woman's laughter. My heart is in disbelief. I paused and stood quietly outside his door. I knew there was someone else in the room, I was pretty sure it was a female. What should I do? Should I turn and leave? Should I never let him know I was here? Am I right, is there a girl in his apartment? Should I knock on the door and let him know I know he was with someone? I wasn't sure! I was so surprised. I knew unless I faced him, face to face, he would never admit it. So, I knocked and knocked again.

Silence, total silence. All the conversation, noise, and laughter just stopped. I waited and knocked again, no answer. I thought, okay, sooner or later, he will have to come out, there is only one exit. I will sit quietly and wait. I did. I don't know how I sat there not saying a word. About 30 minutes had passed. During that time, I kept asking myself, who is the girl? Is it someone I know? What will she look like? Is this really happening? I was so shocked and in disbelief. So, this is why he is acting like he is. He couldn't love her. He just recently started acting like he doesn't love me. When I see her, how will I feel?

I didn't know any of the answers. I did know I had to know what was going on. I had to see her. I had to see what or who was creating this wonderful man into someone I didn't know. Then, finally, I heard some conversation. I got up and looked at the door. The doorknob started turning. I got closer to the door. The door finally opened. When it did, I put my foot in the doorway. I said, "Ronald, I want to talk to you," and I proceeded into the apartment.

I sat down in "our" recliner and calmly said, "I want to see her." He said, "No!" I said, "Yes, I am going to see her! I will not leave until I do." He knew among my good qualities; I was stubborn. He knew I would be determined at this point. He yelled and screamed at me while trying to pull me out of the recliner. He finally succeeded and got me out of the recliner, but I was not going to leave. I was as determined I wasn't going to leave without seeing her as he was determined I was going to leave and not see her. He kept attempting to throw me out of the apartment. I jerked at the furniture and knocked things off the wall while grabbing anything to keep me from leaving the apartment. We were both getting exhausted. At one time, I felt I had physical power over him.

I slipped out of his grasp, and I started down the hallway. I caught a look in his eye, and I knew he was going to shove me into the bathroom. I thought once he had me in the bathroom, he would hold the door shut, and she would slip out. I would never see her. I quickly turned toward the other way. We continued knocking over furniture, and he pushed me down. I came so close to hitting the wood frame of what was now the upside-down recliner, stabbing me in the stomach. I was scared for my life. At this point, seeing her was not even important. I had three children to care for, and I had to live. I dropped my defense, and he pushed me out the door.

I was out of breath, hot, and broken hearted. I went to the next apartment, knocked on the door, and asked for help. A lady answered. She would not open the door. She refused to help me. As I was going downstairs, I saw a door open to an empty apartment. I thought if I could just get some water. I went into the kitchen, where I got a drink of water. A guy from the phone department was there. He asked me, "What

are you doing here? Are you okay, what happened to you?"
He could easily tell I had been in a scuffle and almost totally
out of breath.

I took a deep breath and told him, "My husband was
upstairs with another woman, and we had a fight." He told
me to stay there in the apartment and he was going to call
the police. I told him, "No, not the police, just the security
guard." He immediately went for help. I couldn't just stay at
that apartment, I needed to see this girl. This girl that is
ruining our lives. While he was gone, I went upstairs to see
if Ronald would let me in. Of course, he said, "No!" I told
him, "Fine, I will stand outside until I die if I have to." Why
I thought he would let me in at this point, who knows? I
guess by now, I was as crazy as he was. Surprisingly,
suddenly, and very angrily, he agreed. He said, "Okay, fine,
I will let you see her. Give me a minute." I never intended to
cause any harm to him or her. I only wanted to see her.

While I was waiting for Ronald to finally open the door,
the security guard came upstairs. I explained what had
happened. He advised me, "I had no right to be there. I
wasn't renting the apartment and that I should leave." I asked
him, "Please go with me to the door. I just want my watch,
that got broken in his apartment, and I want to see his
girlfriend." The security guard asked, "If I go with you to the
door, and you get to see her, and you get your watch, will

119

you leave?" "Yes, sir, I sure will. That is all I want, and I promise you, I will turn and leave." He finally said, "Alright."

He went with me to the door. The security guard knocked on the door. Ronald yelled, "Who is it?" "The Police!" Ronald opened the door a little, just enough to see a plain-clothed man and me. "You are not the police," he screamed. "Yes sir, I am, and you best open the door." Ronald asked to see his badge. He got the badge out and showed it to Ronald.

Ronald came outside. He started telling the security guard how I had barged into his apartment. I said, "Ronald, I have already told him that. Just give me my watch and let me see her, and I will leave." Disgustingly, he said, "Okay, just a minute." He closed the door, and I stood there in fear. Would I see someone I knew? Who would it be? What would she look like? Who had taken my place?

A million thoughts must have entered my mind in that brief time. Then the door opened. There stood a girl that looked like a tramp, with dirty tight blue jeans. She had short dark hair. She stood about 5'2". I could tell she was a tramp. Why was Ronald protecting her? Ronald said, "I hope you are satisfied!" I said, "No! And I don't believe our children will be either. Where is my watch?" He handed it to me. I thanked the security guard, and I turned and left.

I went outside and sat in my car. I wanted to sit, rest, and try to decide what to do now. How could all of this happen? He had never even thought about hitting me, let alone hit me. He had never ever pushed me or cursed at me. As a matter of fact, I had never even heard him say a curse word until he called me "....." that night about the towel. He has never been unfaithful to our wedding vows, that I knew for sure. Until now! What has happened to him? Why would he even want another woman in his life? I love him. He has got to know that. I have always been a wife to him, in every way. How much can I take?

I sat in the car, looking up at the apartment. He and his girlfriend came out onto the balcony. They appeared to be having a calm conversation. Ronald was picking some dry skin off his arm. That was something he would do when he got upset or nervous. I wanted to tell him it's okay, just tell her to go away, and we will work it out. Then he kissed her. I couldn't take it anymore. That is something I can never erase from my mind. I should have left as soon as I came downstairs. I should not have put myself under any more emotional stress. I was just so shocked by another woman being there. So shocked by him cursing, pushing, and hitting me. I was so upset; how could I even focus and drive? I wasn't sure, but I knew I had to get home.

Chapter 18

I was sore, upset, and in shock. I knew I had to calm down. I had to face the kids when I got home. I couldn't let them see me like this. I decided to go see a friend, Candice, and her husband, Sam. They didn't live too far away from Ronald's apartment. If I could just focus and calm down to make this short drive. By the time I got to Candice and Sam's, I was hyperventilating. Sam got a paper sack and led me to a chair. He made me breathe into the sack until I calmed down. In a few moments, I was somewhat better. I tried to explain to them how I was going over to see Ronald just to talk to him about spending some more time with the kids. I told Candice how badly they were hurting from their dad's rejection.

I told Candice how I went to the door and knew I should wait until he woke up and he had some coffee. I told her I waited outside the door but instead of hearing him, I heard laughter. I knew a woman was there. I told her about our fight and that I finally got to see her. Candice, my husband, had another woman there. Not just another woman, Candice she looked like a tramp. What is wrong with him? I couldn't talk about it without crying. The crying wasn't from physical pain, just emotional pain. I was just so hurt. How my kind, loving husband could do this? Candice said, "I think we need to take you to the doctor." I said, "Candice, I can't. I am too embarrassed and too afraid to talk to any officials about this. I am just so hurt and upset. I just don't understand. Who is she? Why is he doing this?"

Candice asked about the kids. I said, "Oh my gosh, how will I cover up these bruises and scratches when I see them." I knew I had to go home. She said, "You cannot drive anywhere; you are too upset. The kids need you. You cannot take a chance of having a wreck." I knew she was right. I just couldn't stop the crying, the fast breathing. She said, "I am going to drive you home, and Sam will follow us in your car. You just cannot drive. On the way home, we can talk about how to talk to the kids." She gave me a big hug. Then she prayed with me. She asked God to give me strength, to calm me down, so I could get through all of this. She asked God to take care of the children and to give me strength and wisdom when talking with them.

I hugged her and took a deep breath. I said, "Thank you so much. I can do this." We left her house, and we talked all the way home. We just talked about the kids, their activities, and their school. She kept talking about everything to keep my mind off what had just happened. That is exactly what I needed. I needed to re-focus on the kids. That was the only reason I was at Ronald's apartment in the first place.

I couldn't tell them what had happened, but I knew they could see the scratches and the bruises. I was hoping they would still be asleep. If they were asleep, I would just go inside and go to bed, and maybe the conversation about my bruises would not happen. But when I got home, the kids were all up watching cartoons. I thought cartoons; now this is how a Saturday morning should be. Saturday should be a peaceful, happy day full of joy and relaxation. But here it was, for me anyway, full of loss, sadness, pain, and, unfortunately, reality. The reality that there is another woman in my husband's life. Well, in my life too. She has ruined my and my children's life. Not only another woman but one that looked like a tramp. I can't even call her a woman, only a female. A female with no morals, simply a tramp. That is what I would call any woman messing around with a married man. I should use even worse names, which would identify her even better.

Now I was facing our children, awake, and I knew would be full of questions. I walked in and said, "Hi guys." I just wanted to let them know I was home. I was hoping they would stay focused on the cartoons. I needed time to come to grips with what had happened before I had to answer any questions. But as luck would have it, that is not what happened. They got up and got some cereal to eat. The cartoon ended as I was walking in the door. They jumped up to come and see me, and then I couldn't avoid the situation. Ryder hugged me, when he did, I realized how sore I was going to be.

Ryder said, "Mom, what happened to you?" I said, "I turned my foot wrong and fell." Well, that was sorta true. I did fall. I couldn't, wouldn't tell them the truth. I didn't want to lie. But to have the kids be angry at their dad was not an option. I couldn't hide the way I looked. I had to say something. Anything was better than the truth. Reid said, "Mom, did Dad do this to you?" I said, "No, son." He said, "Yes he did." "No Reid, I really fell. Sweetheart, I am fine. Please don't worry about it." Thankfully, Rachel noticed the new cartoon had started, and that got their attention.

After a couple of hours, I began to get sore. I knew without some type of medication for the pain; I didn't think I would make it. My nerves were shot, and I looked like and hurt like hell. I called my mom. I didn't want to tell her on the phone what had happened. I couldn't take a chance on the kids hearing me. I said, "Mom, if you have time, please come over?" I asked her when she came over and saw me to act like she didn't see anything different. Please ignore how I look, and that I would explain later. I said, "I need a couple of hours of your time if you could just come over and visit and then ask me if I want to go with you somewhere; anywhere, Diane's or church, or anywhere. Then, once we are in the car, I will explain everything." She could tell something strange was up. She came right over and played the role just as I had asked her.

The kids were always excited to see Mom, and she was just as excited to see them. She was a great grandmother. They called her "Grannie!" She always brought some goodies for us. When she saw me, she didn't say a word about how horrible I looked. She just hugged me gently and said, "Good morning."

She is some kind of actress, that gal. She sat and visited with us for a while and then asked if we wanted to see Aunt Diane. She knew the kids probably would not want to go there. This way, it looked innocent and for real. Like we thought, the kids asked if they could go to the neighbors to play while we were gone. I called Marilyn and asked if they could come over and stay for a couple of hours. We were always keeping one another's kids, so I thought it would be okay with her. She said, "Of course, tell the kids to come over." That was a perfect solution for everyone. I told Marilyn I would call just as soon as we got home. The kids left, and Mom and I got in the car to discuss my horrible day.

Mom loved Ronald. Just like she knew my dad wasn't perfect, she knew neither Ronald nor none of her sons-in-law were perfect. Mom was a great Christian lady with a forgiving and understanding heart. She wasn't quite as understanding today. I could tell she was rather angry with her son-in-law, Ronald.

Mom could see I needed some medical attention. As we drove to the doctor, I began to tell her why I went over to Ronald's apartment. I told her what happened while I was there. She was very angry at Ronald for inflicting so much physical pain on me, plus all the emotional pain. When I added the rest of the story about his girlfriend, she was furious and just as confused as I was. She never expected he would hurt me in any way. She asked me so many questions. I went over with her everything that had been going on since mid-May. Ronald's unfaithfulness, his attitude, and lack of attention to the kids would be the very last thing she or anyone would have ever suspected.

We got to Dr. Benson's office, my general practitioner, and checked in. Dr. Benson had been my doctor for several years and was Ronald's doctor as well. So, he knew both of us. Finally, they called me back. Yet, although I was grown, I asked if my mom could come back with me. I think I just needed some moral support and someone there who would remember what the doctor said. My mind was still back at Ronald's apartment.

Dr. Benson looked at me and asked, "Oh my, girl, what has happened?" I briefly explained what had happened at Ronald's apartment. I did not want to go into every detail. I was just so tired of talking about it. Plus, I didn't want him to report this to the officials. He examined me and ordered some X-rays. Thankfully, nothing was broken.

He sat me down to give me a doctor-dad caring conversation. He was shocked Ronald had done this. He said, "Ramona, when a man changes like this, the best thing a woman can do would be to file for divorce and protect the children." Divorce, I did not want a divorce. I just wanted my wonderful husband back like he used to be. Besides, Ronald had already filed for divorce.

He encouraged me to continue with the divorce and to get all the financial help from him I could. He said, "You have three children to care for. You will need all you can get. Honey, with this evidence, you can. Not only has he committed adultery, but he has also assaulted you. He has caused you so much emotional and physical pain. He needs to pay you a lot for all the suffering he has caused you.

I am going to prescribe you something for pain and a mild sedative. Just take them at night. You never know when the children will need you, and I do not want you over-sedated. I want you to come back in 10 days. Apply ice to the areas that are swollen, and do your best to avoid him entirely until you look and feel better."

He gave me a hug and said, "You are a strong young lady. Hold your head high and be proud of yourself. You are only responsible for your actions. No one has ever done anything to ever deserve this treatment. You are not any different. Your pain and suffering are all because of Ronald, his character, and his choices. He and he alone is responsible for his choices."

Funny, that was the same thing Lee from our Sunday School class had been telling me for the last few weeks. I guess maybe someday, I can believe it. Maybe someday, I will stop wondering, what did I do wrong? We both thanked Dr. Benson and left his office with my prescriptions.

Mom drove to the drugstore to get the medicine he prescribed. She reminded me what the doctor had said and told me, "He is right. Honey, Ronald is not the man we have known him to be. We only saw the side he wanted us to see for years. Your main concern now is, just like Dr. Benson said, you and your children. You have got to focus on that."

"Mom, I know y'all are both right. I will take care of the children. But Mom, who will take care of Ronald? Who will take care of his hurt and pain? She won't. She must be so selfish to even be dating a married man. I just hate to see him hurt so badly." She said, "Honey," in firm words, "You stop caring for him right now! You focus on everything you have got to do now to get you and your kids through this ordeal. That is an order from your mom. Do you hear me?" I said, "Yes ma'am, I do."

After we picked up the medicine, she drove me home. I called Marilyn, thanked her for letting the kids come over and taking care of them, and told her I was home. The kids came running across the yard. My mom was outside and was already asking them to come to spend the night with her. They came in with my mom. They ran upstairs to their rooms to pack. My mom said, "They are coming home with me, and you are going to bed. Take the medicine and just go to bed and sleep. You will feel better and will think more clearly in the morning." I agreed. When the kids came down, I gave them gentle hugs, and kisses. I thanked Mom, and I did exactly what she said. I took my medicine and went straight to bed.

Chapter 19

The next few days for me were days of pain, mentally, emotionally, and physically. I was so sore. I could barely move. I loved him so much; how could he have done this to me? Not only was I physically sore, but emotionally, I was a basket case. Had I ruined my chances with a life with him again? What if I had not gone over to his apartment? What if I had just left when I heard the laughter? What if I had never let him know that I knew he was with a female? What if I hadn't been so curious?

I feel so much of the same blame on myself as I did when my dad died. Is this all going to be my fault now if we don't get back together? Will he ever call me again? I guess the time of me doing things with him and the kids is now definitely over. Is he going to be so embarrassed that I know the truth, and now he will cut me off forever? What was worse, knowing or now facing the fear he knows I know?

I do know the truth now. I didn't want to find out this way. The truth was he didn't need time due to stress. He needed time to be with his lover. What if he had just told me the truth? I just wonder how this story could have all been different. At least, I wouldn't have been as confused about the way he was acting. I would have known why. I know I would still have had lots of questions. But hopefully, his answers would have been truthful.

Now I know the truth, only because I had to search for it. I want to know the rest of the story. But he won't tell me. I want to know the entire story, when, where, and how did they meet. But once again, I will have to search it out.

I want to know what he is thinking now. Will he be mad and scream at me and say I was wrong to come over without a warning? Hopefully, he would remember the only phone number we had was his business phone, and he was not at work. Will he wonder what I am even thinking? When would he call again? Would he ever accept my phone calls now? I had so many questions.

I would look in the mirror and see an attractive 34-year-old woman responsible for three children. But he wanted a young 20-something. She looked like a tramp, the way she was dressed and the way she acted. Maybe I should start drinking, cussing, and come down to her level? I want him back. What could I do? Would he call to see if I was okay? Does he still care a little? Is there a chance we can work this out?

I had worked so many places on and off as we needed money during the slow days of the car business when he didn't make much commission. There was one small job I still had. A few months before Ronald even talked about leaving, I saw an ad in the local paper. This North Carolina furniture representative needed someone to be his assistant.

It would be easy, breezy. All he needed was someone to stop by the post office, get his mail, and organize it.

The post office was on the way to and from the kids' school, so that would be easy. He would need me to call him and let him know if anything urgent was in the mail. The other thing he needed was to have a business line of his installed in our house. I would just answer it if it rang, which would be seldom. He needed to establish residency in Tennessee to work in the Tennessee area for his sales. He thought this way; it would appear as though he was a resident. I guess I did interview well. I got the job.

Ronald had met him and seemed a bit jealous of him. The guy's name was Fred Danner. He would stop by the house when he was in town and pick up his mail. Ronald told me to put Fred's mail in an envelope and place it on the front porch. He said, "I don't even want you to answer the door." Fred was handsome and a nice guy. But I would always be faithful to my husband. I know Ronald knew that. I never understood Ronald's concern.

The phone was handy to have in the house. It was an extra phone, so if the kids or Ronald were on our phone, there was an extra phone upstairs. Ronald, of course, knew about the phone and that phone number.

It had been a few days since the fight at Ronald's apartment. I heard Fred's phone ring. I answered it, and I realized it was Ronald. He had never called on that line. After our conversation, I realized why he had this time. Ronald didn't want to talk to the kids until he knew what they knew about our fight. He knew the kids wouldn't answer that phone line.

The first thing he said was, "Did you tell the kids?" I said, "No! I would not ever let them know what had really happened. I wouldn't dare say your dad caused these bruises because he was keeping me away from his girlfriend. I just told them that I turned my ankle and fell." He said, "So, they will be spending the day with me on Sunday as planned?" I immediately replied, "No, they will never, ever be around that type of woman." He told me, "They won't be. I will get them and take them to Opryland." "No, Ronald. If you take them to Opryland, she could show up there too. I wouldn't know about it until after the fact. If you want to see them and take them to Opryland, it is only if I go, to be sure she isn't anywhere around them." He said, "Then I guess I will not be seeing them." "That is your choice. I have made mine." Of course, as usual, he wanted to blame me for him not seeing them. He said, "You can tell the kids you are the reason I cannot see them." "No, Ronald, I can tell them that their dad would rather have a less desirable person in his life instead of his family. You are the reason they are not seeing you." Well, exactly what I had grown accustomed to happened. He hung up on me again.

I was proud I stood up for the kids and stood up for myself. I am beginning to realize that it is all on me. He is not going to put the kids first and for sure not put me first. It is up to me to protect them. It is up to me to see them survive this horrible situation with as little stress and depression as possible.

They are strong, confident, smart children, and it is up to me to reassure them of that every day. It is up to me to be sure that they know they are loved and can be and do anything in this world they want to do. This disaster will not follow them in their life. I will pray and love them every day. While all the time reminding them that their dad loves them, and this situation has nothing to do with them.

I had to remind myself that I didn't cause this either. Yes, I agree it takes two to make a marriage, but it only takes one to end it. In the state of Tennessee, it doesn't matter if you want a divorce or not; if the other spouse does, the judge will grant them the divorce after one year.

I would have done anything he wanted to avoid a divorce. Any changes he wanted me to make, I would have made. Any counseling he wanted to attend, I would have attended. But he would never even talk to me about any problem. He never gave me a chance to see what the problem was. He never let me know where I was failing him or why he turned to another woman. Or was it his ego? His pride?

Or was he just a narcissist? Had it always been all about him, and I never saw that side of him?

Whenever anything negative happened, he started blaming me. When the pine trees he planted earlier in the year died, it was my fault. It didn't matter that we had a drought and heat at 100 almost every day for weeks. According to him, our trees were the only trees in America that died, and it was all my fault. When the pool pump broke, I must have done something that caused it. His not seeing the kids on Sunday, now, is my fault, according to him. I must keep remembering what Lee, my Sunday school teacher, kept saying, "You are responsible only for your decisions. Ronald is responsible for his decisions." This somehow did bring me some comfort. If only I can remember and understand that. Hopefully, someday, I will fully understand what that means.

I have a better reason now to go and see if I can get my old job back. Stan was right. He is having an affair. Or at least, he is seeing other women. Now, he is focused on someone else, it could be more challenging than I thought to convince Ronald that I love him and want him home. It could be that the divorce would happen, and I needed to be prepared.

I called my prior supervisor, Mary Duncan. She was very glad to hear from me. I told her, "Mary, remember in my resignation letter, I wrote how my husband wanted me home with him?" She said, "Yes, I do remember that." I said, "Well, that turned out to evidently to be a lie. He moved out and has filed for divorce. I was calling you in hopes I could get my job back?" She said, "I thought you would never ask. When can you start?" "Thank you so much, Mary. How about next Tuesday?" She said, "Sounds good, I will reinstate you, and see you Tuesday night." Well, Ronald is being so difficult and ruining my life, but it sure seems everyone else is there for me. Now for me to get my life together and return to the hospital to work.

I told the kids that I was going back to work. I think they felt good that I trusted them to be alone, especially Rachel. She seemed to suddenly have more confidence in herself, knowing I trusted her. I called Sybil and told her the good news; after all, this was her idea. I called Mom and told her.

Mom was disappointed I was working the night shift and leaving the kids at home alone. I explained to her that I had talked to my neighbors behind me and beside me, and they both agreed to be a phone call away for Rachel in case she needed them. I reminded her we have an alarm system. I want to be with the kids as much as possible. If I work this shift, they are sleeping, and then I am with them during the day when they are awake. It is best for all of us. Reluctantly, she agreed I might be right.

I didn't mind returning to work. I enjoyed working at the hospital. I didn't want to leave the kids at home alone, no more than my mom wanted me to. Ronald has left me no choice. Lee always told me that I was not responsible for Ronald's choices. But Ronald's choices were impacting my life.

Chapter 20

It had been three days and we had not heard from Ronald. I guess he was busy with his young friend. I guess too busy to see his kids or to even call and talk to them. I was beginning to think about the old saying, out of sight, out of mind. Were we not even going to be a thought in his mind now? There is another saying, absence makes the heart grow fonder. Yes, I thought, it makes his heart grow fonder for someone else. I didn't want to be forgotten. I didn't want the kids to be forgotten.

I thought he was not going to call them. For sure, I can't call. Maybe I could get one of the kids to call him. Perhaps he would be so happy to hear their voice; he would want to take some time to see them. After all, I had told him I didn't tell them he caused my bruises that day. I protected him as always. I asked the kids if they would call their dad. I thought maybe we could go by and visit him at his work while we were out running errands. Rachel said, "I will call Dad." I did want the kids to see their dad, and I guess I wanted to see him too. After all, I hadn't seen him since the fight. I needed to know what his reaction would be to me. I also wanted to be sure he remembered he had a family that loved him. I didn't want him to forget about us. Rachel called, but once again, he wasn't there. She left a message, but once again, there was no return phone call.

As we were out running errands, we went to his work to see if he would have lunch with us. It was noon, the perfect time for a lunch break. We stopped at his work, at least he was there. As usual, he said he was too busy. At least this time, being too busy made sense. He was at work. Other times, when asked and he would say he was too busy; he was off from work. Now I know what that meant. He was too busy with his girlfriend. Before, I didn't understand that.

I told him the kids wanted to talk to him. He said, "I will be able to talk to them after we close tonight. Come by after work." So, we planned to meet him after business hours. Before we went back to his office, we went and got some food at McDonald's for all of us, including him. When we got there, he said, "Go upstairs to the lounge, I will be up in a few minutes." Ryder asked his dad for Coke money, but his dad said he didn't have any money. Perhaps, I thought, if he wasn't spending it all on his mistress, he would have some money for his children. But I kept my mouth shut. I just said, "Ryder, honey, I have some Coke money. Let's go upstairs and wait on Dad." We went upstairs, they turned on the TV, and I got the food out. I gave Ryder and the kids some money for their Cokes, and we waited for their dad.

He finally came upstairs. I couldn't read his attitude. I wasn't sure if he was still mad at me or not. I knew he wouldn't show that in front of the kids, though, and everything would be okay tonight. Reid said, "We have you a sandwich; what do you want to drink?" Ronald said, "Just a Coke." So, with my money, Reid goes to the vending machine to buy his dad a Coke. As we sat there eating, the kids started telling him some of the fun things they had been doing; riding bikes, swimming in the pool, visiting with their friends, and some of the new TV shows they had been watching.

Then Rachel said, "We wish you were home with us. Dad, we miss you and love you." Instead of him being thankful, his kids still wanted and loved him. He says, "The only thing wrong with y'all is y'all are upset because someone else has your toy now. I am not a possession." What kind of comment is that for a dad to say to his kids, to his family? Rachel asked, "Our toy? What do you mean, what toy?" He said, "No, I didn't really mean a toy, I was talking about the grandfather clock." That didn't make any sense, either. The grandfather clock was still at our house. He didn't have it. Reid says, "Dad, we just want you home." We were all getting so upset. His dad got upset with him. Funny, he could leave his family and upset everyone, but Reid or the kids can't express their feelings without him getting upset. Then, he acts like it is okay if he gets upset. And, of course, that is our fault, according to him.

Ronald then accused Reid of saying the word "crap." I didn't hear Reid say that. But it wouldn't have been the end of the world, and not the worse word that he could have said if he had said it. Had the kids been around that woman of their dad's, there is no telling the words they would have heard from her. Another reason, they were not ever going to be around her if I could do anything about it.

Things were going nowhere. The kids had finished eating. Ronald said, "I need to close the dealership, and I have a lot to do when I get to my apartment. Y'all need to leave." Once again, we left alone, without any good conversation or the kids feeling like they mattered. He has got to get away from this terrible woman and come to his senses before things keep getting worse. I do realize now that things can always get worse. As bad as they are now, they can keep going spiraling downhill. We have got to stop this train in motion now.

How could I continue these days? Every day seemed like a crisis without him. It seemed like a crisis with him. I needed him physically, mentally, financially, and emotionally.

I did everything for him. What we ate was always what he wanted. Where we went was always where he wanted to go. I would sit on the side of the tub every morning just to watch him shave. I loved him more than life. Now I was a failure. I had not only ruined my life but the lives of our children. Everything was my fault. I had caused it all, or at least that is what he was saying, and the way I was beginning to feel. Am I responsible for this? I just wish he would just sit and talk to me. You would think with almost 16 years of marriage, he would have at least one conversation with me.

The kids and I got in the car to drive home. Rachel sat up front and turned on the radio, and she just looked out the window. The boys were just as quiet. I wish I could have known what they were thinking. I was almost afraid to say anything. So, I kept quiet too, and everyone was alone in their own thoughts.

We finally got home, and I did my best to console them and get them ready to go to bed. Hugs, kisses, and I love you, and our prayers were our nightly ritual. At the end of Ryder's prayer, he said, "Jesus, please take care of our dad." I wish Ronald could hear his sweet prayer. Here they are going through all this emotional stress themselves, and Ryder is asking Jesus to take care of his dad. What a sweet little boy. His dad doesn't deserve these kind thoughts the kids have for him. The kids are acting more like adults than their dad. They probably think he is all alone and lonely and needs protection. If they only knew just how unlikely he was alone. Although, I do agree he did need protection. Protection from this horrible woman. I guess I should follow Ryder's lead

143

and ask Jesus to protect his dad. His dad is going to need protection.

Once the kids seemed settled into bed and falling asleep, I went to the office and did the work for Fred, the guy from North Carolina that I was working for. But I was so upset; I couldn't work. I was so angry. I picked up my shoe and threw it across the room. Damn him! How could he? How could he? I hate him. He will pay and pay and pay. It will cost him to leave us and have someone else. I will not give up everything for some other woman. No way! I just didn't know what to do anymore. My language and anger weren't anything to be proud of. I hated I was allowing this to make me so angry and using this language. This really wasn't me. For me, screaming at myself was my only venting mechanism. I must remember I am not responsible for what he does. But I am responsible for my choices.

He makes his choices. Lee would say Ronald must suffer the consequences, good or bad, for his choices. But I knew I would suffer the consequences of my choices, too, good or bad. Plus, I am suffering from his choices too. Lee would keep telling me you are not responsible for him. I couldn't understand it. Ronald said it was all my fault. What did he mean? How could I apply Lee's knowledge to my life? When will I finally get it in my head that Ronald is

144

responsible for his decisions? It is not my fault what he chooses in life.

Chapter 21

The sheriff showed up at the door the next day. I knew there was no more delaying the inevitable. I had to accept the papers. I had to accept that Ronald wanted our marriage to end. I decided it is time, time to talk to an attorney. The next morning, I looked at the list of names the sheriff had given me the first time he was here. I knew none of the attorneys' names. I looked in the yellow pages in the phone book. I chose one that had advertised divorce and stated some of the things they had done for their clients.

I chose an attorney by the name of Charles Jackson. I called his office and got an appointment for Friday. I did not want to file for a divorce, but I had to answer the divorce papers I had received from Ronald. I had the divorce papers, and I knew Ronald was having an affair. I needed to figure this out. I knew an attorney would help me.

I hated to call Lee, my Sunday school teacher, over again. He was paralyzed and in a wheelchair. It wasn't easy for him to get into his car and come over, get out, get the wheelchair, and repeat this all as he left. I really don't know how he did it. But he told me to call anytime I needed him. I needed him now. I needed someone to pray with me before I went to see the attorney.

My head just spins with confusion and hurt. I don't want a divorce, but Ronald does. I must protect myself and the kids, but I don't want to hurt Ronald. I want the kids to see their dad, but I can't stand the thought of that woman in their life. I needed to calm down, pray, and feel I was following God's will for my life. Who better to help see me through this but Lee? Who better to pray with me but Lee? So once again, I called him and asked if he could come over and help me. As usual, within the hour, Lee is at the door.

Lee came in and could see I was upset. I chose not to tell him about the fight. I only told him that I had found out Ronald had a girlfriend. He asked me, "Who?" I said, "I didn't know her." "I wonder how they met?" That I didn't know either. Those questions had been haunting me too. I wanted answers. I wanted to know who she was. Lee said, "It would be nice to have answers to those questions before you see the attorney. Do you think Ronald would answer them?" I said, "Are you kidding? He would probably deny I even saw a woman in his apartment. I don't have a clue how to get the information." He said, "Let's just pray about that too. If God wants you to have these answers, he will open the door for you." I agreed with Lee, if God wants me to have the answers, He will show me the way. We then prayed and asked God to give me the guidance I needed.

I felt God in the room and appreciated having such a great friend in Lee. He was someone that I could trust to have my best interest in line with what God would want. Someone I could trust to keep everything confidential and someone who truly cared. Lee agreed with me, the best solution would be for Ronald and me to stay married. He and Connie had been married for 30 years and had a wonderful marriage. That is what I wanted. Just a good marriage, like I thought we had.

Who was the woman in that room? The curiosity was killing me. When did they meet? Where did they meet? Are they still seeing one another? I began a calendar at this point to see if there was a pattern. I would need to pay attention to when or if he mentioned what days of the week he was off. He had always worked long hours and on Saturdays. So, I didn't think he could see her or anyone on Saturdays. What is he doing with all his time? I began to wonder if I should go to the apartment again. I sure found out a lot the first time. It might not be a bad idea, but I should drive a different car. I just don't think I could take a chance on him seeing me. Of course, if he would talk to me, be honest about it, and tell me what was going on, I wouldn't have to sneak around and try to find my answers.

I called Candice and asked if I could borrow her car early the next morning. I told her I just needed to see if they were still an item. She asked me, "How will you find out?" "I'm not sure." I didn't know, but I thought maybe if I just parked in the parking lot and waited until Ronald left the apartment, that would give me a clue. If he left alone, perhaps they had broken up. If she was with him, I would know they were still an item.

I said, "Candice, all this uncertainty of not knowing is just driving me crazy." She said, "I understand. Of course, you can borrow my car whenever you want." "Thank you, so in the morning, if I come by about 6 A.M., will that be okay?" "Sure, that is fine." We talked a little more, and then I let her go to be sure that time would work out okay for me. I knew the kids would be okay. They would probably be asleep until I got back.

By now, the neighbors knew that Ronald had moved out. They were all so supportive. They had told me to let me know anytime they could help me in any way. They also were keeping close tabs on the house in case anything looked suspicious. They knew to contact me or the police department. So, now I had it planned. I would go over in the morning to his apartment and just see if I could pick up any more information. The more information I had under my belt before I met with the attorney, the better it would be for me and the kids.

We still haven't heard from Ronald. I knew he wouldn't know I would be in his apartment complex area. I just had to be sure nothing like the last time happened. I didn't think the security guard would give me another chance. But I was going to go and just keep a low profile. Only Candice would even know I was there.

I got up at 5 A.M., got dressed, and drove over to Candice and Sam's to exchange cars. Then, I drove over to Ronald's apartment. At this point, I wasn't sure what I would do once I got there. Probably no more than just observe.

When I got there, I drove around just like I had done the first time until I saw where he had parked his car. It took only a few minutes, and then I found it. At first, I just parked beside his car and sat there. Then I thought, if I looked in his car, I could tell from the front seat if he had a passenger riding with him. He would usually keep the passenger seat with something in it. If it was empty, it would probably mean she was with him, her, or someone else.

I got out of Candice's car to ease over to look inside Ronald's car. Well, it isn't his car anyway; it is the company car that they loaned him since he is the manager. No one was around the car; fortunately, 6 A.M. is early for most people. The front seat was empty. I thought that would mean she was probably there. As I was looking in the front seat, I noticed his briefcase in the back floorboard. When he lived at the house, he would always bring his briefcase inside. He must have been sidetracked, probably with her, and forgot it.

I thought, man, if I could get it, I bet I could find out something else that was going on with him. I reached for the car door handle; the door was unlocked. So, I "borrowed" a briefcase. I just wonder what I will find inside. I took it and put it in Candice's car. I turned to open the briefcase. Dang, it was locked. Well, I wasn't about to put it back in his car and never know what was inside. I will take it home and figure out the combination or get it opened somehow. I haven't gotten lucky enough to have an unlocked car door, with his briefcase in the back, to leave it now. I thought I should just sit here a little longer to see if they came out to the car. I wondered if she had her car here. With it being so warm today, perhaps they will go outside on the balcony, and then I would know if they were still seeing one another.

As I sat there, my mind wondered about our past weeks. I thought I could go up to his apartment. I could just sit outside the door like I did before. No, second thought, bad idea. I would probably get in trouble. I waited in the car for about 45 minutes and never saw Ronald. I decided to go back to Candice's, exchange cars, and go back home. At least, now, I have his briefcase, and it is possible that a little more insight into what is going on with him will be inside it.

Chapter 22

When I got home, the kids were up. I cooked breakfast. I decided we would do something fun today. I'm not sure what it would be, but we were going to enjoy our day. Our day as a family; even though their dad wasn't with us, we are still a family. The kids watched TV for a while. Then they decided, since it was a beautiful day, that they would love to go to the country club, go swimming, and maybe play some tennis after it cooled off. That sounded good to me.

I went out to the car and got his briefcase while the kids were focused on TV. I just set it in the chair in the dining room. As much as I wanted to see what was inside, I knew I had to wait. I had to wait until the kids went to bed. I needed to be alone and undisturbed when I saw what was inside. I knew it was locked, and it would probably take some time to figure out the combination.

Right now, it was time to focus on my kids. Before leaving the house, we ate lunch. Then, it was time to go to the country club and enjoy our day. I was so glad we had decided to go. Most of their friends were there. The kids loved to swim, and I was hoping this would get their minds off everything going on at home. This way, we could all visit, they could visit with their friends, and I could visit with the moms.

Today was going to be a day just like last year. A year that we were all so very happy. We were living our lives then, not even thinking about the word divorce. That word was never in our brains. The day was so good. After the sun went down, we stayed and went to the restaurant and had the best hamburgers ever. They played a tennis game, the perfect ending to a great day, before we headed home.

We still hadn't heard from Ronald. I think that was pretty good today, anyway. This meant he hadn't noticed his briefcase was gone. For a few days, maybe I wouldn't be his screaming target, or a recipient of a phone being slammed in my ear since tomorrow morning was my appointment with the attorney, Mr. Jackson. I needed today to be a little relaxing and to get a good night's sleep. I needed to be composed and not have a night putting up with Ronald's anger. That is exactly what I did. I had a great day at the pool with the kids. When we got home, I took a long hot shower. I washed my hair and got my clothes out for the next day. Then the kids and I did our nightly ritual of me tucking them into bed, hugs, I love you, and prayers. Then I went and got in my bed.

I woke up rested and ready to meet with my attorney. I told the kids where I was going today, who I was going to talk to, and why I had to talk to him. Reid asked, "Mom, does this mean Daddy will never be home again?" I said, "Honey,

I do not know your dad's plans. I know we still want Dad home if he agrees to it. This is just a meeting for the attorney to explain to me where we go from here and what he needs to do should your dad continue to decide not to come home. This will just be for our information. I said it is much better to know what to expect than to go into something and be shocked because you didn't ask questions. This way, we will be prepared. This will make everything much easier for us." They seemed to understand, and I left for the attorney's office.

I nervously drove into Nashville to meet with Mr. Jackson. I got to his office and told the receptionist who I was and that I had an appointment with Mr. Jackson. I waited only about 5 minutes, then Mr. Jackson came to the lobby and said, "Ramona Jenkins"? I stood up. He said, "Ms. Jenkins, I am Charles Jackson. Thank you for coming into the office today."

I thanked him for his time and told him I was very nervous. I have never spoken with an attorney before. He said, "I think you will find this easy and painless. I will ask you a few questions and see what is going on. Then I will tell you how I can help you." Well, if that is all, it will be easy and painless, I thought to myself.

I sat down in his office in a very comfortable chair. I thought, here I am about to tell a total stranger about my personal life. But I got to do this. I guess he's been through this situation before. I need to take a few breaths, relax, and know he is here to help me. And I am here because I am so confused and need some legal help.

He asked me some questions, and then I explained the situation. I told him that we had always been happy. Then suddenly, Ronald said he needed to be alone, and then, just as suddenly, he said he was moving out. Then he filed for divorce. Then he got an apartment. He never would tell me why. He never wanted to discuss it with me, our pastor, or a counselor.

I have been going crazy trying to figure out why he would want this. Then, last week, I went to his apartment, and when I heard a woman's laughter, I figured out why he wasn't interested in me anymore. He had another woman he was interested in.

Mr. Jackson asked me how I felt about that. I told him how hurt and upset and how rejected I felt. I said, "My main concern is how can I keep her away from my children?" He said, "Well, you can't help who he has around them. During this process, it would be dumb if he did have her around them. You can be pretty sure that will not happen. If he continues to see her, when we go to court for the final divorce, you can talk to the judge about it." I felt better anyway, about that for now. Mr. Jackson convinced me it wouldn't be in Ronald's best interest to have the kids around her during this process. For now, I will allow the kids to see him without me.

I told Mr. Jackson about the scuffle we had that day and about my doctor's appointment. I explained to him I didn't want a divorce. I asked him, "How can we stop it?" He looked puzzled and said, "He is with another woman, and you scuffled, and he has filed for divorce, but you don't want a divorce?"

I said, "No, I don't want a divorce; I love him. I married him for better or worse. I know he will come to his senses if the divorce doesn't go through, and then we can work out our marriage. I want to be a complete family again. I know he loves me and the kids. He is just confused now. I am not sure what is going on with him. But I know I do not want a divorce."

He shook his head. He said, "I don't understand why you would want him back, but I work for you, and I will do whatever you want." That is exactly what I wanted to hear. I was so grateful that I had found an attorney with empathy and an attorney that really had my interest at heart.

I told him what the sheriff had already done for me. He, too, was shocked that he would risk his job to help me. Mr. Jackson said, "I am glad he did. I am sure he could tell, just like I can, how sincere you are about keeping your family together and how much you love your husband. We will do all we can."

We still had to discuss the money issue. My checking account balance was getting low. I had very little in savings. I did have a home equity line of credit I could pull from in case of an emergency. Why should I go into debt with the equity line when Ronald is supposed to support his family? He has a great job and makes good money. It is just that now he is paying for an apartment, spending money on a strange woman, and living like he has no family.

I asked Mr. Jackson, "What can we do about getting Ronald to support his family?" He said, "When I file the answer for divorce from Ronald's attorney, Mrs. Donavan, I will ask for a court date for the judge to order him to pay the bills until the divorce is granted."

He told me should anything come up that he would need to know, just call the office, and he would be back in touch. I told him that sounded good and I would let him know. I shook his hand and left the office. I felt confident about my attorney choice. I even felt confident about Ronald having enough time to decide to come back home, and a divorce would never happen.

That sure took a load off my mind. I knew Ronald wasn't going to like the idea of my attorney talking to the judge about Ronald paying our bills. After all, that was going to cut into his play money. But at the same time, he married me, and we built this family and created these bills together. If he got mad, so be it. He has a financial responsibility to his family.

After my appointment with Mr. Jackson, I felt much better. He was going to take care of the financial situation, and we were going to delay the divorce as long as we could. Mr. Jackson had agreed to do it my way, and we would stall. He would keep putting trial dates off as long as he could, except for the one to get the judge to order Ronald to pay the household bills.

Chapter 23

When I got home, I told the kids the visit went great with the attorney. I explained the information that the attorney gave me about how the court worked with the children. I told them the attorney talked to me about documents and how they are filed. I said, "He is on our side. We decided we would take things slow and see what happens."

Then Rachel said, "Mom, Dad called while you were gone." I asked, "Did he ask for me?" She said, "No, so I didn't tell him that you were gone. He just wanted to see if we could see him on Sunday." I said, "Of course, that is fine with me; what did you tell him?" She said, "I said sure we miss him and would be happy to see him Sunday." "Princess, that was the exact thing to say. Your dad loves y'all, and I bet y'all will have a good time."

Saturday went by uneventfully. Now for Sunday. Ronald and I had not talked since I got his briefcase. I wonder if he has even missed it. Or is he just waiting to scream at me in person? The children haven't seen him in a while either. They were excited, and I was nervous. This time, I hoped he would pull into the driveway and just honk for the kids. Unlike before, I always wanted to see him. Now, I was scared to confront him.

Ronald called the house, and Reid answered. Reid told me his dad called to say he would be at the house in about 10 minutes and that he would be in a hurry. That they need to be ready when he gets here and just come on outside. Well, that means I won't have to listen to him screaming at me. Had he noticed his briefcase was gone? Probably not, or I would be hearing about it. Finally, he was here, and the kids went outside to get into the car.

This big puzzle was still driving me crazy. I still don't know who she is, where they met, what she does, or how long he has known her. What type of connection do they have? I really know nothing! If I knew, perhaps I could at least rest my mind. I decided today to open the briefcase, and hopefully, I would get some answers. I went into the dining room and once again started working on combination number options. I tried everything. Nothing worked. I tried to cut the lock. That didn't work, either. I knew to just wait; someway, somehow, I would come up with the right combination, and when I did, I felt confident I would understand more. I felt sure that inside that briefcase, I would uncover his secrets. I just needed to be patient.

Meanwhile, I knew I needed to find out as much as possible. I had to find some way to do that. I need to just slow down and think and figure out what can I do. I need a quiet, relaxing place to think. I put on my tennis shoes, and

I took my dog for a walk. I walked down to the lake, and I found a beautiful shady spot. There I just sat down and thought and thought, what can I do to get my questions, all of them answered, once and for all?

I was so tired of his games. Sick of his lies, I just wanted to draw a line in the sand and say, Ronald, tell me the truth. I want to know everything. I already know you are involved with another woman, so please, please answer my questions. I need to stop my mind from swirling so I can focus and take care of the kids. I thought to myself. This is what I need to do. I need to just ask!

The next day, I called Ronald. I said, "Ronald, the kids are going to some school events tonight, and I need you to come over and talk to me." He said, "What about?" "Ronald, look, we both know you are involved with someone else. This stress, this pressure with this, the kids, the house, everything is too much for me. I need someone to talk to; that is, you. You have always been my emotional shoulder to lean on and talk to, and I need you to help me through this." He said, "I can't. I am not your emotional shoulder anymore."

I said, "If you can't help me, then you leave me no other choice but to leave the kids and go seek help. I cannot handle this anymore." He said, "I told you I can't come over there."

I said, "Fine, the kids will call you when they get home. They will be alone, and you can raise them by yourself."

He said, "You would do that too. Just stay there; I will be there in 30 minutes." I thought that would change his mind. He didn't want to take on the responsibility of raising the children by himself. Besides, his little mistress wouldn't like to share him with his three children. I was surprised she allowed him to have four to five hours on a Sunday afternoon every other week to see his kids. Why in the world, if he wanted someone else, why someone like that? Why couldn't he have chosen a good woman? Oh yeah, a good woman wouldn't have an affair with a married man. Especially a married man with three children.

I would never leave my children, regardless of my confusion or stress. But I pulled his bluff. Now, hopefully, one on one, face-to-face, maybe, just maybe, he will answer my questions. When Ronald got here, I was lying across the bed, crying. He came into the bedroom and sat in the chair. He asked, "Now, what is wrong?" I just looked at him. I thought, you are going to ask me, now, what is wrong, like you don't have a clue. Let's see whether it could be my husband of almost 16 years has left me, without any reason, for another woman. Do you think that might be it?

I said, "Ronald, my head is spinning. I have so many unanswered questions; please help me. I need to understand some of this. This is the problem; I just can't believe any of this is happening. I don't understand when it happened, how it happened, and now I have the question: who is she? I need your help to understand, please?"

He said, "I didn't mean to hurt you!" I said, "You didn't mean to hurt me?" I felt like I was repeating every word he said. Every word he said was so crazy that I had to say it again for it to register that he was really saying these things. I thought, what's wrong with you? I didn't mean to hurt you; that is crazy. How did you think I would feel? You didn't think it would hurt to have my husband walk off and leave me?

I finally just said, "Ronald, what did you think walking off from our family and getting involved with someone else would do to me? Did you just think I wouldn't notice? Why? Why did you do this?" He says, "You were getting prettier and prettier. Everywhere we went, people would say, Ronald, you better play your cards right, or she will be gone. I knew if you left me after the kids grew up, I would be old and gray, and who would want me? So, I had to leave now."

I couldn't believe what he was saying. Who does this? Who thinks like this? I said, "Ronald, I love you so much; how in the world would I ever want to leave you?" I just shook my head and then started asking questions about her.

I just hoped his answers were honest and made more sense than he had made so far.

I asked him, "Where did you meet her?" He said, "At Shoney's, just the night before you had seen us together." "Have you seen her since that day?" He said, "Yeah, a few times. She has a rich father." I thought, so, you meet a girl with a rich father. Is that a reason to stay away from your wife and your children? I was beginning to think the man was totally crazy.

When you are living in a world of events you never saw coming, you need some answers. But how many of his answers were even true? By now, he was getting antsy. He was only humoring me to try to calm me down so he could leave.

After almost 16 years, you can almost read someone's next move. At least, before, I thought I could. Guess I was wrong. I never saw any of this coming. I could never tell he was making these moves. I must have been living in my own little world with a mask on my eyes or something. I didn't think I was; I think he missed his calling as an actor.

He totally made me think before he left me in May, that he loved me and only me. He told me that constantly. And I thought he showed me that constantly. How could I have ever been so blind and naive? How will I ever be able to trust myself in the future to see someone for who they really are?

I feel he has ruined every chance in my life to ever trust him or anyone ever again. But here, I want him back. If he comes back, I have got to learn to trust him. I have got to learn to trust my gut again.

He calmed me down, and as soon as he saw he had, he was out the door. I needed to know I could still lean on him. I needed to know that he would come over if I really needed him. I had to know we could talk like before, and I was not totally discarded, even if I felt like I had to threaten to leave the house before he would come over. Plus, I had so many questions about her. But his answers, they were probably lies. I still don't know any more than I did before he came over to the house. Except maybe he did meet her at Shoney's.

Chapter 24

The following week, I was scheduled for surgery. I had a tumor in my throat. I knew Ronald still loved me. He had to love me. There is no way you can be with someone from the time you are 16 to 34, love them, build a family and life together, and just turn all of it off. It is not possible. I know I cannot do that. Surely, he could not do it either.

I called and told him of the surgery. He asked, "Is your mom keeping the kids?" I said, "No, Mom isn't keeping the kids. You are keeping them; you are their dad." What was he thinking? That the only ones that took care of the kids were me or my mom? Where was his duty? I guess he thought that Mom would keep the kids so he could continue his affair. After all, it appeared that was what I was doing.

He said, "How long are you talking about?" Throughout this conversation, never once, how are you? What kind of tumor? Are you scared? It was just like it had been for the last two months. All about him! I answered him and said, "Ronald, it is only one day and one night." I wanted to say, I am sure I will be just fine. I won't need any rest or anything. I can take care of the kids without your help.

Why couldn't he just say, you focus on yourself and take care of yourself, and I will take care of the kids as long as you need me to? Why? Ok, he had left me. Ok, he had found someone else. But what about a little consideration for his wife and the mother of his children? It is a good thing I wasn't on my deathbed. At that point, though, I didn't know that for sure. This might have been my deathbed. I had a tumor; was it cancer? Was I going to die? I hoped not. I didn't think so, but I didn't know for sure.

Then he says, "I will pick them up at the hospital." At the hospital! I guess he thinks I am supposed to get ready for surgery, get three kids ready and out the door, have them sit with me in the waiting room, and then leave them alone in the waiting room when they call me back to get me ready for surgery. I am beginning to wonder how this man can move from A to B. He has lost his mind, even worse than I thought before. You would think he would at least come and take me to the hospital and then keep the kids with him. I figured surely he would realize how horrible he was sounding and what he was saying. I just knew he would call back and be kind and considerate. No, that never happened. He didn't.

The following day, I got up and got dressed and ready to go to the hospital. I drove myself and my children to the hospital. I thought Ronald sounded tough, but when he sees me in the hospital, he will have a different attitude. He will care, and he will send flowers like he always had, and everything will be fine. This will be just like every time I have been in the hospital in the previous years.

I finally got checked in by 3 P.M. The kids waited downstairs in the waiting room all that time. I stayed with them until about 2 P.M. I told the nurse about the situation and that their dad would be there to pick them up. I asked if she thought they would be okay. She said, "I will ask the receptionist to bring them over to where she is, and she will keep an eye on them. Hopefully, he will be here soon." I said, "I sure hope so." The kids were so tired. I am sure they were probably concerned and confused too. They let Rachel come up to where I was to tell me her dad was here and that they were leaving.

I asked Rachel to please ask her dad to come up before he left. She left to go get him, and he came up within minutes. Boy, was I wrong about him having a concerned attitude? He was rude, arrogant, and hostile. Here, I lay in a hospital bed, facing surgery. He acted like this was my fault and I was causing him too much inconvenience.

When did he get so selfish? His personality has totally changed. I had to wonder whether he was doing drugs. Maybe that is why he left me. Maybe he had gotten mixed up with this girl, and she did drugs, and maybe she was blackmailing him. He loves me. He is just not being himself. As he was leaving, at least he said, "Take care, and I will take the kids to your moms in the morning." Then he left. There I was, just lying in the bed, thinking how and why over and over. I think even at that time, facing surgery, all I could think about was Ronald and our divorce that was pending.

I started crying, crying, and crying. I was hyperventilating again. I rang for the nurse. When she came into the room, she saw me in distress. She said, "I will call the doctor and see if he will prescribe something to help you calm down." She immediately left the room. She wasn't gone very long. When she returned, she gave me a shot and two pills to calm me.

The medication did calm me down. But I still couldn't sleep. I looked over at the clock; it was 1 A.M., and I was still awake. Confused about Ronald and still upset, but at least I wasn't hyperventilating. I called and talked to Sybil. What would I have done without my friends and my mom? Sweet Sybil would stay up and listen to me anytime I needed her. And my dear mom, God bless her, she would answer the phone at all hours and let me talk about whatever was on my mind at the time.

In a few short hours, the anesthesiologist came into my room, asked me some questions, and started the IV. I was feeling scared and sorry for myself. I had never had to go through something like this. Now, I am going through it alone. As they rolled me out of the room into the surgical room, I think even then, I thought I would turn and see Ronald standing there. But no, he never came back. No, he didn't send any flowers. No, not even a phone call after surgery checking on me. It is like he doesn't care. Yet, I wouldn't accept that.

The surgery went just fine. The doctor said he thought the tumor was benign. He would send it off to the lab to be sure. He wanted me to make an appointment to see him in a week. Then he released me. That whole day, I thought Ronald would call. He didn't. He didn't even care if I had cancer or if I didn't. I guess he didn't care if I had died. I just still couldn't believe this was happening. It was just a horrible dream, and I knew I would wake up and everything would be fine. How in the world does someone change so much, so quickly? For what reason could this happen?

Chapter 25

I called and talked to Sybil. I told Sybil my theory. That the only way Ronald would act like he was acting was if he was on drugs. Knowingly, he would not ever act this way. I told her about me thinking maybe he was being blackmailed. I knew I had to find out more.

He said he had met her at Shoney's. I wonder if she was a waitress there. My previous investigation skills have got to kick in. I thought, what if when he had the kids on Sundays, I checked out Shoney's to see if she was there? Sunday is the only time he will see the kids, so she must not be available to him then. If she isn't available, then perhaps she is working. I really don't know what I am looking for if she is there. I just need to know something about her.

I wasn't sure what I would have done if I had seen her there. I really had no clue. I guess I thought, at the very least, I could get her name. I decided that is what my Sunday would be, investigating, a day of truth!

Sunday finally got here, and Ronald picked up the kids. I got in the car and drove to Shoney's. There were a lot of people in front of me. That was good. That gave me time to look around. I couldn't go to every restaurant to eat. So, after being there waiting for a table for 20 minutes, I realized that his mistress wasn't there. I told the girl at the front desk that

I couldn't wait any longer. I turned, and I left. I thought of some other restaurants he had talked about over the last six months. Po Folks Restaurant was one of them he liked.

I got in my car and drove down the road to the Po Folks Restaurant. I went into the restaurant. I thought I had heard Ronald say something about her name being Rose. When I arrived, they asked, "How many?" I said, "Just one. Oh, by the way, can I sit in Rose's section?" They said, "Sure." I said, "So she is here today?" They said, "Yes." Oh my gosh, I was a nervous wreck. It is amazing what you will do when you feel desperate.

They seated me, and I sat there shaking. The waitress came by. I knew this Rose was not the girl I was looking for. This girl did have a name tag on that said, Rose. But it was not her. I was relieved and disappointed all at the same time. I just sat there looking at every waitress and employee that was there. I did not see anyone who reminded me of the girl at Ronald's apartment that awful Saturday morning!

As I sat there eating, I kept thinking about that Saturday morning. I thought I only saw that girl briefly. Will I even recognize her if I was to see her? Am I just spinning my wheels and wasting my day? I sure would love to find out something. But seriously, what are the odds? I will probably just go home empty-handed and disappointed.

I kept trying to think of some other restaurants he had talked about. I thought I had time to try a couple more before I had to get to the house by the time the kids got there. Since I am already out in the area, I might as well give it a try. I finished eating, paid my bill, and left.

When I left there, I drove down the street and went to another restaurant. By now, I had had so many failures trying to find her. I had assumed this would be the same result. I wasn't even very nervous by now. Now it was, go in, look around and leave.

I get there, park the car, and casually walk in. I looked around, and I had a flashback to that Saturday morning. There she was. She was standing behind the counter accepting the drink orders. My stomach was turning; I was sick. I stood frozen. After I settled down, I asked another waitress, "What is the girl's name that is behind the counter?" She said, "Her name is Barbara, Barbara McCloud." I was sick. I just wanted to go home and forget it all. But the more I knew, the more I wanted to know. Just who is she? Who is this girl, Barbara McCloud? How could I find out? Her name wasn't Rose. Here I was, face to face with her. Do I leave the restaurant now or do I stay? I was beginning to panic.

The waitress asked, "Would you like to sit at the table or at the bar?" I said, "A table, please, but I need to go to the restroom first." I was sick. I wanted to hide. I didn't want her to see me. I needed to think about my next step. I went to the restroom, feeling like I was going to throw up. I got myself a paper towel, got it wet, then went into one of the stalls. I just needed to wipe my face, cool off and think. What now? I soon realized I needed to find an escape from the restaurant before she saw me. I quickly left the restroom and just headed for my car.

I made it; the coast was clear, and she didn't see me. At least, I didn't think so. I knew if she did see me, she would tell Ronald, and then I would never hear the end of that conversation. He would accuse me of stalking her when I wasn't. I didn't know she would even be there. I was just trying to find out if she was there. But once again, in everything he was doing, he would turn it around and blame me for it. This would not be any different.

I just sat in my car thinking, do I just sit here and see if she leaves and follow her to see where she goes? I wondered how long that would take. Ronald would bring the kids back home at 5 P.M., and I had to be home. He would always be punctual too. Well, punctual when it came to when he brought them home. So many times, the kids would sit at the window, waiting and watching for him to get there. He was often late picking them up. And, of course, he always came with his excuses.

As I sat there in the car, thinking, the time was ticking. I knew I just needed to leave and find another way to find out more. I'm not sure how, but I was determined to find out what I could. I would use every private investigation tool that I had been taught. Although I didn't have much experience in investigation, I had only done it for a few weeks. I learned a lot. And I would use everything I had learned to find out everything I could. I would leave no stone unturned. My future and my kid's future depend on me right now. Or at least, that is the way I felt, and that was what was motivating me.

I made it home by 4:35 P.M., just in time to be sure I was there when the kids got home. As usual, he was right on time; at 5 P.M., Ronald pulled into the driveway, and the kids got out of the car. If only I could count on him in other areas of our lives right now. But that isn't happening. And I am going to find out why!

After the kids went to bed that night, I sat up thinking of a plan to find out who this girl, Barbara, was. I had my red phone upstairs that I used with my job working for Fred. I would use it in the morning and do my research. If anyone traced the number, it would go back to Fred. I would be in the clear.

The next morning, before the kids got up, I went upstairs. I used the red phone. I called the restaurant where she worked. When an employee answered, I said, "Hello, I need to verify some employment, please." The girl who answered said, "I will have someone in the Human Resources Department call you back." I thanked her. I knew everything would be okay. I was going to use a fake name and a fake business name. She would never know who I really was or why I was really calling. I would answer the phone, using the business name when it rang. Fred's phone was just there for proof he lived in the area. I would be fine. I said, "Yes, if you could ask them to call me back at 615-737-9989; my name is Josie at Dr. Doak's office." She said, "Yes, it would be a couple of hours." I said, "Sounds good, thank you." This was natural for me since I had worked for a doctor before and knew how to verify employment. I could do it in my sleep. I just had to wait until the phone rang.

Finally, here was my call. I answered the phone, Dr. Doak's office; how may I help you? The girl said, "I need to talk to Josie." I said, "This is she." She identified herself and said she was calling from the Human Resources department. I am returning your call. I said, "Yes, ma'am, I just need to verify the employment of a Barbara McCloud. She works in Nashville, TN." She put me on a brief hold and came back and said, "She is employed with us. Her full name is Barbara Jean McCloud from Murfreesboro." "Okay," I said, "Thank you, that is all I need. Have a good day."

There, I now have a full name, and I know where she is from. This is a start. I might have gotten a little more information. But I wanted to keep it simple, and hopefully, I would sound like other companies verifying employment, and no one would be suspicious.

I just kept wondering if I could find her family. If I could find a relative, I would ask them to talk to her. Hopefully, they would, and they would tell her she shouldn't be dating a married man, especially a married man with children. Maybe, just maybe, they would, and she would leave Ronald alone. Murfreesboro is a big town. Fortunately, her last name wasn't Smith or Jones. Possibly, I could find them. If I did, would they talk to her? Or would Ronald hate me because they broke up?

I was going crazy trying to figure out how to get her to leave him alone. How could I figure this out? I didn't know how a 20-ish girl even thought. How did they even process anything? I remember Ronald told me her father was rich. That didn't matter. She wasn't rich. She was a waitress. I bet Ronald looked rich to her. There he was, driving a brand-new Volvo car, not his, but she didn't know that. He dressed to the nines because I would buy for him to be sure he did. He had a diamond ring that I had bought him. To her, I bet he really looked like a catch. She evidently doesn't care if he is married. Or, possibly, he told her he was single. Who knows? I wish he would just be honest and tell me everything. I shouldn't be left to figure this out on my own.

I would randomly call a business number. When they answered, I would ask to speak to an employee about 21 years old. I am sure they thought I was crazy. I just needed to talk to someone her age and ask them how I should handle this. I wanted them to tell me what I would need to do to stop her from seeing him. I just could not relate to anyone her age.

I would be at an office or a restaurant and just strike up a conversation and talk to people that I didn't know and ask them what I should do. I would be at a gas station, post office, or anywhere anybody would listen. I was desperate for answers. How could I get my husband back? That was the only thing on my mind. I guess I thought if I kept asking enough people, finally, someone would give me the vital information that I needed.

I need her address. I have got to find a way to get it. When I worked with the private investigator, we would take the license plate number to the state. They would run the plates, tell us who the car belonged to, and give us their address. I need to get her license plate number. Then, I will go to the state courthouse and get her address.

I knew there was a restaurant beside the restaurant where she worked. If I got there before she did, I could wait until she got there. I would see what she drives, and I can get her license plate number. It might be a long wait, but it would be worth the wait. The kids were starting school the following week. I decided that after I took the kids to school, I would drive to the restaurant and wait and see what I could find out.

I wanted the kid's last week before school to be a fun week. The swimming pool at the country club was still open, and we would go every pretty day. The boys would ride their bikes, and Rachel would ride with me to the club. On rainy days, we went to see a movie. It didn't matter to them if it was a new release or one they had seen before. They would always enjoy a good movie over and over.

We had to shop and get school clothes. Of course, the boys wouldn't have fun shopping, but since they were growing up like weeds, they would need to be with me to try on clothes. Ryder would tell me his legs weren't made for shopping. We went to several stores and finally ended up at our local department store. The clerk totaled the items, and I was $180.00 short. Oh no, I didn't have that much money, and I didn't have a credit card, and I didn't get paid until Friday. The kids had their hearts set on these clothes. I should have been more careful when I was letting them pick things up. That total just got up before I realized it. The clerk said she could hold the clothes for 24 hours.

I called Ronald at the office, but he wasn't there. I left a message to have him call me back. I also told Martha, the receptionist, what I was calling about, that I needed some money for the kids' school clothes. I knew if she knew it was for the kids, she would be sure he called me back. I could always count on her. She would go out of her way for the kids. He never called me back. Evidently, he never returned to work. The kids called him at work and at his mom's, and there were no return calls. I told the kids not to worry.

I told them I would ask and see if I could borrow the money from my mom, their Grannie. I called the store and asked if they could hold the clothes for a few more hours. They agreed. I called Mom and told her the situation. Like a champ, she agreed to loan me the money. She didn't want the kids to be disappointed again. They had already had so many disappointments. The kids were so excited when I told them Grannie said okay. We stopped by Mom's, got the money, went straight to the store, and picked up their clothes.

When Monday came for the kids' first day of school, everything went great. They were still in the private school they had attended the year before. They were all dressed cute and already to start the new year. I prayed it would all go well, just like they had hoped. I prayed the schoolteachers would be understanding and someone they liked. I prayed they would get into the classes with some of their favorite friends.

If the school year went well, then hopefully, any other disappointments they may have to endure would be easier on them. For sure, I had no idea what was ahead for us down the road. I knew God said, "In all things, give thanks." And I knew whatever came down our path, He would hold our hands through it. Earthly fathers may disappoint, but our Heavenly Father never disappoints us. We can always count on Him. He was, and I knew, would be our strength in the coming days.

With the kids settled into school, I set out to start my investigation. I wanted to see what this girl Barbara drove to work and to get her license plate number. After I got that information and her address, what then? Possibly, I just wanted to know where she lived so I could see if Ronald was spending a lot of time there. Then, I might know the seriousness of this girl and my husband. I wasn't sure. I just knew I needed to know more than I knew.

I got to the restaurant, the restaurant beside where she worked. They opened early for breakfast. I ordered some food, picked it up from the counter, and sat down. I sat where I had a good view of the restaurant's parking lot where she worked. As I was eating and watching the parking lot, I saw a new Volvo car pull into a parking spot. I thought that looked like Ronald's car. I kept watching. The car parked, and a guy gets out of the driver's side. It is Ronald. I thought, what is he doing here? They aren't open for lunch yet. Then I see him walk around to the passenger side and open the door where this lady gets out. Well, let's stop there, no lady, where Barbara gets out. I couldn't believe it; Ronald was bringing her to work.

I just sat there in disbelief and watched as he put his hand into his pocket and gave her something. I could only assume money. He has no money to buy the kids a drink for supper, and he gives her money! Then, as I sat there restraining myself, I saw him kiss her. She then turns and waves to him, and he gets in the car and leaves. What just happened here? What is going on?

There was a gentleman sitting there eating breakfast. I just started talking to him. I said, "Sir, I cannot believe it. I am sitting here and looking out the window, and I see my husband bring this girl to work and kiss her bye. How can a man do this to his wife?" I asked him, "Please look at me and be honest. Am I ugly? Fat? What is it? What is wrong with me? Why doesn't my husband want me anymore? Why would he turn to someone else?"

He told me I was beautiful, classy, and very attractive. He had no idea why any man would walk away from me. He said, "I think your husband is crazy." But he was probably thinking I was the crazy one. Just starting up a conversation like this with a stranger. By now, I think I was crazy. I appreciated his kind words, but I still left in tears as I drove home. I was even more desperate than ever to find out who is this woman. To find out what kind of spell does she have on him? I will find out, but how? How? I didn't know.

I have got to get her address. But how will I get it now? My husband drives her to work. I can't even get her address from her license plate. Now, how will I find out the information I need? I still have his briefcase if only I could get it open. Ronald has never asked me about it. Possibly, he thinks he lost it, or someone stole it. I got lucky there. He may not even know it is missing.

Chapter 26

When I got home, I called Sybil. Oh my gosh, what would I do without that girl? I told her what had happened and told her I must find out what was going on before I lost my mind. I told her I couldn't believe the restraint I had, just sitting there. I said, "It was like an out-of-body experience. Just like I was watching someone else, but I knew it was Ronald."

"Sybil, I have got to find out who she is. I have got to figure out a way to get Ronald back home." She told me to just breathe and assured me we would find out. I didn't know what we would come up with, but for now, I had to rely on myself and my determination. Hopefully, Sybil can help me.

I was just so angry all day. I was tired of putting myself down. I was tired of him putting me down. I was tired of all his rejection. There he is, helping her, giving her money, kissing her. The rejection is so hard to deal with. I just felt like a thrown-away old crumpled-up dollar bill. I guess if I didn't know about it. If I wasn't watching it right in front of my eyes. Maybe I wouldn't feel the rejection as much. But then I wouldn't know the truth either. I have got to know the truth. As God says, the truth shall set you free.

Ronald called the next day; I panicked when I heard his voice. Did he see me yesterday at Bojangles? Did he see the car? I surely hope not. I need to get all the information I can so I will know the truth. If he starts suspecting, I know. He will start getting even more sneaky about it, and I might not find out anything.

He didn't know I saw him; if he did, he didn't mention it. He called to tell me he was attending a writing seminar in Atlanta. Why was he even calling me and telling me this? He hadn't been telling me anything else. Why not just go?

Perhaps he was trying to throw me off base. Trying to make me think he was going to this writing seminar to learn more about writing, his passion. Trying to make me think he wasn't spending his time with other women, but he was spending his time writing and trying to find success with it.

After all, his original reason for needing alone time was due to rejections in writing. He needed time to relax because he was so stressed by all the publisher's rejections. Or was it like he said, he left me because I was getting prettier every day, and he was getting uglier? What will he come up with next?

He said he would be in Atlanta for the weekend and wouldn't be seeing the children. I didn't believe a word of his writing seminar story. I thought I would call around and, just by mere chance, see if he was telling me the truth. I really did want to believe him. I wanted to be able to trust him again. After all, should he come home, we needed trust in our marriage.

He had left information at the house on writing seminars, so I had a list of them to contact. There was a seminar in Jekyll Island, Georgia, the following week. I wondered, had they changed the date? Was he telling me the truth or lying? I wouldn't know until I checked. I called and asked about the seminar. It was still going to be in Jekyll Island, and they had not changed the date. I knew that was not the one he was going to. I called some others on the list, and no one knew of any seminar in Atlanta for that weekend. Here it is again, another lie. Why does Ronald have to lie to me constantly?

I decided to follow him. At least this way, I would find out if he was getting on the Interstate toward Atlanta and if he was alone. Mom came over to stay with the kids. She was so scared for me to do this. She had already had to take me to the doctor for the last fight. But at the same time, she understood why the truth was so important to me.

I went over to his apartment and parked on a side street with his apartment in view. I waited and waited. Then I saw him walking out of the breezeway of his apartment. He got into his car alone and drove onto the Interstate to northeast Nashville. I am thinking this is not the way to Atlanta. Where is he going? Would I be able to keep up with him without him seeing me? One thing I learned from the detective is that

186

people are so interested in what they are doing that they usually pay no attention to what is happening around them. This was exactly what was happening tonight. I don't think he ever saw me or even suspected I was following him.

He drives into a grocery store parking lot on the opposite side of town from where he lives. I would have thought that if he had to go to a grocery, he would have gone to one a couple of miles from his apartment. He gets out of the car, enters the store, gets a grocery cart, and comes out. He didn't even get any groceries. What is he doing? He brings the empty cart to the back of the car. He opens the trunk, gets something out, and places it into the cart. He takes it inside the store, and then he buys some groceries.

He returns to the car with the groceries, but first, he gets something out of the front seat and places it in the trunk. He looks around like he does wonder if he is being watched at this point. Then, he proceeds to put the groceries in the front seat. Why does he need groceries anyway at a seminar? Seminars provide breakfast, lunch, and sometimes even dinner. And why drive so far from where he lived to go to a grocery store? Nothing made any sense. I knew he must be lying to me.

As he left there, he drove to a motel just down the road from this grocery. He parks, gets out, enters the lobby, and sits on the couch. In about twenty minutes, he came out with

187

what appeared to be some towels. He then drives back to his apartment. It was 11:19 P.M. He never picked up anyone. What is he doing? This is so very strange. Driving to the far side of town, 30 minutes away, to get groceries and towels from some dump motel? What is he doing?

I waited out the evening. At 6:08 A.M., he left the apartment with an ice chest. He placed it in the car. Once again, he was alone. I followed him to the Interstate toward Chattanooga. So, was he telling me the truth? Or did he? Is he going to Atlanta? This would be the most direct route, unlike his drive last night. By now, I was so exhausted, with no sleep, I knew I couldn't follow him anymore. I just had to go home and attempt to rest for a while. My mind was spinning. I still needed to know about this Barbara Jean McCloud.

It was a long ride home. I got home. I told Mom about the crazy night I had just had. She hugged me and told me I needed to get some sleep. She was so right. I hated that I was a burden to her during all this time. I keep her up at night talking when I can't sleep. Plus, she was my babysitter when I wanted to make crazy runs like this last one. I was grateful she understood me.

Luckily, the kids slept in this Saturday, and I could catch up on the sleep I missed last night. I got up at about 10:30 A.M., got the kids up, and we ate breakfast. While I was cleaning up the kitchen, I thought Ronald was supposedly out of town, and this would be a good investigative day. I could take the kids on a drive to Murfreesboro, where the human resource personnel said Barbara lived. I wondered if I could find out anything.

At that time, Murfreesboro was a rural town, and it seemed like people knew one another. Perhaps someone would know her and would talk to me. I just hope that I don't talk to the wrong person and that Ronald finds out I am investigating her.

All I need to do is rely on my training and my instincts and see where it takes me. With my private investigation skills, my determination, and God being with me, I set out to find out everything I could. I set out to find out why Ronald was really leaving me. Who was this woman? What was really going on? I was a little afraid of what I would find out. But what could be worse than not knowing?

Even if Ronald did find out, hopefully, that would just let him know how very much I still loved him. That, among the other reasons, was just another reason he said he left. He didn't think I loved him. Look at all the effort I am putting forth to try to save my marriage, and hopefully, it will make him realize the depth of love I have for him. Although I showed it every day we were married, if he couldn't see it then, whatever made me think this would do any good, and he would see it now.

I told the kids it was a pretty day. It would be a good day for a drive and to stop by Shoney's and get some famous hot fudge cake. We all loved chocolate; selling them on the idea didn't take much. We got in the car, bound for Murfreesboro. The kids played some games on the way. While driving, I was thinking and trying to decide what I would do when I got there. I had no idea.

Then it came to me with a name, McCloud. I could check the phone book there and see how many, if any, were listed in the phone book. If I found anyone, would I have the nerve to call? I didn't know. If I did call and they answered, what would I say? So many decisions, and I had so many questions. We reached the city; it was about 40 minutes from our house, and we saw Shoney's. I said, "There is Shoney's. Is everybody ready for some good chocolate hot fudge cake?" At about the same time, they all said, "Yes."

We walked in, and the waitress seated us. We all got some water, and then I ordered three hot fudge cakes. I would just take a bite of each of theirs. We talked about their school while we were waiting. The school year had started well. They all liked their teachers and had several friends in each of their classes. It wouldn't be long until they were in full gear there. I prayed that our life would become somewhat normal now they were back in school, and we got on a regular routine.

"Here comes the cake," Ryder said. Reid says, "Wow, they look good." Rachel noticed the waitress had put a lot of chocolate fudge on the cakes. She could probably tell we all liked chocolate. The kids started eating, and then I thought, well, I drove up here to get some information, so let's see what I can find out.

I asked the kids to sit there and told them I had to make a few phone calls. I told them I would be on the pay phone up front where they could see me, and I could keep my eyes on them too.

I walked up front and got the phone book. I opened it to the "M's" and then to "Mc's." I started down the list, and there it was, "McCloud." The first was H.M. McCloud. My hands shook as I dialed the number. A guy answered, and I asked, "Is Barbara at home?" He said, "I do not know anyone named Barbara." I said, "Thank you. Sorry to bother you; I must have the wrong number." The next was T.B. McCloud, and that phone had been disconnected. I then called the next one, W. Sadie McCloud. I was losing all courage, my hands still shaking, when this elderly lady answered, "Hello." I said, "Hello, ma'am. I am trying to locate Barbara McCloud; do you know her?" She said, "No, I don't know her, but I know some McCloud's. Why are you trying to locate her?"

The way she asked that question, I thought maybe she did know her. I thought I would tell her exactly why. I did. I said, "I am married, my husband and I have three wonderful children, and she is having an affair with my husband." She said, "Oh my honey, you come to my house, and we will talk. She is a distant relative of mine. She is always in trouble. You come right over here, and I will tell you what I know." I was intrigued and ready to talk to this lady.

She gave me her address and said, "Just call me Aunt Sadie." I said, "Okay, thank you, Aunt Sadie. We will see you soon. I am not familiar with this area. I am at Shoney's in Murfreesboro now. How would I get to your house?" She said, "When you leave Shoney's, cross over the bridge and take a right. There is an old mailbox, and I live on a farm on the dirt road." "Okay, I will be there soon."

My first thought was, is this safe? A farm on a dirt road, and she had already told me that Barbara was trouble. Is this a setup? This Sadie lady had already told me she was related. Is Barbara there? Is she dangerous? What should I do? My second thought was that I needed to talk to her. Here is my chance to find out what I need to know. I must go. I wanted to talk to someone who knew her. I need someone that could tell me something about this, Barbara. I felt I had no choice but to go. I knew I would not endanger my children in any way. I could drive out where she said she lived. If it in any way looked dangerous, I would turn around and leave.

I hung up the phone and walked back to the kids. "How's the cake?" "Yummy," they said. "Well, it looks like you have just about eaten everything but the plate. Are you ready to leave?" They said, "Yes, are we going home now?" I said, "Not just yet. A lady, Aunt Sadie, lives just down the road. She asked that we stop by and talk to her." They looked at me like I was crazy. I guess I was.

"Aunt Sadie?" Rachel asked, "Who is Aunt Sadie?" I said, "She is an aunt of a friend of your dad's." I wished I hadn't said that as soon as I said it. What if one of the kids tells their dad? I thought I needed to be sure they didn't say anything to their dad. I said, "Dad would probably be mad if we saw her; he doesn't like her. Please never say a word to him about it, okay?" They agreed. I just bet they all wanted to know the whys, but they didn't ask.

"We will only be there for a few minutes." We got in the car, and I followed Aunt Sadie's directions. I soon saw an old mailbox beside a dirt road. My heart sank, and my hands were sweaty. Not the sweat from the heat, either. I said, "Kids, we are here." Ryder said, "Mom, it is a dump. Look at the cows and the horse." Rachel said, "Look, there are pigs." I said, "Please, remember, do not tell your dad we came here."

There were animals everywhere, it took only a glance for me to know I was not getting out of the car. When Reid saw the big dogs, I knew he was not getting out of the car either. Reid had been bitten by a dog when he was about three years old. He was not afraid of them but just preferred to stay away from them, especially big dogs he didn't know. The dogs were barking. I knew their barking would arouse Aunt Sadie unless she was totally deaf.

It was only seconds before Aunt Sadie stood in the doorway. She was an elderly lady living in a dump, but she was clean. She came outside and walked over to my car. I introduced myself and the children. I immediately thanked her for seeing me and apologized for taking her time. She said, "Honey, that is quite all right. Let's go sit on the porch where we can talk privately?" I got out of the car and told the kids I wouldn't be long. I anxiously walked to her front porch. We sat on the swing.

After we sat down, she asked, "Why don't you tell me what has happened?" I told her that Barbara was seeing my husband and that he had moved out of our home. She quickly responded, "You get a divorce and get it as fast as you can. That girl will drain you of everything you have." I said, "But Aunt Sadie, I love him; I do not want a divorce. I just want him to come home." Aunt Sadie said, "Then you get a legal separation. With a legal separation, he will be ordered to pay the bills. Then you follow up and be sure he is paying them."

I asked her, "What do you know about Barbara?" "Honey," she said, "Those kids are in trouble all the time. Barbara's parents divorced, and there were four kids. There were two boys and two girls. The boys are in and out of jail all the time. They live with their grandmother on East Woodland Street here in Murfreesboro. Barbara's mother married a man whose last name is "White," and they moved to Nashville."

She said again, "You need to get rid of your husband; Barbara will ruin him. When she gets through with him, you will not want him." I kept thinking, how could he have met someone like this? How could he be attracted to her? She must be blackmailing him for something. How could this even have happened? What had he done? I now had more questions about Ronald and his decision-making than I did about this girl, Barbara.

I thanked Aunt Sadie for her help and asked for her prayers. I walked to the car, and the kids had so many questions. "What did she say? Does she know Dad? Who is she? Why did she want to talk to you?" I was very vague. I told them she wanted to talk to me about her niece. I wanted to answer the kid's questions. After all, I had told them to always come to me if they wanted to talk. I was too upset by what Aunt Sadie had told me to even think clearly to answer their questions.

I just kept hearing Aunt Sadie saying, "Get rid of your husband; Barbara is trouble." I couldn't understand, but I knew I had to find some way to save my marriage, or at least what was left of it. I had to find some way to get Barbara out of his life, out of our life. How could I do this?

We drove home. I was so drained when we got home. I just wanted to sleep, but I couldn't. I just kept thinking. I knew I had to talk through this with someone. Although I was tired, I had to stay up talking to someone, anyone who would listen, until I felt better or fell asleep. Especially tonight after what Aunt Sadie had told me. I drove to Murfreesboro hoping I would get some information, but never in my wildest dreams did I think I would get this type of information.

Chapter 27

I decided to call Sybil. Sybil always had great advice and would know what to do. We talked for two hours about my day. I was always talking about me, my day, my problems. This whole situation had consumed me. I couldn't seem to think about anything but Ronald. I was so desperate for some answers. I needed to find someone to make this nightmare end. She was a great friend to listen to me, if only she could stop this nightmare. She would always help me through and never once complained. She reminded me of my private investigation training. Part of the training was how to research public records at the courthouse. She suggested I go to Murfreesboro courthouse to see if Barbara or her siblings have criminal arrest records.

"Sybil," I said, "I never thought trouble would mean criminal. Surely, nothing criminal. Surely, that is not the trouble Aunt Sadie was talking about." Now, Sybil had me really thinking. What could it be? I had been wondering if Barbara had gotten Ronald into some drugs and was blackmailing him. But it was just a passing thought, only because I couldn't figure out why Ronald was acting this way. But could it be true? Do I need to do this? Sybil agreed to go with me if I wanted to go. I told her I would, as they say, sleep on it. We hung up, and I think I was more concerned when I hung up than when I called her. I had just never thought about criminals. Was Ronald involved with a criminal? No, not my sweet Christian husband. That could not be the trouble Aunt Sadie meant.

Everyone had advice, and their advice was always different than what I wanted to hear. I wanted my husband and our marriage. I was willing to keep a commitment to him, although he wasn't perfect. Why couldn't he keep one to me? I could not believe that he could have or would have ever walked away from me, our children, our home. The way he was looking at it, this wasn't his home. He told me that. He said he would rather live in a tent. How could he feel that way?

Why couldn't he just have told me what the problem was? If I only knew what I had done? What did I do that made him act like this? If he would just tell me. I would change anything to make him happy. He had to know that. But no, he wouldn't tell me a word; we had no conversation at all about any problems. Without some conversation, I didn't know what to fix.

All of this came out of the blue. Just the year before, he was happy. He spent thousands on an inground pool in the backyard. That Christmas, he bought me two fur coats. The card on one of the coats said, "To the prettiest woman in the world, to the only woman I have ever or will ever love, to the woman of my life, Love your husband, Ronald. Now, I

198

am supposed to believe we have problems. Here we are going through this. What is happening? How has this happened? Why? Why? I just wished I knew.

Even less than a month before he left me, April 22, is the date he took me out for a romantic night and gave me diamond earrings. He was so romantic. I know he still loves me. Then I ask myself, why is he gone? Why did he leave me if he loved me? I always thought, just like everyone else thought, that we had the perfect life. We adored one another. It wasn't fake. We showed it at home just like we did outside the home. We always laughed and enjoyed one another's company so much. Even when he said he needed some alone time, I still thought we had the perfect relationship, family, and life. We were living a good life. And now ... he is gone.

Now, he was involved with Barbara McCloud, and her Aunt Sadie had just told me how much trouble she was. All during the night, I kept hearing Aunt Sadie's words, "Trouble." I thought, how much trouble could she cause? How much trouble had her brothers been in? Was Aunt Sadie, right? Or was she just a woman wanting someone to talk to?

I thought about what Aunt Sadie had said all weekend. I thought about Sybil's suggestions, checking out the courthouse records. I decided I needed to clear my head, thoughts, and suspicions. I needed to put the idea of a criminal to bed. I had to check that off my list and move on.

On Monday morning, I called Sybil and said, "Let's do it. Let's drive to Murfreesboro and check out the courthouse records." She said, "Come get me, I am ready. I am eager for you to teach me how to check records and see what we find." I said, "I was eager to look, but I don't think we will find anything." I drove the kids to school and went to pick up Sybil.

It wasn't long before we were in Murfreesboro. We went straight to the County Courthouse. We walked in, and I asked the clerk where the criminal court dockets were for the last four years. She walked us back into this small room where there were books and more books. When researching, I explained to Sybil that you take one book at a time. Each book will usually include four to six months of records. In the large book, you will find the name, date, and docket number. In the back of the book, you will find the docket number and a little about the arrest.

We just started in the first book. One book led us to the next book. As we were going through the pages, we kept seeing the name McCloud. Usually, four different first names would show up. The names would come up with different types of arrests. The records would come up with DUI, public arrest, speeding, and then I saw rape. Then I saw burglary. I was beginning to get scared. Is this her? Is this Barbara's family? What has Ronald gotten himself into? Then I saw her name, Barbara Jean McCloud, armed robbery, and drug charges!

My gosh, I thought, his mistress was arrested for armed robbery. I cannot believe it. Ronald is a good man. He and I were teaching the youth group at our church when he left me in May. He had been the President of our children's private school booster club. He had been the ball team commissioner, and now, who is he? I can't believe he would be involved with a woman who has been arrested for armed robbery and drug charges. This woman has a brother charged with rape. This must all be wrong. This cannot be the girl that he is seeing. It just cannot be. This makes no sense at all. How can I find out if this is right? I must find a way to link this all together or, better yet, where it is not linked at all.

Sybil and I left the courthouse with this information. I just had to leave. This is more than I can comprehend. I need a break from it all. Besides, I work tonight at 11 P.M., and I need some sleep. I'm not eating or sleeping, and my mind will not slow down. A break from all of it will do me good. I have been going through all this crazy stuff for almost four months, just trying to understand and figure everything out. Sometimes, I think someone is in front of me, just putting this stuff out there to throw me totally off track. There is no way this courthouse information can be right. Or could this be God one step in front of me, showing me the truth?

I took Sybil home and was determined to take a break. When I got home, I had a phone call from my attorney. He had obtained a court date for three weeks from Friday. It was a date to talk with the judge about Ronald paying the bills. This is some good news. I know Ronald is not going to be happy. Hopefully, he will understand that he still has responsibilities.

Knowing I was taking him to court was stressful for me. I knew if I agitated him, he would never come home. I decided to go talk to him before the court date. I knew I had to be wrong with all this research I had been doing. Perhaps, maybe, he wasn't even seeing that same girl anymore. Yeah, I know he took her to work the other day. But then he called me and told me about going to Atlanta for the writing seminar. Although he did some crazy things that night when I followed him, he did eventually head out toward the correct Interstate for Atlanta, and he was alone.

Perhaps after I saw him taking her to work, he got mad at her and wasn't going to see her anymore. Maybe that is why he was nice to me when he called to tell me about the seminar. Yes, here I am, maybe this and maybe that? I feel so desperate and lost without him. I want to believe he is thinking about coming home. I sure didn't want to ruin his thoughts by taking him to court for money. I have three weeks before the court date, and three weeks to do my best to convince him to come home.

Chapter 28

Our anniversary was coming up. He had to remember it, just like I had. This would be the perfect time to go and talk to him. I called his office, and he answered. Once again, he was very nice to me. So, maybe he wasn't seeing her or anyone. I asked him, "Can I come over and talk with you?" He said, "Sure, let's go for lunch." I said, "Okay, sounds great, what time?" "About 11:30 A.M., does that sound okay?" I said, "Sounds great. Where do you want me to meet you." He said, "What about Shoney's?" I knew it was down the road from his work. I was feeling really encouraged. Not only was he going to talk to me, but he was taking me to lunch. I said, "Shoney's is great. I will see you there at 11:30 A.M." My hopes were high. I just knew this was the beginning, the beginning of the end of all this divorce talk.

I got dressed and wanted to look my best. I might look even better than when we were married since I hadn't been eating and had lost so much weight. I drove over, and there was my handsome husband sitting there waiting for me. He smiled and said, "Ready to eat?" I said, "Yeah, I am hungry." I kept thinking about the recent wedding at our church, the same church where Ronald and I got married. I thought I would try to bring that up along with our anniversary. I was feeling so positive that this was all perfect timing.

The waitress came by and took our order. We sat there talking about the weather, talking about the kids. Then, I asked him how the writing seminar was?" He said, "It was great. I learned a lot." I encouraged him to continue writing because I knew he had a real passion for it. I reminded him what a good time we had working on his first novel. He said, "Yeah, too bad I couldn't get it published." I said, "Yes, it is. Possibly someday, don't give up."

He said, "I was afraid I was going to have to miss the seminar since we were so busy at work." "Yes, I remember how busy this time of the year has always been. It was always hard to find a day to celebrate our anniversary due to the busy season." He said, "Oh yeah, our anniversary is coming up." I said, "Yes, 16 years. Ronald, you know I still love you. I know if we wanted to, we could work everything out." He said, "I am impressed with your persistence. Things were winding down. If you will give me a couple of weeks to think, I will be home." I said, "Of course I will. I love you."

He said, "For two weeks, let's just not talk so I can think." I said, "No problem, I will be sure to be out of sight when you see the kids." They are so excited about seeing you this weekend. He said, "Yeah, I think we will go to Opryland Park. It will be closing soon." "They will love that. They always love anything they do with you." He said, "I will talk

205

to you in a couple of weeks." He gave me a slight hug as he left.

Finally, this ordeal is almost over, just two weeks. I kept remembering the two-week period when he first left. I did not even answer the phone because I was afraid that if he heard my voice, he would not come home. Of course, I did stick to his two-week request then, only to meet him and listen to him say he wanted a divorce. I was apprehensive about this two-week request since the last request ended as it did. But I had to remain positive. I have got to believe him.

For the next two weeks, I stayed busy with the kids. I tried not to think about Aunt Sadie and the day of research at the courthouse. I tried to just remain focused on the future. I had to be patient, be positive, and wait and see if he would be home at the end of the two weeks. Ronald hadn't called the kids in a few days. They were afraid something would come up to keep him from seeing them on Sunday. I tried to explain to them. I said, "Dad has a lot on his mind right now and is just busy. He loves you, and I am sure he will see you on Sunday." Reid said, "Sure, he loves us Mom, that is why he does not call." I repeated, "Yes, he does love you. I am sure he is just very busy."

I asked, "Reid, why don't you try to call your dad?" No way, Reid said. He knows our number; we always call him, and he never calls us. I said, "Reid, just call your dad, please.

I will pay you fifty cents just to call." Reid finally said, "Okay." Reid dialed the number, his dad's office number. It rang six or seven times before he gave up.

Reid said, "He didn't answer Mom, as usual. Do I still get my fifty cents?" "Sure, you do. I stick to my word." At least Reid saw the humor in all of this. Ronald called him back the next day, and they set up their Sunday visit. That phone call seemed to help their spirits. I had to keep their spirits up without telling them about their dad and me talking at Shoney's about him coming home. I was hopeful. But I couldn't tell them and get their hopes up. What if something happened and Ronald changed his mind? That would crush the kids again. I couldn't say a word about it.

Two weeks had passed when Ronald said he did not want to talk to me. I could not stand it any longer. He said he would call, and he hadn't. I called him. I asked, "Are you coming home?" He said, "What are you talking about?" I said, "Ronald, you said that if we did not talk for two weeks, you would come home." He denied saying that. I said, "Then, what did you say when we met at Shoney's?" He said, "I just said, leave me alone!"

Again, deceit, lies, how long will this last? How long would I keep believing and keep getting hurt? He said, "You will be glad to know that she is moving out." I said, "Yes, I am. Where is she moving to?" "I am not sure," he told me.

But could I believe him? Of course, I couldn't. I couldn't believe anything he said. He was constantly lying to me. I guess he thought if I thought she was moving out that the divorce would go smoother. That I would think that maybe we would have a chance after all. Who knows what he was thinking?

Chapter 29

Well, the next time I see him will be in court. The date my attorney scheduled for the judge to hear the case and order him to pay the bills until the divorce comes up. My savings are about gone, and I am beginning to get behind on the bills. One bill that I will pay if I must clean out commodes is the bill for the fur coats. The fur coats he got me for Christmas. Ronald had put them on a payment plan. He has not been paying the bill since he left me in May. I will not let them be repossessed. I will not give up everything while she has my everything.

The collection agency keeps calling me about the payment. Not only could I not make them, but I couldn't even remember to pay them if I had the money. When the bill collector called, I told him I would start making payments. I asked him if he would please call me each month to remind me. A collection agency had probably never had that request before. The collection agency guy agreed he would call me each month, and I agreed to make the payments. Now the court is going to order Ronald to pay me at least some money, I hope.

Mr. Jackson called and asked that I send him a list of all the bills. I got them together and sent them to him. I thought Friday would never get here. Now, I didn't care how mad Ronald got about going to court. I was mad too. I was tired of his lies and him not taking any responsibility when I had all the responsibility.

Finally, on Friday, I get to court and see Mr. Jackson. He said, "Now, it is sit and wait until our docket is called." I thought, fortunately, with the last name of Jenkins, if they go in alphabetical order, it shouldn't take too long. I spent some time talking to my attorney, and then he got the call that it was our time. Nervously, I entered the front area of the courtroom. I had never been in a courtroom. For the first time, it had to be a time that I was depending on a judge to hopefully see my needs and order Ronald to pay the bills.

My attorney presented our case. Ronald's attorney, of course, he got a female. She had little to say. The judge issued a judgement for Ronald to pay the bills, just like Aunt Sadie said he should. I felt that since the judge ordered him to pay, Ronald would surely pay as he was ordered. The judge ordered Ronald to pay me the money, and I would be responsible for paying the bills. That was good. I knew I would pay them, and this way, I didn't have to go behind him every month to be sure that they got paid like Aunt Sadie had told me to do.

I had taken some time off from my investigation. I felt I was on the wrong track, and I was focusing on Ronald coming home, which didn't happen. Now, since he had lied again and he had told me she was moving out, I was more curious than ever to see if he was still seeing her. If he was, then I needed to go back to the Murfreesboro courthouse to see those documents. I didn't believe it was the same girl, but I had just enough doubt to pursue the search if they were still an item.

He has no idea I know where she works or that I have ever seen him take her to work. I have had good restraint to keep my mouth shut about all of it. I am glad I have. By doing so, it will help me in the future. Then, I can check again, and he doesn't suspect anything.

The following Monday, I drove to the restaurant, sat, and waited to see if my husband was still hauling his girlfriend to work. I needed to find out if they were still an item. I sure couldn't believe anything he said. As I sat there, waiting, I couldn't get my mind off those arrest records I had seen.

If he were still involved with her, I would be in Murfreesboro the next day. I looked up, and there he was, just like before, in his new Volvo, pulling into the parking lot. Just like before, he gets out of the car and goes around and opens her door. Just like before she gets out, they kiss, and she goes into the building. That liar, she is not moving out. Why would he even say that?

Well, tomorrow couldn't come soon enough. I will be in Murfreesboro first thing in the morning after I take the kids to school. This time, I will look closer at the notes. I will verify the spelling of the names. I will check addresses more thoroughly so I will know for sure who they were referring to. I would be sure I was accurate about everything before I left. I would go alone; this way, I can take more time and ask more questions. This is too important. If this is her, Ronald has got to know. I sure don't want to tell him his girlfriend is a criminal if it's not true.

It was a stressful drive this morning, but after I drove the kids to school. I was on my way. This time, when I reached the courthouse, I knew exactly where the room with the information I needed was located. I started where I did a few weeks ago, one document at a time. To be sure, I had all the actual information.

What Sybil and I uncovered was accurate. The names, the dates, and the events, now to see the actual arrest record. First, I asked the clerk to make me a copy. Then I started scrutinizing every word. Barbara was with her boyfriend and brother when they robbed the local drugstore with a loaded gun. When the police went to make the arrest, they were at a motel. This motel was just down the street from where Ronald was working. The police called for them to come out. The men came out, but Barbara stayed inside. Per the record, when the police opened the door, a syringe and drugs were clearly seen, and they found the loaded gun in Barbara's purse. This arrest was two years before Ronald left me. This woman should have been in prison today, but I knew Ronald's girlfriend was working at the restaurant. I must be wrong about the name or something. I saw the date in the court records that she was to be released from jail on parole, March 20. It could possibly be her. But if it is, I just can't understand how in the world Ronald got caught up with her. How would it even be possible?

I have got to find out! But how? I am not a professional investigator. I have only had minimal training, but boy, am I invested in finding the truth. I have got to protect Ronald and my family. If this is true, no one in her family can be around me, Ronald, or my children. But I have got to be sure before I say anything. Aunt Sadie mentioned that the boys lived with their grandmother on East Woodland Street in Murfreesboro, TN. The police records also have East Woodland Street in Murfreesboro, TN, as the address. I have got to do this. I have got to find this grandmother. I have got to go into the house and see if she has a picture of Barbara, then I will know if this is the same Barbara, the same family. Surely, I am wrong. I have got to be wrong.

Chapter 30

I called Sybil and asked if she would go with me to Murfreesboro again. I told her I wanted to find the grandmother and talk to her. We both knew this could be dangerous, but at least there is safety in numbers. At least, I hope there is safety in numbers. The court records state loaded guns, drugs, and rape. I knew we had to be extremely careful. I felt I had no choice. Sybil had a choice. This wasn't her family. She didn't feel the urgency as I did. She could tell me no, that she can't go, and she can protect herself. I was so glad she was a good friend and agreed to go with me. We planned the trip for the next day.

I got up, got dressed, and drove the children to school. Then, I nervously drove to pick up Sybil. We arrived in Murfreesboro. First, I drove to the post office, went inside, and asked where East Woodland Street was located. The guy I was talking to knew the area well. He said it was two streets down from the funeral home on Main Street. We left the post office and drove around until I saw 122 East Woodland Street. That was the address on the rape report of one of the McCloud boys. There was an old frame house situated on the corner, neat and clean but small.

It had a screened-in front porch, and a motorcycle was parked outside in the yard. It looks like maybe one of the boys might have been there. I wondered, what if they were home? What if it was the one boy that had been charged with rape? What if Barbara was here and recognized me? Would she have a loaded gun today? I was second-guessing my idea of even stopping here. This could go wrong, fast, very fast! Once again, I felt I had no choice.

Sybil was now second-guessing this idea too. She reminded me that during the drugstore robbery, shots were fired. She thought we needed to leave. That probably would have been the best idea for our safety. If we left, how would I find out the truth? This was my best opportunity to talk directly with the grandmother. I have got to follow through and see if her granddaughter is the same girl in the police report. Is this the same girl that Ronald is having an affair with? If it is? My children can never be around her. They can't be around a family of rape, drugs, theft, guns. I just pray that if she or her brother is here, they don't come to the door with a gun. If they brought a gun with them to the door, I knew the chances were high that it would be loaded.

I took a deep breath. I told Sybil, "I want you to stay safe in the car with the car keys. If you see any sign of trouble, leave, and go for help." I was scared, but I had to do this. None of the dangers mattered to me at the time. I just had to find out and protect Ronald and my children from this family. With that thought in mind, I handed Sybil the keys and got out of the car. I drew in a deep breath, said a prayer, and walked up to the door, and knocked. No one answered. I knocked a second time, and I could hear someone coming to the door. I was terrified of who it would be. I waited, and an older female opened the door.

I smiled and said, "Hi. Is Barbara here?" She said, "No, she is not here right now." I said, "Oh, I hate that I missed her. I went to school with her, and I am passing through from Florida. I was hoping she would be home." What made me think she would believe I went to school with her? I was 13 years older than Barbara. But at the time, I had to say something. I should have been prepared for what I would say.

She said, "She has gone out of town with her fiancée." I said, "Fiancée, I guess she is getting married." "Yes, she is getting married in December." I said, "That is wonderful. Is it anyone that I would know?" "I don't know if you would know him; he is from Nashville." My stomach was turning in knots. I tried to contain my composure. I didn't want to add suspicion to my story. I calmly said, "Really? What type of work does he do?" Then she said, "He owns a car business." I knew then she was talking about my husband. Ronald did not own a car business, but he was the General Manager of a car business.

I wanted to think this was a coincidence, but was it? Could all of this be a coincidence? I said, "Wow, that's great.

How old is he?" She said, "I think about thirty-four." Ronald was thirty-four. Somehow, I got the nerve to ask, "What is his name?" She answered, "Ronald George." I realized it was a coincidence; it was the wrong name. I was relieved.

She invited me inside and asked me about some of Barbara's friends. I stumbled through, and I thought I had left her unaware of who I was. I asked her, "If she had a recent picture of Barbara." I could tell that excited her that I asked. "Yes, I will go get it." She came out with an 8 x 10 and said, "This was a couple of years ago." I thought it was her, but I wasn't 100 percent sure.

She said, "You should visit Barbara's mother. She would be glad to see you." I told her, "I will; that is a great idea. Where does she live now?" She told me she had her phone number and address in her purse. She left the room. I took some deep breaths and prayed. Lord, just give me strength to sit here, and Lord, please protect me.

She came back with a piece of paper and a pencil. I wrote it down, Juanita White 673 794 2867. I thought I should call. If I called, maybe I would find out that I had the wrong person. I thanked her for her time, and I left. As much as all the puzzle pieces fit, I still did not want to believe it. I just could not believe Ronald would be involved with someone in prison for armed robbery and drugs. Her brother is in prison for rape. I couldn't believe it. If he knew this, he wouldn't be. He must not know.

I walked out and got into the car. I quickly pulled out of the driveway. Sybil said, "Is Barbara, Ronald's girlfriend, this lady's granddaughter? Is this the girl that Ronald is having an affair with?" I said, "I do not know. I thought so until she said the name of Barbara's fiancé is Ronald George." Sybil said, "Fiancée! What?" I said, "Yes, the grandmother said Barbara was out of town with her fiancée. Then she said his name was Ronald George." Sybil said, "Perhaps they did not want Grandma to know the real name because he was married. This way, he would be protected in case anyone asked." Maybe Sybil is right. I just didn't want to believe it.

I told Sybil that she gave me the name, address, and phone number of Barbara's mother. The last name is the same last name that Aunt Sadie gave me, "White." I may call her. I just really don't believe I have figured out who the girl in his apartment was and is the girl, the same girl, the granddaughter of the lady I just went to visit. This is not Ronald's character. If this was her and her family, if he knows, perhaps they are blackmailing him for something. Maybe I have been right all this time. This gave me even more determination to find out. I have got to protect him. If this was her, she could rob him. She could even kill him.

After all, this could be the same woman who had robbed the drugstore with a loaded gun when shots were fired.

I can't stop my investigation yet. I have got to be sure one way or the other. Our family depends on me right now. I need to protect all of us.

Chapter 31

Confused, anxious, and angry, I drove back to Nashville. I took Sybil to her house, and then I went home. I had decided to call Barbara's mother, Juanita. When I did call, I would use the same storyline I had with Barbara's grandmother. I was a friend of Barbara's, visiting here from Florida. When I worked with the investigations, I would use the name "Dee Stewart." If Juanita asked me my name, that was going to be my reply.

I called, and a lady answered the phone; Dray's Health Studio, this is Juanita. When she answered, I identified myself and why I was calling. We talked for a few minutes. Then I said, "Barbara's grandmother said Barbara was out of town." "Yes, she is. She went to Gatlinburg with her fiancée." I said, "That is wonderful. I am sorry I missed her. What will Barbara's new name be when she gets married?" She answered and said, "Jenkins."

It felt like my heart had just stopped. I caught my breath and asked her, "When are they getting married?" She said, "December." I attempted to be calm. I said, "So in December, she is marrying Ronald Jenkins. What a beautiful time of the year. Will she be having a large wedding?" "Probably not too big." My puzzle is complete. I had all the information. But does Ronald know who Barbara is, what

Barbara is? A robber, a druggie, in prison? Does he know he is marrying a criminal?

He is planning on marrying this girl. But marrying her in December did not make any sense. He left me in May. Was she still in prison, then? I bet she got the job at the restaurant on a work release program. Did Ronald meet her there? Had he met her before she went to prison, and had he just been waiting for her to be released? Had he been living a lie with me for the last couple of years? I know the truth about her now. What about the truth about my husband? That I didn't know.

Did he already know her? Had he been visiting her in prison? Her parole date was Mar 20. How could he have met her in late March and, by late May, ready to leave his family? There is no way he could have met her the day she got out of prison, fell in love, left his family, and planned in June to marry her in December, ninety days! He had to know her before. The police report said the guy was her boyfriend. I bet it wasn't her boyfriend; I bet it was her brother's friend.

After Ronald wrote the story about Bigfoot, I remember he started another novel. It was about this family in Murfreesboro. We had never been to Murfreesboro. I remember thinking back then, that it was strange that he chose a town we didn't know anything about. Now, this all makes sense, I think.

These questions were all a puzzle to me. I want to know exactly when he met her and where. But for now, I must stay focused on Ronald and his safety. I must remain focused on finding a way to get the information to him. He has got to know all about her before it is too late.

My husband was not only having an affair but with an ex-convict, and he was planning on marrying her in December. Now I know why he told me that night at Tempo's Restaurant that he had to have everything final by December. He said he did not want to be in the middle of a divorce during the holidays. The deceit, the lies, I just cannot believe this is happening.

That night, telling me we had to get divorced. After the divorce, we might start dating and even get married again. It was lies, all lies.

Does he know about her criminal record?

Surely, he does not know she was arrested for armed robbery and drug possession. What should I do with this information? Should I go directly to Ronald? Will he listen to me? Will he believe me? I have the proof; I have the police records. He will have to believe me, if he gives me the time to talk to him.

On second thought, he won't listen to me. I need to go tell his parents. They will talk some sense into him. Once they know, he will end this whole mess. Ronald will come home, and once again, we will have our family together. Our family, just like it was supposed to be.

Tonight, I just hugged my kids and loved them. My mind has been so focused on finding out the truth, now I have it. I have got to focus on being a mom, a mom of three children who are hurting as much as I am. We played games, laughed, ate dinner, and had as good of a time as we could. I got them settled into bed. I went downstairs to go to bed. I got into bed and just kept thinking about my decision to tell his parents. Yep, that was the right decision. His parents are where I needed to go with this information. They loved me and would know what a tragic situation their son had gotten into. They will take care of everything.

The next morning, I drove the children to school. Then, I started my drive to his parents. As I drove over, everything went through my mind, Rachel was fourteen, and Ronald was planning on marrying a girl whose brother had been arrested for "rape." Surely, he does not know. As I got closer, I got to thinking about Ronald's mom. She was not in the best of health. Would this cause her to have a heart attack?

I loved her and would not want anything bad to happen to her, especially not because of this situation. As I got closer to their house, I passed the South Station police department. I noticed a police officer in the parking lot. I pulled in and asked if he had a moment to talk to me. Nothing had changed for me; I was still constantly talking to anyone and trying to decide what to do. He said, "Sure!" He was a middle-aged man, very distinguished-looking, and I hoped he would be compassionate. I felt if he was, he would be exactly the type of person I needed to talk to.

"Sir, thank you for your time; I won't keep you long. I just need some advice." He said, "No problem, I have some time. What type of advice do you need?" I proceeded to tell him, "Well, sir, my husband has left me, and he is involved with a woman who has been arrested for armed robbery, and I don't think he knows." He said, "Surely, he does." "But, sir, he would not stoop to a convict." He asked, "Are you going to tell him?" "Yes, he has got to know. She could kill him or steal everything he has. He has got to protect himself from her and her family."

I told the policeman, "My husband is out of town with her now, so I thought about going to his parents and telling them, but they are in poor health. I wouldn't want to cause them any additional health problems." He said, "You are right. It would be best if you did not tell them. You need to take everything you have to your attorney and let him handle it. He will know what to do." "I don't know why I didn't think of that." "You are upset, and it is hard to think straight when you are close to the situation." He said, "Be careful driving." "Yes, sir, I will. Thank you!"

Ronald didn't live far from here. I kept thinking I would just tell him. I drove over to his apartment. I thought maybe he would be home from Gatlinburg, and we could have a conversation uninterrupted, face-to-face. When I got there, I looked around and did not see his car. I knew that sometimes he drives other vehicles from the car dealership. He could have done that today and be home. I thought I would go upstairs and knock on the door. I did. I got there, and I knocked and knocked, and no one answered.

As I came down the stairs, I just kept thinking I have got to do something with this information today. Time was of the essence. If I waited, anything could happen to him since he is mixed up with this type of family. I have no choice; I must do it today. Coming down the stairs, I thought if I had a phone, I would call Mr. Jackson, just like the police officer suggested.

There was an apartment at the bottom of the stairs, and I heard the TV on. I thought maybe I could use their phone. I knocked on the door, and this large guy came to the door. I said, "I needed to call my attorney; can I please use your phone?" He said, "Sure, come on in." I entered his apartment. He locked the door behind me. I thought, oh no, I have just made a "huge" mistake. But there I was, in the apartment of a guy that I didn't know, and he was three times my size, and he just locked the door. I knew I had to use his phone and get out of there as fast as possible. Hopefully, he will let me out of here.

I called Mr. Jackson, and fortunately, he was in the office. His assistant sent me right to his phone. I said, "Mr. Jackson, I hate to bother you today. You asked me if I had any pertinent information to contact you." He said, "Yes, what is going on?" "Mr. Jackson, I have found out that the girl Ronald is having an affair with, Barbara McCloud, has been in prison for armed robbery and drugs. She may be out on work release; perhaps that is why he can see her. I don't know. But her brother has been in jail for rape. I feel like this is a very dangerous family. I am sure Ronald would never have been involved with her if he had known this. We must get this information to him before something horrible happens."

He was as shocked about this information as I was. He might have even thought I made it all up. I wish I had. I wished it had been a story. But it wasn't. It was all true, and I had all the documentation to prove it. He asked me, "Are you sure this is the same person?" "Yes, I am sure. I didn't want to believe it either. I have verified it all with her grandmother and her mother. I am very sorry to say, but it is her. She is a convict.

I talked to her mother. She said they were in Gatlinburg. I didn't ask her when they would be home. He has got to get this information as soon as possible. How in the world does the prison system work? How could she even go out of town to Gatlinburg?" He didn't understand that either. He told me he would call Ronald's attorney the next day. He felt that Ms. Donavan would talk with Ronald about the situation. I said, "Okay, I guess that's all we can do now. Thank you."

Now, to get out of this apartment. I was trying to be very quick. I didn't want to be rude and make this guy mad. I just had to get out safely. As I turned and started walking toward the door, I was once again praying. Please, Lord, please let me get out of here so I can go home to my children.

I got to the door, and I reached for the knob. I wanted to open the door as quickly as possible and quickly walk out. As my hand grasped the doorknob, I realized I was right; he had locked the door. I panicked, and my heart was racing. Ramona, I thought, just unlock the door, open it, and get out of here. I quickly reached for the lock; about that time, I heard him walking up behind me. I thought, no, please don't touch me. I was scared. I didn't know what he was going to do. Suddenly, I heard him say, "I will unlock it for you." I politely and gratefully said, "Okay, thank you." He unlocked the door. I said, "Thank you for letting me use your phone." I quickly turned and left. What a relief to get to my car. I think I was so worried about myself that I had forgotten about Ronald for a moment.

When that big guy answered the door, I probably should have said, "I am sorry, I have the wrong apartment and left immediately." I should have never asked to use his phone. I never thought about safety until he locked the door. I just had gone through so much the last few days with all this information I just wasn't thinking straight. I was trying desperately to get this information to Ronald to protect him.

I was so glad; I had called Mr. Jackson. I knew he would contact Ronald's attorney. Ronald would get the information, and now he would be safe. I knew I had done the right thing with this investigation. Without it, Ronald would not have known. No telling what she would do to him. I knew that once he knew, he would end it. He would want out of that dangerous situation and away from her and her family. I would hope he would come back home. But should he decide not to, I would have to accept that. At least he would be safe.

He evidently thinks he loves her. After all, he left everything he had for her. He will be devastated, and I will need to be there for him. I will be strong. I will listen to him when he wants to talk about it. Listen as a friend, not an upset wife. No judgment. I can't imagine how hurt and angry he is going to be. She knowingly has been lying and deceiving him all these months. I don't think any other wife would give their husband a second chance and let him come back home. I will. I will be strong as we get through this. All the time, remembering my go-to scripture where God says, "In all things give thanks, for this is the will of the Lord!"

Chapter 32

It has been a few days, and I haven't heard a word from my attorney or from Ronald. I was afraid maybe he couldn't be reached. Afraid Ronald still didn't know, and he was still in danger. What is happening? How long will it take for the information to get to him? What if her old boyfriend had gotten out of prison and found out about her engagement? What if he is the jealous type? He could kill them both.

All these thoughts of her ex-boyfriend out of prison and looking for Ronald were whirling through my head. Then I thought about me and the kids. What if her family found out it was me, his wife, doing the investigation, and they wanted me out of the picture? Perhaps they would get someone to kill me so I wouldn't be a threat to their relationship. I was afraid they would take revenge. Every car that slowed down in front of the house, I wondered, who was that? Every time the phone rang, and if they hung up on me, I would wonder if that was her brother. Was he checking to see if I was home? What have I done? This all must end. We have all got to get away from her and her family. None of us are safe.

I decided it was time for Ronald to know. I couldn't wait any longer. I called his work, and he answered. "Ronald, I must talk to you." He said, "Okay, come on over." He seemed calm and even nice, just like before when I met him at the restaurant. I wondered why? It did not matter. I just need to go and tell him and show him the documents. I had made extra copies so I would be sure to have a copy for myself. I drove over to his work. When I got there, I went straight into his office. I sat down in the chair directly across from him.

"Ronald, I have something I must tell you. I am not sure where to start, and I don't want to upset you. There is something you must know." I couldn't find the words, so I just handed him the documents. The documents of her arrest and her brother's arrest for rape. He sat there calmly reading them. He would turn to the next page and keep reading. All the time, remaining calm and without any reaction.

Before I got to his office, he didn't even know I knew her name. Let alone all the information I had obtained. If the documents didn't get a reaction, him knowing I knew it all, that would have been enough for some type of reaction from him. I knew he would be shocked about the documents. I also wondered if he would be mad at me for doing the research that found the documents in the first place? But what I wasn't prepared for was his response. After he read all of it, he was still very calm. He then looked up and said, "So?"

I was so shocked by his response, that all I could say was, "What do you mean? So? She is a convict! Her brother has been arrested for rape! We have a fourteen-year-old daughter. And all you can say is, So?" He then says, as if he was proud to say it, "She was framed, and her brother never got convicted." I said, "You knew! You have known all this time." So shocked he knew and so disgusted with him, I just got up and left.

I got in my car and drove down Murfreesboro Road. I just kept saying, "He knew, He knew!" I was getting more and more upset. I couldn't stop crying and screaming, "He knew! He knew!" I was so upset I knew I had to stop the car. I had to safely get home to my three children and protect them. Ronald wasn't going to protect them. That he just proved to me. He knew he was involved with a violent criminal family. He knew this could hurt our children. He didn't care.

I was almost at the dealership where my former neighbor, Paul, worked. It was down the street from Ronald's company. I knew Paul would help me. Paul and his wife, Glenda, were our neighbors when Rachel was born. His wife was the one who would help me with Rachel when she was a baby. I knew I could confide in and talk to Paul. I just prayed he was there and had time to listen. I got there and drove around to the body shop of the dealership. He was the body shop manager. He knew what a great man Ronald was and would understand why I was so upset.

He got me some Kleenex and sat there and just listened to me. He was shocked. "Ramona," he said, "I can't understand what has happened to him. I do know you are a good woman and a great mom. You know God will take care of you and the children." "Yes, I know He will." I knew God had been with us through all of this. God had opened doors and windows for me to see what was going on. God knew this information would help us. Paul was right. God would not let us down.

I finally calmed down enough to drive home. I felt like a zombie. I could not believe he knew this information and still got into a relationship with her. I didn't understand how or why he would do that. What did she have that was so wonderful for him to overlook all of that? I went back to my thoughts. Is she blackmailing him about something? Is he on drugs?

I got into my car and started driving. I drove and drove, not even realizing where I was driving. I knew I was going to go home, but it was as if the car knew the way. Suddenly, blue lights were behind me, and a siren blaring. I pulled over. The police officer came to the window. He could visibly see how upset I was. I said, "Sir, I am so upset I can barely breathe. My husband has left me for a convict. I just found out he knew about her police record and got involved with her anyway."

He never asked for my driver's license, insurance card, or anything. He just asked me, "Do you want me to drive you home? Or I can lead the way to be sure you get home safely." I wasn't even thinking. I was a danger to myself and everyone else on the road. He said, "I can't leave the area right now, but when I finish my shift in about an hour, I could escort you home." I sat there, and he talked to me. It seemed more than an hour had passed. He finally talked enough to calm me down. I told him, "I think I am okay to drive now. I am much calmer. Thank you for talking with me and your concern."

He must have agreed. He let me leave to drive home. I did make it home safely. You know how sometimes the news is upsetting? After you absorb it, the upset turns to anger. That is what happened to me. I was now angry. I was still shocked he knew and stayed with her. Now I was angry he even left me for the convict. It was a good thing I searched for the truth. I am sure he thought I would never know the truth. He probably thought he would get a divorce and marry her in December. If he thought he would get a divorce, we would sell the house, and she would get half of the money for drugs. He could think again. I loved him, but I was not stupid.

This whole time, he knew he was planning on marrying her in December, knowing she was a convict. That is why, at Tempos, he told me we had to be divorced by December. That S.O.B. He didn't have the nerve to say, we need to get a divorce by December because I am engaged to get married, and we want to get married in December. No, that would ruin his plan. He just says go along with my divorce plan, then, I will be nice to you. You can go with me and the kids when we go somewhere. Do that, he says, or things will get dirty. The nerve of him and what a coward at the same time. He was playing his cards, thinking he had a stacked hand; he had just forgotten what a good card player I was.

Chapter 33

Now, I was even more curious about the stuff inside his briefcase. When I got home, I went straight to the dining room, where I had put it in the chair. I had tried so many dates and combinations before, trying to open it. Nothing worked. Then I thought about her parole date. I thought, surely not, surely, he didn't use her scheduled parole date. I entered that date. Bingo, that was it. He had put her parole date as the code for his briefcase. Just how long has he known her? How long has he been playing me for a fool?

I got it opened. Inside were hotel receipts and hotel keys. That was a real eye-opener. But the real eye-opener were the letters inside that she had written to him. She probably had written them while she was in the big house. She dated them. The date was before he left me. How long had this been going on? For her to say how much she loved him, and she couldn't wait until they could be together, all dated with a date in May before he ever left the house, May 21. It had to have been going on for a while. Had he been going to prison to visit her? How did they even meet? Did they meet before she got arrested? Is this the family in Murfreesboro he started writing his 2nd book about? I am so sick of wondering, questioning, and trying to understand. But I need to know. I have found out a lot. I need to find out the answers to these questions too.

There is a guy at our church who works at the lady's prison. I wanted to ask him to look at the prison visitation records. At the same time, I did not want to involve him. I didn't want him or other church members to hear about what Ronald was doing and what type of person he was involved with. Why did it really matter if I got that information anyway? I have enough information to protect me and my kids financially. Hopefully, there is enough information for the judge to agree to place an order where she and her family can never be around my kids.

I was just curious. Was she out on work release, and he met her at the restaurant where she worked? Perhaps she flirted with him. If she could get her nails into him, her life would turn from prison to a new home and car. She had everything to gain by playing up to him where he had everything to lose.

He was such a fool to think she cared about him. She loved herself. She was trying to find herself a sugar daddy. And buddy, he looked the part. Maybe that is what Ronald meant when he told me she had a rich daddy. Was he referring to himself? He constantly was talking in circles. She had nothing. If she just got a little bit from him, it was more than she had. Was he so stupid he didn't realize what she was doing?

Yeah, he might have looked like a rich sugar daddy. But he had a mortgage, bills, a wife, and three kids he was responsible for. What he forgot was not only did he have a wife, but a smart wife. I guess he thought he could play me, and he tried. He thought he would have his little affair, and take everything from me for her. But that is NOT going to happen.

Is that why he wanted me to quit my job? So, I would be poor like her, so I could see how it felt? Is that why he sold my car so that I would be like her with nothing? Did he want me to know how that felt? Well, he won that. I quit my job because he said he couldn't sleep without me. I did say yes, you can sell my car, when he said you have a company car. He tricked me then. But the trickery is over. I now have the upper hand. Now that I know the truth. God is so right, "The truth will set you free!"

Did he think I would never find out? What about the kids? Did he think they would accept this convict as a stepmother? Did he believe having an accused rapist around our children was okay? I don't know what he was thinking, nor do I care. I know everything now, and no way that is ever going to happen! No way will she or her family ever be around my children. I would move to China first. He would never see his children before I would let that happen. She is

NEVER going to be a part of their life. I will not allow it. I will find a way! Someway!

I called my attorney and told him to name her in the divorce papers. I told him to include she is NEVER to be around my children. Mr. Jackson knew I was adamant about it. He said, "We could name her in the divorce. However, we can only request the judge to order that she can't be around them. I don't know if the judge will do that." I said, "Then, there will not be a divorce. I will take care of my kids and be sure she is never around them. I did not want a divorce anyway."

He tried to talk me down from my anger. But I thought he probably didn't have children. Anyone who had children would feel the same way. Hopefully, the judge had children, and he would understand. He had to honor this. I cannot allow a criminal and a criminal's family to hurt my children. If they didn't hurt them physically, they for sure would emotionally and financially. All the money would be going on drugs and whatever else criminals spend their money on. It isn't going to happen. I will protect them to the day I die. Aunt Sadie was right. She will drain him.

This was just too upsetting to me. I couldn't handle this anymore. What had happened to him? What had happened to our life? And why? Why would he stoop to a convict? Why leave his family at all, especially for a criminal? All he had to do was just talk to me. We could fix whatever it was that he wasn't happy about. He had to know this. Almost 16 years of marriage, and this is how it will end?

Chapter 34

I needed to talk to someone. I called Lee again, our Sunday School teacher. I felt he would keep this confidential and could help me understand. He said, "I am on my way." I don't know how he got here so fast. He had to get his wheelchair out, load it somehow in the car, and then drive over. He does all this and makes it look effortless. It is amazing.

When he got here, I opened the door, and we started talking. I told him the whole story. Of course, he was shocked. Anyone who knew Ronald would be. He was shocked Ronald had left us, and now this. "Ramona, I understand why you would be so upset. You have every right to be. This is extremely shocking and totally out of character for Ronald. God will help you through this.

Ramona, you are strong. The kids need your support and protection now. You must accept the Ronald you knew doesn't exist right now. He is operating from a totally different mindset. We can pray that soon he will snap back to himself. For now, you cannot give up. You must hold God and his word close right now. You must keep remembering the verse you told me about. The verse God revealed to you on the day Ronald left in May. Remember it daily, "In all things, give thanks, for this is the will of the Lord!"

Lee was right. I was strong, and God was going to help me. The kids needed me, and I needed to focus on them. Once again, I took a deep breath and gained control of my thoughts. Lee prayed with me, and then he left. I went into my bedroom and started reading the bible. The scripture I wanted to read about was on marriage.

I needed to read what God said about divorce. I had married for better or worse. Brother Adams had always preached about working things out and communicating. I knew he thought divorce was wrong. What did God say? In Matthew 5:32, "If a man leaves his wife except for adultery. He 'causes' her to commit adultery." I thought that was good. Ronald will now be responsible for my sins. Not really, but it was rewarding to know that Ronald was going to be responsible. He will have to answer for all the damage he has caused to me and the kids. He is responsible for his choices and the consequences that come from his choices. By now, I knew Ronald had committed adultery.

It was time for the kids to get home from school. Marilyn and I had started carpooling. She knew Ronald had moved out and how much I had going on. She didn't know, thank goodness, about Barbara. Marilyn offered to take the kids to and from school each day. I wouldn't let her do that. I insisted let's just alternate. I will drive for one week, and you can drive the following week. This will still help me so much. I went into the kitchen to make them their favorite cookies, chocolate oatmeal. They all loved them. Hot chocolate oatmeal cookies and a big glass of cold milk would be the best snack after school.

I was making cookies and thinking. I was so grateful I could be home after they got out of school. I always thought the first minutes you saw them were the best. The school day was fresh on their mind, and they would have so much to share. At least for now, I could work part-time, and that was at night while they were asleep. I could still be home when they got home or pick them up after school on my carpool days. I would be here to hear about their days. I would be here to share the joys, and the ups and the downs. I would be here to help them with their homework. I would be here, and they would know I would be. They would know they could depend on me. They would know just how important they are to me. And how much I loved them, and that I would always protect them. For now, I will be home. I hope it will stay that way. But God will be with me and with them should the day come that I need to work full-time.

I kept thinking about the conversation at Ronald's office. I thought possibly now that he knew I knew, possibly he would reconsider the whole affair. Maybe he did not know until I told him she was a convict. Perhaps he just acted like he knew, because he did not want me to think I knew more than he did. Maybe it was just his ego and pride? He just could not continue a relationship with a convict. What kind of life did he think he would have?

Every time the news came on and there was a drug bust, I would grinch. I would stand there glued to the TV until they called the names of the ones involved. I would read the newspaper articles, afraid one day I would see Ronald's name. I called the police department and asked for signs to look for when someone was doing drugs. He advised me they would have red eyes and varying personalities, and they would be different. Whenever I would see Ronald, I would look at his eyes. They would be red. I would say your eyes sure are red. He would say, I haven't been sleeping much. He could have red eyes from lack of sleep. His personality would change daily. How will I ever know if he is doing drugs? I wished I knew more about the signs. I didn't want to believe he was on drugs. I just wanted the truth. I wanted to know the truth about their relationship. I wanted to know the truth about his habits. I wanted to know the truth about the possibility of us staying married.

I will stay focused on my kids. Focus on their day and what happened at school. I would have the cookies ready, so when they came through the door, they could smell them. About that time, I heard Marilyn pull into the driveway. I went to the door to greet them, "Kiddos, cookies are ready."

They dropped their backpacks and ran into the kitchen. I followed them and got out glasses, and poured them some milk. I asked them, "How was your day?" Each one began telling me. Rachel was excited. She was on the cheerleading team last year, and she had decided to go out for the team again this year. She was so talented, so smart, and so friendly. Although she hadn't had professional training or classes like some of the girls, I knew she would get to be a cheerleader this year too. It would be a great way to keep her mind off her dad. The boys didn't have as much to talk about. Except for Ryder, they had signups for the Cub Scouts, and he wanted to join. I asked them both to get the papers out. I would look over them and get them signed right then. That way, they could turn the papers in to the teacher's first thing tomorrow morning. The cookies and milk were gone, conversations were done, and now they wanted to go and visit with their friends.

Kids have so much they want to do and so much on their minds. That is why I hope I can stay home with them until they are grown. These moments are the best. I think the best for them and for me. They are just such a joy.

Chapter 35

The next few weeks seemed a bit easier. The judge had ordered Ronald to pay the bills. I had completed all the investigations that I could and knew what was really happening. The children had been back in school for a few weeks and seemed to be adjusting. There were school activities and homework that were taking our minds off these last few months.

Fall was in the air, and fall meant my birthday. We had always made a big deal of birthdays, especially with my children. The week of your birthday would be your birthday week. You wouldn't have to do any chores, and you got to decide the menu for the week. It was all about you. Of course, when it was my birthday, it was recognized, but I still had chores to do.

When Ronald and I were together, we would all go to Gatlinburg to celebrate my birthday. With my birthday being in October, it was the best place to go celebrate. The leaves of East Tennessee are gorgeous that time of year. The temperature would usually be around 70. Halloween decorations would be everywhere: caramel apples, apple cider, witches, and goblins. We would always have the best time. This year would be different. The kids and I could not afford a trip. It was literally dime to dime to get through each day. Fortunately, my mom had taught me how to manage with little money. My mom was a queen at stretching a dollar. I want to think I learned how to do it too. That knowledge will come in handy.

After the kids left for school the next day, I sat at the breakfast table, and the phone rang. I answered it, it was Russ, the assistant manager at the company where Ronald worked. He asked me, "Do you know where Ronald is?" I said, "No, I haven't talked to him in a few days." I thought Russ was calling me to locate Ronald for something going on at work. But that wasn't it at all.

He said, "I thought you might want to know where he is if you didn't know." I said, "Yes, where is he?" He told me Ronald had won an all-expense trip to Gatlinburg, including a chalet. Shocked, I said, "Really? Is he there now?" He said, "I am not sure if he is, but he is on vacation. Russ went on to tell me, "Ramona, watch out for yourself. Ronald is telling everyone that you are a bitch. You need to be sure to protect yourself."

I think everyone at the dealership knew he was having an affair. They probably knew the way he had been treating me too. They all liked me and respected me. I thanked Russ for the information. He said, "I just thought you should know." I did need to know. I appreciated him watching out and telling me too. The very idea that Ronald is with a convict. He has left me and the kids, and he is telling everyone I am a bitch. They knew that wasn't the case. They knew me.

I could not believe it. He had won a trip to Gatlinburg, all expenses paid. This is the place he takes me to every year for my birthday. Of course, we never get a chalet. He had not said a word to me about winning this trip. Of course, he is not going to tell me. What was I thinking?

There is no way she will go to Gatlinburg and not me and the kids. Once again, I had to put my investigation skills to work. The kids and I are going to Gatlinburg. If anyone is going to be in Gatlinburg on a chalet all-expense paid trip, it is going to be me and the kids. His boss would not want Ronald and Barbara to use it while the kids and I were at home. That, I knew for sure! His boss, Mr. Dennis, liked me. So did Russ and the rest of the guys there. I was always supportive of Ronald and his work at any dealership where he worked.

While the kids were at school, I started packing. When they got home. I told them, "Kiddos, you know, the other day, we talked about my birthday and going out of town this year to celebrate. I know I said then that we wouldn't go anywhere. Well, I have been thinking about it; I think we should go to Gatlinburg. We are going to the mountains, after all." They were so excited. I said, "We would get up early in the morning and head out." Reid asked, "Mom, what about school?" I said, "You will only miss one day since fall break starts on Friday. I decided y'all could miss one day for this vacation."

We drove to the store to get some snacks and drinks for the ride. We always packed a cooler for road trips. That way, the kids have plenty without getting hungry on the road. I said, "We should get a good night's sleep. Tomorrow will be a busy day."

The following day couldn't come soon enough for me. Boy, was Ronald going to be in the shock of his life. If he thought me knowing about Barbara and confronting him was a shock. Well, he didn't know the meaning of shock. Once again, God has opened the door for me. He used Russ to let me know about the trip. Thank you, Jesus. I mean that literally, and thank you, Russ.

Without Jesus, where would my ship be? That was a song we sang in church. If it wasn't for the lighthouse, where would my ship be? That is so very true. I know that had it not been for God constantly opening doors, one by one, Ronald would have been successful and gotten his divorce by December. I had God on my side. None of Ronald's trickery would win. Not only was God opening doors for me to see the truth. He protected me every day as I searched for the truth.

Morning finally came, and we got in the car and were on the road. On the road to Gatlinburg to celebrate my birthday. We will need to find the chalet where Ronald is staying, and I am sure staying with Barbara. If they are there alone, they won't be for long. I will find the chalet, and the kids and I will use the chalet. It won't be their dad and Barbara using it unless they stay with us. And that is not going to happen. That is something none of us would want. Oh boy, will they be in for a shock?

I had no idea the challenge I would face to find the chalet. I had faced challenges before. I will find it. I would have to find it. I realized I hadn't thought this through very well. Here, I am driving to Gatlinburg with the kids. I had very little money and no credit card. If we didn't find the chalet, we would be on the side of the road, sleeping in the car. It was fall, the busiest time of the year. If I had a credit card, it wouldn't do me any good. There would not be any rooms anywhere to rent. Well, so be it. Ronald and Barbara can sleep on the side of the road. This is going to get interesting.

Now, to focus on finding the chalet. On the drive up there, I got to thinking about the area and recalled there is a central location for cabin rental. I could go there and show my I.D. since my last name and Ronald's last name are the same. After all, I am his wife. I would tell the clerk the kids just got out of school, and we are to meet their dad at the cabin. I don't have any way to reach him. I don't remember the cabin name or number. Can you help me?

That was easier than I thought. Who wouldn't feel sorry for a mom with three kids trying to find the cabin where their dad was waiting for them? That worked. He gave me the information. I said, "May I please have a key in case he isn't there right now? I know he had some business meetings." He said, "Yes, ma'am, just a moment." Then he came back with a key and a map and said, "Enjoy your stay." Since there were no cell phones in 1983, he knew I wouldn't have a way to get in touch with Ronald. Fortunately, he believed me and my story and gave me the information I needed.

The kids took the map. Even though they were kids, they were probably better at reading a map than I was. I always had trouble reading maps and have never had any sense of direction. Plus, I was driving in the mountains and had to keep my eyes on the roads. They are very curvy and are huge drop-offs on the side of the mountains. The map is in good hands with the kids.

Rachel had a great sense of direction. I knew they would find it. I just didn't know what I would do when we got there. What if they were there? Would she have a loaded gun with her? Sometimes, my desperation seemed like it took me to places I didn't need to go. This very well could have been another place I didn't need to go. I guess it was all about the principle for me. I was always big on principle. Right is right, and wrong is wrong, regardless of who it is. And Ronald was wrong; he should have offered this chalet to the kids and me to use, to begin with. If he had done the right thing, we wouldn't be in this situation right now. Once again, just like Lee said, Ronald is responsible for his choices. Boy, he made a wrong choice this time. He was not going to like the consequences.

We drove about five minutes through the winding roads. Rachel gave me directions while the boys were trying to help her, while the whole time, they were looking for bears. Before we got to the chalet, I thought I needed to tell the children about the possibility of seeing their dad there. It was going to be hard to explain. Even harder for an explanation if Barbara is there. I knew I should not subject the kids to all of this. I couldn't leave them at home. I thought, whether I should have or not, I had already told them about Barbara. I had told them about the divorce. I had tried as best as I could to explain things to them. But explain it to them in a simple conversation. The way you would talk to the children when you first explain the birds and bees. You tell the story without details.

After I found out she was a convict, I told the kids about her, not that she was a convict. I wanted to tell them, just in case the kids were with their dad, and she showed up. I had to keep tabs on who and what they were being exposed to when they were with him. It wasn't about their dad's character; it was about their protection. I simply told them, "You know that your dad has filed for divorce. I have found out that he has a girlfriend. I do not want you to ever be around her. His attorney is supposed to have told your dad that. I want you to tell me if she is ever there. I want you to tell me if she is ever anywhere y'all are. If she is at your grandmother's, a restaurant, or anywhere. This is very important for y'all to remember this and to tell me." They seemed to understand. They didn't even ask questions. They just said, "Okay." At least, they know, so when we get there, and she is there, they will probably understand why she is there.

Rachel shouted, "Mom, there it is." The boys started clapping and were so excited. We had always had a great time in Gatlinburg but never stayed in a chalet. This chalet was beautiful. It was huge and had a perfect view of the mountains. I could see there was a big deck out back overlooking the mountains. I knew the boys would love looking out over the mountains in hopes of seeing a bear.

We pulled into the driveway. There wasn't another car there. That was good. I felt good about that. I didn't think they were there. I was nervous but determined. This chalet was ours for the weekend. We got out of the car, the kids each grabbing their suitcases. We went to the door; I got the key the clerk had given me. I placed the key into the door lock and turned it, and the door opened. Once I was inside, I knew no one else was there. This was great. This will give us time to unpack and scout out the place.

The view from the deck was better than I thought. This would be a great place to look and probably see some bears. We were going to celebrate my birthday and have a great weekend. I just could not wait for Ronald to return to the chalet so I could thank him for winning this trip. Not!

After looking out over the mountains, we stepped back inside the chalet to unpack. I went into the bedroom first, and there I saw her stuff: her lingerie, her toys, her pictures. I was sick to my stomach. I threw them in the trash. I couldn't take a chance on the kids to see any of that stuff.

What a low life! Of course, she is, she is a convict. I wouldn't want Ronald now if he wanted to come home. I had all their stuff in the trash and the bedroom cleaned when the kids came in to unpack. I didn't throw away Ronald's or Barbara's clothes. I packed them. I just threw the personal stuff away. Trashed, just like her.

We couldn't believe how big the room was. We then went upstairs to the loft to see the other bedrooms. They each found the room they wanted. I didn't know if they would decide to sleep there once it got dark. A cabin in the woods at night might get scary. We had never been in a chalet before, so we weren't sure what to expect. For now, they were happy. They were happy to be in Gatlinburg and to be in a chalet. That was all I needed. To see their smiles and enthusiasm was enough for me. I didn't need him.

Of course, I knew it would not be long until we had visitors. I didn't mean bears, either. It wouldn't be long before Ronald would return. The kids and I played games and watched TV while waiting for them. It wasn't long before I heard a car. I peeped out the window and saw Ronald's Volvo. I saw them both jump out of the car. There wasn't any walking around opening her door this time. They were both in a hurry to get inside. I guess he recognized my car too.

Boy, was he shocked when he saw us there? He had to recognize the car before he came in. Why didn't he keep going down the road and avoid the whole confrontation? He unlocked the door, opened it, and came into the chalet. He never acknowledged the kids. He said, "You have got to leave!" I said, "No, not me and the kids. We are not going anywhere. Your boss would like the kids and me to enjoy this chalet this weekend. How do you think I knew where you were?" "Get out!" he screamed. "Scream all you want, but we are not going anywhere. It looks like you and Barbara need to find a place to stay."

Oh my gosh, Ronald was mad, but his girlfriend was furious. She picked up a chair and started to throw it at me. Ronald stopped her. I was glad it wasn't a gun. I thought, girl, with your criminal record, that is not a good idea. I wouldn't have pressed charges for fear of revenge from her family. But she didn't know that. Had it not been for revenge from her family, had I pressed charges, that would have sent her back where she belonged, Prison! Without another word, they got what was left of their stuff and left.

The kids and I checked out the refrigerator. They had it stocked well. We were going to have plenty to eat. I guess they had planned to have plenty of food and no need to leave to go out to eat. They thought they would have a good fire, good food, and a good time. Instead, they had no fire, no room, and no food. Oh well, we had plenty of food, and we were going to have a good time, just like Mr. Dennis would have wanted. That is precisely what I bet he had planned when he offered the trip. It would be family time for whoever won it.

I am sure he had no idea Ronald would use it for a convict. He probably thought this would be an excellent weekend for Ronald and his family. I am sure he never suspected the domestic scene that would have occurred. I knew when I got home, I would go and thank Mr. Dennis for a beautiful weekend. I will tell him about the great weekend the kids, and I had and how much we appreciated the trip.

Chapter 36

The following day, the kids and I got up, ready to start our wonderful weekend in the mountains. Ronald had packed the refrigerator with so much food, so I asked the kids, "How would you like to have a picnic lunch this afternoon by a beautiful creek." Reid said, "Mom, what if the bears are hungry?" I assured him we would stop at a safe place. Of course, anytime in the mountains, if there are bears and you have food, you must be careful.

We got dressed. We packed our picnic basket full. For breakfast, we are going to our favorite place, The Pancake Pantry. It was only a short drive down to the restaurant. Nothing is better than chocolate chip pancakes and hot chocolate on a crisp October morning. We ate our breakfast and were ready to go to the park and to the waterfalls.

It took a little bit of time until we reached Laurel Falls. Once we did, we had about a mile hike down to the falls. We had had a lot of rain this year, so I thought the falls would probably be the best. They were always beautiful. I was right. When we reached the falls, the water was gushing over the rocks, absolutely beautiful! We stayed down there for a while. It was tough trying to keep Reid and Ryder out of the water. But we had a fun time. We hiked back to the car to drive over the mountains to Cherokee, NC. The drive through the mountains was gorgeous. The leaves were changing colors. As you drove through the mountains, seeing God's beautiful creation was amazing and so peaceful.

We reached Cherokee, NC. It wasn't long until we were at the Cherokee Village. We could see the ladies sitting outside the teepees, making their crafts. The guys were performing the Native American dances. We parked the car and started walking around. It was only a short time until we saw their small zoo. They had bears in a confined area. The kids enjoyed watching the bears play and climb around. It had been a fun day. Before we left the area, we found the perfect creek to sit by for our lunch. We felt it would be safe from bears. It was at the edge of a bridge just outside the village. We spread out our blankets and had a great late lunch.

After we ate, it was time to drive back across the mountain to return to our chalet before it got too dark. Rachel reminded me about the fudge in Pigeon Forge. We drove there and went directly to the fudge shop. We bought fudge and caramel apples. It was a perfect end to our day. It's the ideal place to celebrate my birthday. As we drove back to the chalet, we rolled down the windows. The air was so cool and clean. We could smell fall in the air.

We got to the chalet and decided to sit outside for a while. It was such a beautiful night. We just sat outside on the deck, looking at the stars and listening to the night sounds. Then it was time for bed. Tomorrow morning would be a busy morning, and we had to get our sleep.

When morning came, I cooked breakfast at the chalet. We packed our clothes, drove down to Pigeon Forge, and spent the day there before it was time to drive back home. We couldn't leave the area without a visit to our friends Carol, Gary, and their son Chip. They lived only 30 minutes south of Gatlinburg; it was on our way home. By the time we finished visiting with their family, it was like the kids had put the episode of their dad out of their minds. It was time to go home.

Fall was in the air, for sure. Fall break at school was over, but the fall weather had just begun. The leaves were falling off the trees. You could smell the logs being burnt in the neighbors' fireplaces. It was almost like our world had settled down into a peaceful place, as if the chaos was over. I would do my best with God's help to keep the children in a happy place. I had learned to take one day at a time. I was stubborn, and I was going to show Ronald he wasn't going to take our happiness with him.

Our neighbors and friends were the best. Lee listens during the day, and Sybil listens to me at all hours of the night. My guy neighbors, Stan and Al, had kept my lawn mower running and in good shape. Stan's wife, Marilyn, was helping with the carpooling to school. We had another neighbor, Burke, who knew about heat and air. He kept my home air conditioning up and running. The unit had a freon leak, and he would refill it every season. Chrissie lived across the street; she kept me encouraged and was determined to keep me going. Chrissie told me a story that helped me so much. It was a potter's story:

"A guy had some clay that wasn't good for anything; for him anyway, he was going to throw it away. A potter came by and asked him how much he wanted for the clay. The old man said you can have it. It is of no value to me. The potter took the clay home. He molded the clay, spun the clay, and painted the clay. It wasn't long before he had a beautiful, valuable cup."

Chrissie then told me, "Ramona, you may feel invaluable now and thrown away for someone else. God will pick you up, and you will be more beautiful and valuable than ever when he is through with you. Never give up on God, and never give up on yourself."

Chrissie taught me so much through that story. She would help me with advice on dealing with the children. So many people were there for me. I genuinely feel that God placed each one in my path.

Although their dad didn't or wouldn't help with anything around the house. We were going to be okay. I felt like

Ronald was trying to break me in every way, mentally, emotionally, and financially. So far, I was still standing. I was going to keep standing too.

Chapter 37

This next week at school was going to be fun. Rachel had cheerleading tryouts. Football games were gearing back up. The kids were going to have Halloween dress-up days at school. We had a lot to look forward to.

Just when you think things cannot get worse. Trust me, they can. Last May, when I backed into Ronald's car, I thought things could not get worse. But things got a whole lot worse quickly when he left me two weeks later. Yes, things can always be worse. I was about to be reminded of that again.

We had only been home from Gatlinburg for a week when I got some devastating news. Russ, the assistant manager from Ronald's work, called to tell me that Ronald had gotten fired. I couldn't help but wonder if it was because I went up to the chalet. Had Ronald come back to his office screaming that somebody ratted on him and possibly he caused a scene? I didn't know. I just knew things were about to get worse. Here again, Ronald could have made a different choice.

I knew his job loss would lead to all kinds of problems, my income, for one. I had a feeling he would want to take me back to court and try not to be required to pay the bills since he didn't have a job now. Russ told me when Ronald lost his job, he lost his company car. He said, "Ramona, I am so sorry that someone from the company will have to come get your car too, at some point. I will do what I can to delay it as long as I can. I know Ronald sold your car right before he left you. I know when we take the company car, you won't have a car at all. I wanted to warn you and give you some heads-up time to figure out something else." Like I would have a way to figure out how to get a car with only a part-time job. I was grateful he had called me and gave me the warning. That would give me some time. Plus, it made me aware of Ronald's job loss so that I can plan for the repercussions.

My personal car, Ronald sold. Now, when I lose the business car, how would I even take care of the kids? How could I get food? Take them to school? To Church? How would I even find a full-time job to buy a car without a car? Although growing up, my family didn't have a car. It wasn't too bad, then. I was only a kid and had no responsibility. Plus, we always lived on the city bus line. Dad managed to work and support us. This time, I didn't live on the city bus line. I couldn't walk to the bus stop. The kids went to a private school several miles away and couldn't walk to school. It seemed just when I got over one hurdle, I had another to jump.

That same week, Rachel found out she didn't make the cheerleading team. She called me crying. I couldn't understand what could have happened. When I got there, my sweet princess came outside broken-hearted and told me what had happened that day.

After lunch, the girls had the afternoon to practice their cheers and then were the tryouts. She was dressed as cute as a bug. She had her hair pulled back in a ponytail, a big bow with the school colors, gold and blue. She knew her cheers; after all, she was a cheerleader last year. She had charm. She had everything. I thought she would be the best cheerleader on the team. What happened next blindsided her, and it came right before her tryouts; no wonder she couldn't do her best.

School had ended for the day. The girls were in the locker room to get ready for the tryouts. When a friend of hers, Amy, says, "I saw your dad at Opryland this weekend. Rachel, he wasn't alone. He had a woman with him." Rachel says, "Mom, I was so embarrassed; I just wanted to run away. I couldn't, Mom. I had to go out there and do my best to cheer to make the team. Mom, I just couldn't do it. I didn't make the team. It is all dad's fault. He is ruining my life." That was a lot for any fourteen-year-old to endure.

She was brokenhearted. So embarrassed. I didn't even know how to console her. She was so upset she didn't make the team. So angry at her dad for leaving and having an affair. Angry, he had taken Barbara to Opryland, where he would be seen. She was so embarrassed and upset that her friend had seen her dad with Barbara. She kept asking, "Mom, who else knows?" I just hugged her, wanting to cry with her, and said, "Baby, I don't know." She said, " I wish I could kill Barbara." I knew she didn't mean it, but she said it. How much anger did she have with her dad and Barbara? Had I been so wrapped up in my pain that I had overlooked her pain, her feelings, and her anger? I sure couldn't fuss at her for saying it. I wanted to say it too. I was so angry. Angry that Ronald had created so much anxiety for all of us. Right now, I had to push thoughts of Ronald out of my head and focus all my energy on Rachel. I had to console her.

I was sure I had made my share of mistakes with the kids. When I told them about Barbara, I wasn't sure it was the right thing to do. I didn't want them to be angry with their dad. But, today, I was glad I had told them. I couldn't imagine Rachel's shock, pain, and embarrassment if the first time she had heard of Barbara was from her friend, Amy. That would have been way worse. At this point, I just had to help her. I wasn't sure how. With love, attention, and time, I was hoping it would resolve itself. I wasn't sure.

I just knew I had to be strong. I knew it was up to me to get her and the boys through this horrible ordeal. She had no idea that, in addition to everything else, we were about to be without a car. I had a lot to figure out.

It was horrible. Ronald had already sold my Thunderbird. What was I going to do? Here I sat with three children; their school year had just started. I had to get to the grocery store to feed them. I had to get to my part-time job and find a full-time job. I had to keep them in church. How would I do this without a car? My world was crumbling! How could this happen? How could I go from happiness with a wonderful husband to suddenly a divorce? Now, here I am, a mom with no money, soon-to-be no car, three children to care for, and no husband to help me. How in the world has this happened? This is exactly what I found myself asking: How? How? How? Not to mention, I felt sure Ronald would try to take me back to court to reduce payments. Was this his final goal, to see me alone, with no money and struggling?

Chapter 38

It was time to get resourceful. It was a time to be tough. It was time to call Mom. She had two cars. One was hers, and one was her husband's. My stepfather had a stroke, and he couldn't drive anymore. I knew Mom didn't need two cars. I knew she would loan me one of theirs. I felt comfortable driving the worst of the two. At least it was a vehicle and would get me from point A to point B.

I called and told her that Ronald had lost his job, and they were going to come pick up my company car. Could she let me borrow a car? I needed to find a full-time job so I could qualify for a car loan. Another shocker, she said, "No honey, I have two cars, but what if one doesn't start one day? Then I will be stranded." I thought, are you kidding me? Mom, "I have three kids here; I have got to have a car." She agreed with me and said, "I know you do. But I need my cars now." What a blow to my gut. My own mother had always been available to help me, even financially. She is telling me no; she would not let me borrow a car. Where else could I turn if my own mom said no? What friend or stranger would help me? What will I do? I didn't know where to turn.

I only had a few more days to figure this out. They had scheduled to pick up the car at the end of next week. I still had no idea what I was going to do. It was my day to pick up the children at school. While I was waiting in line for them.

I saw Amy's mom, Sue. I didn't want to avoid her. I knew she must have known about Ronald's affair. She probably was with Amy when Amy saw Ronald and Barbara.

Sue saw me and came over. She smiled and asked, "How are you doing?" "I am okay, how about you?" "Doing good." I then brought the skeleton in the room up. "Sue, I am sure you heard that Ronald has moved out and is having an affair." "Ramona, I didn't know it, but when we saw him at Opryland, we knew then. I am so sorry. I had no idea what you were going through."

I thanked her and said, "Yep, it is going to get worse." She said, "What do you mean?" I told her, "I found out Ronald has lost his job, our only cars were company cars. That means they are coming to pick up this company car soon, and I have got to find a car." "Oh my gosh, Ramona, what will you do? That is going to be tough. Wait, I have an idea. Our son, Toby, isn't using his car. Toby is back at college, and his car is in the driveway. You can use it." I asked her, "Are you serious?" "Yes, I am very serious. He won't need it until he comes home for Christmas break."

God was a step ahead of me again. Amy and her mom seeing Ronald was a blessing in disguise. God knew about Toby's car being available. God knew I would need a car. This was, once again, God helping me when I couldn't see any light. Yes, it was disastrous for Rachel. Now we have an idea why it all happened like it did.

Rachel now had one of her friends who knew what she was going through. She had a friend she could talk to. Amy's mom had a solution to my car problem. Lee is so right; God does and will take care of us. Sue said, "Just call me when they come and get your car. Eric and I will bring you the car." Oh my, what a friend and what a great God I have.

Chapter 39

I wonder what his poor little convict thought about her rich fiancée now. Now, he didn't have a job, and he didn't have a brand-new Volvo. Her great Gatlinburg vacation had just been interrupted. Let's see how much you love him now. How long will you stay with him now? I bet things around his house might just be getting a little uncomfortable. Welcome to the real world, Barbara.

We had not heard from Ronald since the Gatlinburg incident. I knew he was furious with me. Well, now we were even. I was furious with him too. He has almost destroyed our lives with his affair. Knowing the truth about her and her family, now we must live in constant fear too. He has screwed around, literally, and has lost his job. Now, we won't even have a car. Now, he was flaunting his affair to the world. About that time, the phone rang. I answered, "Hello." It was Ronald. He started out screaming, "You made me lose my job. If you think I will pay you now, you are crazier than I thought." Slam went the phone, as usual. This time, I didn't get to say anything but hello.

As usual, he can make bad decisions, but when things go wrong, he blames me. If he got fired over the Gatlinburg deal, it would have been how he handled it. He made a choice to use it for himself and his convict. Mr. Dennis would not have tolerated that. Ronald and his poor judgment just didn't think he would get caught using it with her. Things hadn't changed since the day he had left. By now, I am convinced they never will. He could have been doing other things that caused him to lose his job. That might have just been the final straw.

I knew I had to call Mr. Jackson and let him know of Ronald's job loss. I called his office and asked for Mr. Jackson. The receptionist said, "Can you hold for a minute? I think he was going to call you a little later. I know he will want to talk with you." "Sure, I will hold; thank you." She placed me on hold, and Mr. Jackson came to the phone. "Ramona, thank you for holding. I got a call from Ms. Donavan: Ronald has lost his job. She has filed an injunction to stop all payments to you until we go to court. The court date is next Wednesday." I told Mr. Jackson, "Yes, I found out about his job. Ronald called me this morning screaming and blaming me and threatening me not to give me any more money."

Mr. Jackson asked me, "Have you been harassing him at work?" "Absolutely not!" I told him boldly. "Okay, try not to worry too much, Ramona. We will prove that in court. Harassment is what she had put on the documents." "Mr. Jackson, he is lying to her." He assured me the judge would pick up on that and probably even make things better for me.

I was anxious for my day in court. Ronald could scream and lie. But the truth will come out.

I drove to the courthouse on Wednesday, ready to defend myself against his lies. I parked, went to the main floor, and waited for Mr. Jackson. Strangely, today, I wasn't even nervous. I was angry. Angry, Ronald lied and blamed me. Angry that he wants to take away support for the kids and give what money he has to that convict.

While waiting for Mr. Jackson, I am keeping my eyes on the elevator for him and Ronald. The elevator doors opened, but it was neither of them. It was the owner of the auto dealership, Mr. Dennis. He walked over to me and said, "Ramona, how are you?" I said, "I am okay." He then told me he was sorry for what I was going through. I thanked him and told him I appreciated his concern; it would all be okay. I asked him why he was here. He said, "Ms. Donavan, Ronald's attorney, subpoenaed him to testify as to why Ronald got fired." "Yes, Ramona," he said, "Things will be okay today. I know why Ronald was fired, and it had nothing to do with you. I am here for you, young lady. You have always been so supportive of Ronald and his job at the office. I have nothing but the best regards where you are concerned."

Mr. Dennis reached over and grabbed my hand and said, "Don't worry." He was standing beside me, holding my hand, when the elevator door opened, and Ronald got off the elevator. Ronald looked like he was thinking, oh my gosh! He was seeing his former boss standing here, holding his soon-to-be ex's hand. He had to know this was not going to go well for him. He should have known his lies would catch up with him.

Our docket was called, and we entered the courtroom. Judge Wiser was residing. We all stood and then sat down, and the proceedings started. Ronald's attorney, Ms. Donavan, called Mr. Dennis to the stand. She proceeded to ask questions. She asked him about Ronald's position at the company, or should I say former position at the company. Mr. Dennis stated, "Ronald no longer works for me."

"Mr. Dennis, isn't it true that you had to let him go due to his wife, Ramona, being a nuisance at the company?" Mr. Dennis did not hesitate to tell her that I was well-liked. He said to her that I was very supportive of anything that was needed. He proceeded to tell her that I had been a positive influence on the company staff. Then she says, "Isn't it true that Mr. Jenkins lost his job because his wife was harassing him at work?" He replied, "No, Ma'am. Mr. Jenkins lost his job after several warnings that he had to stay present at the office. He was leaving for hours at a time, and I finally had to let him go. His dismissal had absolutely nothing to do with his wife."

I am sure this is not what Ronald or his attorney wanted to be told in court by the owner of the company. I knew I had not done anything. I just didn't understand why he lost his job until then. Now, I was curious why he was leaving his job for hours at a time. What was going on? I could only assume he was spending time with Barbara every chance he could.

Ronald seems to have the attitude, lie until you die. Ms. Donavan looked shocked and probably felt awkward, and If I had been her, I would have been annoyed that my client had lied to me. I wanted to say, well, Ms. Donavan, how does it feel to have Ronald lie to you? Now you know a little of what my life has been like. Ronald would rather lie when the truth sounds better.

Now, it was our time. I had Ronald's checks he had written to me and had bounced. I had copies of the checks he had written that were for less than the amount Judge Wiser had ordered him to pay. It had gotten so bad. I had to learn a few bank tricks to save myself a little grief. After several bounced checks, I went to his bank to verify the funds. Then, if there were sufficient funds, I would cash the check and deposit the money into my bank. If there wasn't enough money to cover the check he had written, I would ask the teller how much I would need to deposit into his account to clear his check. I decided giving him $50.00 or $75.00 was worth it for me to cash his check.

Mr. Jackson showed the Judge proof of his insufficient funds on the checks he gave me. The checks also showed a new address for Ronald, and he had added Barbara to his checking account. Surely, the judge would see that as well. But what did the judge do? He just said, "I don't know what you think the man can do. He doesn't have a job. You can't get blood out of a turnip." What? I thought. I have three kids to support. I looked over at Ronald, and he was smirking.

My attorney says, "Judge, may I approach the bench?" The judge says, "Yes sir, come on up." I could hear Mr. Jackson as he fought for me and the kids. "Your Honor, Mr. Jenkins is a healthy young man. There is no reason he can't get a job, keep it, and pay support to his family. Your honor, the last check Mrs. Jenkins got from Mr. Jenkins shows he is living with another woman and supporting her. He needs to support his own family."

At that time, I felt the eyes of the bailiff in the courtroom looking at me. I looked up, and he was saying, as I read his lips, "You should have shot him." I thought that might have been a good idea. If he was dead, I wouldn't be going through this. If he was dead, I would have a life insurance policy, and the kids would have social security payments; that money would have helped. Not to mention all the emotional pain. When someone dies, people bring food to your house, and they have sympathy for you. Killing him might have been a better option.

Until I thought back about my sweet neighbor, Anna Rose, what she went through when she shot her husband. Anna Rose was my neighbor when Ryder was born. She was married to a very mean and evil man. She had decided to divorce him. She was at her house packing her personal items and moving out when he came home unexpectedly. He came in and threatened her. She felt she had no choice but to defend herself. She didn't intend to kill him. She only wanted to get out alive. But the shot was fatal. After his death, the emotional pain she went through with her guilt and others blaming her wasn't anything I would have wanted to live with. If she had gotten out of the house and just gotten a divorce, her life would have been much better than the way it turned out for her. Besides, I loved Ronald too much and wanted our wonderful family back like it should have been. Just like I thought it was before all this happened.

The Judge turned to Ms. Donavan and asked if she wanted to add anything. She said, "No sir." The judge ruled. He finally ordered Ronald to pay $600.00 a month, $200.00 a child, until the divorce was granted. We could resubmit evidence then, and he would make his final decision.

Well, Ronald got what he wanted. Now, he is only required to pay half of what he was paying. I couldn't believe this Judge. If I had the female Judge in the county, I just imagine this would have turned out differently. She had no problem telling guys you would pay child support or go to jail. I heard one guy cry that he couldn't pay child support because he had to pay his electric bill; she told him he would need to shave by candlelight. Judge Wiser should have had a concern for the children. Not a concern for a young, healthy man who is shacked up with his young, healthy girlfriend.

I was not happy at all with the Judge's decision when I left the court. Nor was I happy looking at Ronald's smirks, like he got by with something. At least he didn't get by with lying about me. Mr. Dennis was not going to let that happen. He stood up for me. My money was being adjusted, which was going to be hard for me. At least I didn't have to worry about where I would get a car since Sue was lending me a car for now. I had to look at every bright spot I could. I knew just like God was a step ahead of me in being sure I had a car. God would take care of me with the money and a job situation. I had to do my part and trust God to do the rest.

Chapter 40

I was so tired of Ronald getting by with everything. I had all the stress and all the responsibility. While he was free as a bird, traveling and living his life with a girlfriend, without a care in the world. The next morning, it finally got to me. I thought no more; he was going to take some responsibility. He is going to take the kids to school today. He didn't know it, but he was going to drive them today. I was going to drive to his apartment and tell him, today is your carpool day, buddy.

I was driving over to Madison, where he and Barbara were living. I don't know what I was thinking. The children's school was about 10 miles west of our house. Ronald and Barbara lived about 15 miles east of our house. I was driving in the totally wrong direction for them to go to school. I didn't care. I was tired of him walking all over me. I was tired of him dumping all the responsibility onto me. It wasn't fair. I just told the kids that I was going to drive them to their dad's, and he would take them to school today.

I was driving down Gallatin Rd toward his apartment in Madison when blue lights and sirens came up behind me. I pulled over. I didn't know I was speeding. My mind was in a tunnel. My mind was on Ronald, telling him to get out of bed, and he had to take the kids to school today.

If I had been thinking clearly, I would have never done that. Barbara was at the apartment. I would have never allowed her to be around them. I was just so totally stressed I had forgotten about her living there.

The policeman came to the window and said, "Ma'am, did you realize you were driving 50 in a 35-mile speed zone?" "No sir, I didn't, but I don't care. I am taking my children to their dad for him to take them to school. I have been driving them to school all year, and it is time for him to do it at least once." He said, "Ma'am, I understand your frustration, but…" I interrupted him, "No, you don't understand my frustrations. Do you have kids?" "Yes, ma'am, I do have children. I have four." I asked him, "Are you divorced?" When he said, "No." I yelled back at him, "See what I am talking about? You don't understand my frustration. If you were divorced, you probably wouldn't take responsibility for your kids either."

I couldn't believe I was talking this way to this police officer. I really was so upset I don't think I realized what I was even saying. He finally stopped me from talking when he said, "You don't have to have this responsibility now; I can take your kids." I started crying and said, "No, sir, please do not do that. I want my kids." He said, "Well then, does your mom live nearby?" I told him it was only a few miles away. He said, "I suggest you calm down, drive to your mom's, and try to relax. Let her drive the kids to school. Will you do this?" "Yes sir, I will." "Okay, if you go there right now, I won't give you a ticket." "I will. I will go there right now." I couldn't believe he would take my kids. He got me to straighten up. At this point, I didn't care if I ever saw Ronald again. I didn't care if Ronald ever took any responsibility. I only knew I didn't want anyone to take my kids away from me, regardless of how much responsibility I had.

I did exactly as he asked. I drove to Mom's; I told her what had happened. She said, "I want you to sit down, relax and watch some TV. I will take the kids to school. When I get back, we will go for a walk, eat lunch, and talk for a while." "That sounds perfect, Mom, thank you." She might have let me down when I asked to borrow a car, but at least today, she was there for me.

Just time to sit and do nothing is what I needed. When I was at home, I couldn't do that. I would always see something I had to do. I would see things reminding me of Ronald, my happiness, and my anger. I couldn't seem to relax at home anymore at all. So today, just sitting at Mom's and getting away was a tremendous help.

I had been going to Mom's once a week since Ronald left, but I wouldn't stay for long. I was trying to cut out some expenses at the house. I would take the kids to school and then, once a week, continue my drive to Mom's to take my trash. That saved me a monthly trash bill. Every penny I could save would help me. That also gave me an opportunity to visit with her and Papa.

But our visit today was a long visit and a good one. It was nice for someone to wait on me, to spoil me a little. She made the best chicken salad sandwiches, and then she made my favorite cookie, chocolate oatmeal. I just sat at the table while she spoiled me like she did when I was a child. It felt good to be taken care of. I felt loved and wanted. The rejection I had been going through with Ronald was surmountable.

Now, I felt like myself a little more. I left Mom's house just in time to go to school and get the kids. I know I had totally upset them this morning. I didn't even think about what I was doing to them. I was really being selfish. I didn't know how they would be when I picked them up. I got there early; I was first in line. I wanted to pick them up as soon as possible, so we had time to stop by Shoney's, get a hot fudge cake, and talk before we went home. I felt they needed this attention and a treat as much as I had needed it earlier.

They were troopers. They were too young to be so understanding. But they were. I apologized to them and said, "It will never happen again. I love you so very much. I would never let anyone take you from me." They said, "We know that, Mom. You were tired. We get tired and do silly things too." Ryder said, "Yes, Mom, like when I didn't feed Beau when I was supposed to."

I smiled sweetly and, in a funny way, said, "Yeah, I remember that." His sweet comment seemed to be what we all needed to hear. We needed laughter. We could always count on Ryder to do that for us. We finished our cake at Shoney's, drove home, and life was normal again. I hoped this time it could stay normal or better.

Chapter 41

One day, out of the blue, I received a call from Mr. Bryant. He owned the dealership where Ronald had worked a year earlier. Mr. Bryant liked and respected me too. I always did my best to be supportive of Ronald, and just like Mr. Dennis, Mr. Bryant knew that too. Mr. Bryant and I both had birthdays in October. I don't know why I remembered people's birthdays. Mom could do that too. I remembered his birthday each year and would send him a card. He couldn't believe that I remembered. He would say I will remember yours soon, and it will surprise you. He did. I was working for an orthopedic. I looked up from my desk at a florist delivering flowers. I smiled and said, "Who are they for?" She said, "They are for Ms. Ramona Jenkins." "That is me!" Excitingly, I thought Ronald had sent them; that was when we were still married. But no, they weren't from Ronald. They were from Mr. Bryant, his boss. I was shocked. He really did surprise me.

When I heard Mr. Bryant's voice today, I panicked. I wondered why he was calling me. Had he heard about Ronald, Ronald's affair, and Ronald getting fired? Was he calling for Ronald here, and I would have to tell him he didn't live here anymore? Ronald had worked at various dealerships, and he knew a lot of car people over his 15-year car career. Just like in any business place, there is always gossip going around.

When he called me, he said, "This is Ken Bryant, Ramona, how are you doing?" I said, "Hi, Mr. Bryant I am doing good. How are you? Did you have a good birthday?" I could hear the surprise in his voice that, once again, I had remembered. He said, "Yes, I did have a good birthday. How about you? Did you enjoy your birthday?" I guess he remembered how we shared birthdays in October. I said, "Yes sir, I did. The kids and I spent it in Gatlinburg. October is a beautiful time of year to spend some time in Gatlinburg." "Yes," he responded, "It sure is."

"Well, Ramona, the reason I am calling you is to let you know I would like you to come and work for me." He said, "I am aware of the situation Ronald has put you in. I know you have not been treated fairly. You know the car business, and you will be a great salesman."

"Mr. Bryant, I appreciate you offering me a position and your kind words. I am not sure if I can do the job. I don't want you to offer it to me out of pity." "I'm not Ramona. I know you will do a great job. I am going to hire two people the first of the year. I want you to be one of my two. This job will also give you a car. I think you should think about it." "You are right! I should think about it. I will. I will let you know my decision in the morning." I told him again how very much I appreciated his generous offer.

This decision was really a no-brainer. I would get a job and a car. How could I say no? I called him the following morning and accepted the position. "Ramona, I am glad you have made your decision to come to work here. Although you will not start working until Jan. 2, I would like you to come over and complete the paperwork before then. The paperwork will include insurance for a car. Once you have completed all the paperwork, you will be assigned a car. Call me whenever you are ready to come over, and I will have my service manager pick you up."

Wow, I was going to get a car with the salesman job, and he was going to give it to me early. I will have my car for Christmas. That is perfect timing since Sue's family will need their car back when their son gets home from college. It amazes me the steps in front of me that God works out constantly. I said, "I can come tomorrow." "Great, I can have Joe pick you up at about 10 A.M.. Will that work for you?" "Yes, that gives me time to get my kids to school. I will be home and ready to go when Joe gets here. Thank you so much."

After I talked to Mr. Bryant, I had to call Sybil and tell her the great news. She was so excited for me. She said,

"Ramona, God is taking care of you." She was right. He is sure all my needs are being met. His timing is always perfect.

Joe was here at 10 A.M. to take me to complete all the paperwork for the salesman job. I was so excited and relieved. I was going to get a car and make some more money. My part-time job was a great source and had came in handy. With the Judge cutting back my payments, I needed more money to survive. I would keep both jobs and somehow make it work. When we got there, Joe showed me where the office was located. I went in, introduced myself, and explained why I was here. Karen was so gracious. She said, "Welcome aboard. You will like it here." She pulled out the paperwork and walked me through it as I completed it step by step. She asked, "Have you seen Mr. Bryant today?" I told her, " No, we checked when we got here, but he had just left for lunch." She called and told him I was in her office and had completed all the paperwork. He had just returned from lunch; he asked her to bring me to his office.

When I got there, I greeted him, we shook hands, and I sat down. Since we already knew one another, this was easy. He did not mention Ronald, and of course, I did not either. He asked me what my favorite color car was and what kind of car I would like. I recalled what Ronald had told me when he got the job at the Volvo dealership. I told Ronald I wanted the owner's car. He said, "You think you can have any car you want." Here, Mr. Bryant was asking me what kind of car I wanted. I was getting more respect than I did from Ronald even before he left me. I told him, "I wasn't picky. I just needed an automatic. It would be nice if it was a larger car to have plenty of room for the kids. I am just so grateful for you and any car that I get."

He says, "Let's go out on the lot." We walked over to the larger Volkswagens, and he said, "How about this pretty blue one?" "That is perfect. It is just perfect." We turned, and he walked me into the service department. He asked Joe to pull out the blue car, fill it up, and bring it to the front of the building. I couldn't believe it. I was being treated like a princess. It had been so long since I had this respect; my heart could barely handle it.

While we were waiting for Joe, we walked around, and Mr. Bryant introduced me to the other salesman. After I had met them, my blue car was parked and waiting for me. Mr. Bryant says, "I see your car is ready. I believe he left the keys in the ignition. Enjoy your holidays, and I will see you on January 2." I said, "Yes sir. I will enjoy them now; thank you so very much. I will see you on January 2. I hope you enjoy your holidays too." He looked and said to me again, "I am glad you made this decision; you will be a great asset to our company." I couldn't believe the respect and gratitude he was showing me. I had been put down and squashed down by Ronald for the last eight months. I was feeling I had no worth. Now, someone sees me. They see me for who I am, and they respect me.

I took the car home and waited until it was time to pick up my children from school. Once again, I decided to be first in line. When they came outside, I got out of my car and called them over. They were ecstatic. They said, "Mom, whose car is this? It is beautiful!" I said, "This is our car!" "Mom, our car, where did you get it?" I explained that I had accepted a position at the car dealership in sales, and he gave me a car. Reid says, "Mom, instead of going home, can we just ride around for a while?" "Sure, I think we need to go get some ice cream." Ryder says, "Me too." Rachel chimed in, "I agree. Ice cream sounds good." There we were, smiles again. We now had a car. I now have a full-time job. Now, I can depend on myself. If Ronald didn't pay or Judge Wiser didn't order it, we would be okay. I had my three healthy kids, my health, a car, a home, and a job. And I had my employer's respect.

I called Sue and told her my great news. "Sue, I know you have been praying for us. I had a call yesterday and was offered a job. I don't start until Jan. 2. The job comes with a company car. Although I don't start until Jan., the owner gave me the car today. I have a car now; can you believe it?" "That is great news, Ramona." "Yes, it is Sue. Now, I have a full-time job and can return Toby's car." She said, "Don't worry about it; Eric and I will pick it up this weekend. You enjoy your new car. Ramona, you will be a great employee." "Thank you, Sue. I will work hard and do my best."

She knew how stressful this car situation was for me. I was so grateful to her and her family for lending me one of their cars. It took a lot of faith for them to do that. They had to trust I would take care of it. Oh sure, they had insurance on it if something happened. But they didn't have insurance on the car for minor dings that I could have caused or extra scratches. I was so careful with it. I treated it like it was mine. I guess they knew me well enough to know I would do that. They came by and picked up their son's car and looked at my beautiful blue car. They were proud of me and the kids. It is wonderful to know when things get you down, have faith, and it will work out. I learned that, and I also learned to never give up.

Chapter 42

I will have a car now for all the holidays, starting on Thanksgiving. I didn't know how Mom felt telling me no; I couldn't use her car. I didn't know if she felt bad about it or just felt she couldn't do it. I didn't want to brag too much to Mom about me getting a car, just in case she felt guilty. I would just wait and show her when we drove over for Thanksgiving.

I was going to be strong. I was going to go forward. I was going to raise my children by myself. If they turned out bad, shame on me. If they turned out good, I would thank God and pat myself on the back. I had no extra money, but I would give them all my love and attention. I would keep them in the church and do my best to raise three model successful children. I was dreading questions my siblings were going to have about my marriage. But at the same time, I needed my family and their love. I wish they knew how badly I needed their support.

When a sibling is going through such a loss, as I was, you would think the family would rally around them. They loved Ronald; I know they did. They all thought, just like I did, he could do very little wrong. I couldn't or just wouldn't tell them all the truth and have them think less of him. What if we did get back together, then all the family would have bad feelings for him? I would go tomorrow and accept their blame if they said anything. I would accept their comfort or love if they offered it.

We got to Mom's, and I wondered if Mom had told them anything about my last several months. I had no idea what had been said. All I knew was that I needed their support. Most of the family was there when we arrived. I went in and acted like everything was the same. Except for the fact I had a new car. I went into the kitchen and saw Mom. She gave me a big hug. When she did, I whispered, "Mom, I got a job, and it comes with a new car. Do you want to go see it?" She stopped everything she was doing, and we walked outside. I could tell she was very proud of my perseverance and determination to keep pushing through and to get back on my feet. She smiled and said, "I knew you would figure this out. I am very proud of you." We hugged again and then went inside for dinner.

Dinner was great, and we had a good time. The questions they asked were few and far between. Now, to prepare for Thanksgiving Day alone while Ronald takes the kids to his parents. Holidays will be hard alone, but I want the kids to see their dad and grandparents for Thanksgiving. Ronald said he would pick up the children at noon.

Ronald picked up the kids the next day, and surprisedly, he was on time. There sat my new blue car. I bet he would probably ask the kids a ton of questions about it. I would think for a guy's ego, that would probably sting. Here, his wife, whom he was trying to get rid of, was offered a job by his former boss. She was given a new car to drive. She was still living in the house they had built. I always felt he was trying to break me and reduce me to crumbs. I was determined to remain strong and show him what I was made of.

They went to his parents for Thanksgiving Day dinner. I was sure Ronald would have his family's support. They knew nothing about Barbara. I knew the kids would be happy playing with their cousins, and the grandparents would be excited to see them.

I had only hoped we could get our lives back to normal somehow. How? At this point, I didn't even know for sure what normal even looked like anymore. What is normal for a family that has been left behind by a spouse? When your spouse has gone from going to church with you to living with a convict? What was or could even be normal when he is acting like her, talking filth like her, and treating his family like a convict probably treats their family? So disrespectful.

Regardless of what the situation would ever be between a husband and a wife, how in the world can a dad even think about treating his children the way Ronald had been treating our three children? He had just become such an irresponsible, self-centered jerk. What else could I expect from someone living with a convict? He needs to look in the mirror and see what he has become. It is like we told the kids for years, "You need to pick good friends. When you don't, if they get into trouble and you are there, this could get you in trouble. Sometimes, people start acting like the people they hang around with." Here he was, living with a convict, acting crazy, acting like her. He should have followed the advice he had given to his children for the last several years.

Possibly, if he had listened to his own words, we would not be going through these holidays with our marriage suffering now. Although Ronald wanted a divorce, this could have all been so different. Other people get a divorce and get along, and all this drama doesn't occur, especially on the holidays. This was our divorce, though, with drama on every corner. I sure didn't want drama on our holidays. I wanted peace, tranquility, and happiness. I would do everything in my power to see that is exactly what we had.

I knew I had to get some Christmas shopping done, and money would be tight. I had to look at the checkbook closely. I got it out of my purse, and I had to get the recent bank statements to reconcile; it had been a while. I couldn't even remember the last time I had reconciled the checkbook. I looked and looked for my bank statements. The last statement I could find was the May statement. I had no idea where they could be.

I went to the bank and explained to them I hadn't gotten any bank statements since May. They asked me, "Have you changed addresses?" "No, I haven't. Where have you been sending them?" I asked the clerk with deep concern. Then she checked the address and told me they were sending them to Ronald Jenkins at a different address. Why his address? She looked up the records and said, "Ronald requested it in May, and since his name was on the account, they changed it."

I had been so upset since May I hadn't even noticed I wasn't getting them. He had changed the address so he would get them. I guess he wanted to know where the money was going. He knew me; he knew I wouldn't waste any money. I couldn't think of any other reason for him to change it.

I immediately told them. I need to open a new checking account in my name only! I explained that is "not" my address. I need to be sure the correct address is on "my" checking account. This is not the way I wanted to start our holiday season. Of course, none of this was the way last year I had envisioned this Christmas would be.

Last year at Christmas, Ronald and I were talking about going to Disney for next Christmas and possibly even a cruise. That sure changed. There wouldn't be a Disney trip this Christmas, nor a cruise. I would work hard to make it a good Christmas without a vacation and without Ronald being home for Christmas for the kids and me.

I wanted to start decorating the house early. I was hoping that once I got the decorations up, hopefully, it would bring some joy and normalcy into our home once again. This year I didn't have the money like last year. I might not be able to decorate like I used to. But I did know how to decorate. I could sew. I decided to get the wreaths and sew fabric around them. I could make a wreath for every door in the house. This would keep our spirits boosted.

Susan, our pastor's daughter, had told me where you can get wreaths for free. Now, I knew I could do this if the wreaths were free. She told me, "The cemeteries take the wreaths off the graves when the flowers die and just throw them in the dumpsters." I had no idea. It looked like I was going to become a dumpster diver.

The kids and I drove out to the local cemetery. The dumpster was located on the far side of the cemetery. "Yes, kids, I know this is creepy, but it will make us happy once I get the wreaths on all the doors." They looked at me with rolled eyes, that only kids can do. When we reached the dumpster, I climbed up on the step and looked over into it. It had already been dumped. It was empty. I said, "That is okay. Let's go to the cemetery where my grandmother is buried; it is on Gallatin Road." We drove there and couldn't find a big dumpster. We couldn't even find trash cans that had any wreaths.

Then I spotted one. The kids said, "Where?" I pointed and said, "There." Rachel said, "Mom, it says grandmother on the flowers, and it is still on the grave. Mom, we can't take that wreath." I said, "The flowers are dead. I bet they will be by tomorrow to throw it away. We are just helping them out. That would at least give me one wreath." Reid and Ryder were in the backseat and couldn't see what I was talking about. When they did, they agreed with Rachel. I kept saying it was just one dead wreath. There are a lot of wreaths on the grave. From the looks they gave me; I knew I should just leave it alone. But I couldn't. I gave in and grabbed it. I got home and got the sewing machine out and made a beautiful wreath for the front door. We had some wreaths I could use from last year. I kept sewing, and before long, we had wreaths on almost every door, including their bedroom doors. I just knew that would make us feel better. They liked them, and it put a beautiful smile on their faces.

We were trying to accept our current life. Their dad saw them every other week on Sundays from one to five. The divorce was scheduled and going as planned. We had a car, and I had a full-time job. I was starting in January. We just had to get through this tough part, the holidays. We could do this. One thing wasn't going to happen, Barbara wasn't going to have her wedding this December. Ronald was still married to me.

We had always gone to my mom's for Christmas Eve dinner. When we left Moms, we would stop and get a live Christmas tree. We would take it home and spend the evening decorating it. On Christmas day, the kids would go to Ronald's parents' home. I didn't want this Christmas to be any different for the kids or for their grandparents. Although, this wasn't as hard on the grandparents as it was for me and the kids. I knew they would like to see the kids just like they had every year.

When Christmas Eve came, we packed up the gifts we had gotten and drove to Mom's house. I always say Mom's house even though she had remarried, but since Dad had passed away, I always thought about her house as just going to Mom's.

It was different this year without Ronald, just like it was on Thanksgiving. Yes, they missed Ronald not being there; we all did. After all, he had been in the family for almost 18 years, counting our dating time. They knew how much I loved him, and they loved him too. While at Mom's, it always seemed the kids would go play, the ladies would sit and talk, and the guys would do the same.

For us, it really didn't seem too different going there except for the drive to and from, without their dad. That was lonely, especially on Christmas Eve. On an exciting note, we were driving my new company car. That made me proud that I had brought myself up from the hole I felt I had sunk into, where he had tried to strip me of everything.

When we were driving home, the kids said, "Mom, we have got to get our live tree." I said, "Guys, I just cannot do that; I can't." "Mom, yes you can. We always do." They insisted. I wasn't sure how I would get it into the house if we got it. I wasn't sure I knew how to even get it into the tree stand if I got it in the house. Not to mention, by now, my fake, better mood was slipping away.

With their insistence and encouragement, we drove to the Christmas tree lot. The lot where we had been going for the last 6 years. We had done this since we moved into our beautiful home in Lake Estates. We looked until we all agreed we had found the perfect tree. I always made sure each child was included in decisions like this. I wanted them to know they were important and their decision mattered.

The guy picked it up and loaded it on top of my new car. I paid for it, and off we went, just like in the Christmas Vacation movie. We got home and went inside, but I couldn't find the tree stand. There I was with a beautiful live tree to get off the top of the car. I had to get it into the house, and I couldn't find the tree stand. I had to improvise. I found an umbrella stand in the garage. We got the tree off the car and inside the house as a team. The boys helped to get it off the top of the car, and Rachel held the door open. We had become a great team.

I set the tree in the umbrella stand. Well, that wasn't the best idea. It kept falling over. Once again, creativity had to kick in. I had a hook in the ceiling where I had hung a plant. I got a ladder and a rope. I tied the top of the tree to the hook in the ceiling. Not the best solution, but the only solution I could figure out. At least when the boys ran through the house, it didn't fall.

Now for the decorations, Christmas music, and the wonderful smell of homemade cookies. Rachel turned on the Christmas music, and the boys got the ornaments out of the attic. I went into the kitchen to get out the ingredients for cookies. I hated the fact that the boys had to do the things their dad used to do. When their dad left, Reid told me his dad said to him, "Reid, you are the man of the house now." I told Reid then; "You are not the man of this house. You are a child. We don't have a man in this house." We have gone through months without their dad at home. We are going to survive our first Christmas without him.

We decorated the tree; I think it was even more fun this year. Rachel could get a job putting Christmas lights on the trees. She was a pro. The kids also took charge of the ornaments, and they seemed like they liked it. This was going to be our new tradition. It would be just me and the three kiddos. I had decided if I would ever get married again. I would not do it until they were all grown. Why? First and foremost, I didn't want to worry about a stepdad entering the home and possibly hurting one of my children. Secondly, I didn't want a stepdad in their life telling me how to raise the children. I would do the very best I could at bringing them up in a Christian home, keep them in church and give them all the love and attention that anyone could do. I prayed that when they were grown, they would all be on equal ground spiritually, emotionally, and financially.

Chapter 43

We got up Christmas morning. They had what Santa had brought to them, and they opened one of their gifts. It was different this year with Ronald not being here, but we had each other. Each other would be how we learned to live our lives. I told the kids we need to be honest with one another and love and respect one another. We are family. I told them I would always be here for anything and everything you need. I knew I would be there for them day or night if there was breath in my body. We ate breakfast, and then we opened the rest of our gifts. This is how we did it every year. Keeping everything the same, I felt, was important for them.

It was time for Ronald to pick up the kids. I stood in the window watching. I wanted to go out before the kids did to ask him If I needed to get batteries for anything he or his parents were getting them for Christmas. That would be good for the kids to have them and give me something to do while he was gone. My first Christmas sitting at home was not going to be easy.

As I stood there waiting, getting a little nervous, he pulled into the driveway. I went outside. I asked Ronald, "Do I need to go pick up any batteries for any of the kid's things?" He only answered me, saying, "Where are the kids?" "They are on their way out. I just wanted to know if you had gotten them something that needed batteries. I can go get them while you are with your parents."

He yelled, " I didn't come here to see you." He started his car, revved up the engine, and backed out of the driveway. It was at that moment that it clicked in my head, finally. It finally clicked what Lee had been telling me, "Ramona, you are not responsible for his decisions. You are only responsible for your decisions." I realized that day I am not responsible for what Ronald does.

Ronald could have simply said yes or no. He had a choice. But no, he made the choice to storm out of the drive. His choice kept the kids from seeing him or his parents on Christmas day. His choice upset the kids again. His choice made them feel rejected again. The kids were on their way out the door. He could have waited for them. But he didn't! That was his choice. His choice that he and he alone was responsible for making. Finally, after 34 years, I understand what that means.

I now realize I am only responsible for my choices. I have no control over him or what he chooses to do. Life is all about choices. Looks like Ronald had made his, and he has to live with them and the consequences of them, good or bad.

I felt for the longest, because of his accusations and blame, that this was all my fault. I felt like I had to fix everything since he kept telling me it was my fault to begin with. In the end, I realized that I made my choice to try to convince him for us to work on our marriage. I asked him over and over what did I do wrong, what I had done that had him so upset. I got all kinds of excuses. The last one, he said, "When your dad died, you said it should have been my dad." I told him I remembered saying that. I also remember that whole ordeal like yesterday. We thought the whole day his dad would die, but suddenly my dad died. At the time, it did feel like his dad should have died and not my dad. That was what we were told that his dad was dying. The doctor said they didn't think his dad would make it through the night. That is why I said it. I also was very upset about losing my dad suddenly.

I even talked to my pastor about this excuse Ronald gave me. Brother Adams said, "Honey, he is making up excuses and blaming you for the decisions he is making. You hold your head high and keep your eyes on the Lord." Brother Adams had never steered me wrong before. This wasn't any different. Although he didn't believe in divorce, he never said that to me to this day. I just think he knew I was trying to hold my marriage together. Ronald was doing all he could to make me feel guilty for what he was doing. I was going to follow Brother Adams's advice on this. I would choose to keep my eyes on the Lord, to lean on the Lord as I raised my children and try to be the best mom I could be.

Chapter 44

It was time for me to start working as a car salesman at the dealership for Mr. Bryant. I started training with a guy named Hal. He had graduated from a very elite University. That didn't mean his family was wealthy; he could have gotten a scholarship. Mom always told us we put our pants on the same way that rich people do, one foot at a time. That we were just as good. I always felt I was just as good as anyone else. Perhaps poorer, especially growing up, but just as good. I guess what my mom had taught me is why it was so easy to live in the Lake neighborhood with doctors, lawyers, and judges. I was never intimidated by them.

I didn't know if I would be as smart; I didn't have any college. Hal graduated from one of the best Universities in the nation. I knew he would be smart. I knew I was kind, considerate, and nice to people, and I would do whatever I could to help someone. That included helping someone find a car that they wanted.

It was easy for me to communicate and work with Hal. He was about 10 years younger, but the age difference didn't create any problems. We got along great. The job was fun and easy. I had been around the car business just like Ronald for the last 15 years. I knew the management staff at this dealership since Ronald had been a manager. It felt very comfortable working here.

It seemed like the guys here felt like they had to protect me from something. I was never sure what it was. I think they thought I had poor judgment sometimes. I probably did. Did I have poor judgment at seventeen when I married Ronald? I didn't think so. Maybe I did and just didn't want to admit I had made a mistake. I loved him. Maybe they were just protective due to the fact I was the only female on the sales force.

Phillip Perry was the manager now. He knew Ronald and me both. I had told him that I had been invited to go to the comedy club down the street to listen to a comedian, Sinbad. He came unglued. He said, "You are going to do what?" I didn't know why he was talking to me like that. I repeated it, "I have been invited to go to the comedy club. Phillip, if you know something about the club that I need to know, please tell me. If I don't need to go, tell me that." He would just say, "I can't believe you are going. It is your decision to make."

I asked the salesman their opinion. No one had any reason why I shouldn't go. So, I went. Sinbad was funny, nothing was out of line in his jokes at all. I had a good time. It was fun to get out, good to laugh. It was a good thing I had that one good night because the divorce was the next week. I knew that week would be anything but fun.

Chapter 45

I had tried and tried to delay the divorce to give Ronald time to come to his senses. Regardless of what I said or did, the date came. By now, we had agreed on everything. Of course, he would agree. I had him over a barrel. I had named Barbara in the divorce. If we hadn't agreed, that meant we would have had to go in front of the Judge. My attorney would subpoena Barbara.

Ronald and Barbara would not have wanted that to happen. If she had gotten on the witness stand, she could have said something that might have incriminated her. She could have possibly been sent back to prison. Well, Ronald wouldn't have allowed that. We knew he would probably be agreeable, unless I asked for money. He wouldn't give up any money to me if he didn't have to. He had Barbara he wanted to support and care for.

I had told him I wanted the house, which had little equity. I wanted the bills; I knew I would pay them. If he got control of the bills and didn't pay them, then I would lose the house, and things would get repossessed. After all, he had been threatening me he would leave the country. If he did, nothing would have been paid. I had to take responsibility for the bills. I told him I wanted full custody of the children. I didn't want him to have any control over decisions concerning them. He wasn't even thinking straight enough to control his life, much less three minor children. He could still see them anytime he wanted if Barbara wasn't present.

He agreed to everything I asked for if I would give him the grandfather clock. I said, "No, he cannot have it." It wasn't because I cared and even wanted the grandfather clock. I didn't care if he had it, except for one simple fact. After he had removed our furniture from our home, he sold it. I knew he would sell the grandfather clock, too, if I gave it to him.

When we purchased it, we made the decision the clock would be a family heirloom. We would give it to our first son. If I had given it to Ronald, he would have sold it, our son would have never gotten it. Here I go again, all about the principal.

My attorney said, "Ramona, if you do not give him the clock, then you will have to go in front of the Judge. He will decide what you get. He may not give you what you are getting now. You need to give it to him." I said, "No." I explained why no was my answer. Mr. Jackson repeated himself, "Ramona, you really need to think about this." " I have thought about it, and my answer is no. He cannot have it."

He went over to Ronald's attorney, Ms. Donavan. He told her I would not budge; Ronald couldn't have it. Ms. Donavan told Ronald that I said, "No." She also told Ronald we could let the Judge decide. I already knew he didn't want that. Ronald said, "Fine, let her keep it. Just give me my divorce!"

That is exactly what happened. The Judge accepted our agreement. He ordered continued payments of child support of $200.00 for each child, a total of $600.00 a month. Despite the agreement we had signed, and the judge signed, I knew I was accepting a lot of financial responsibility. The private school and the house were going to be the biggest expenses.

I had gotten the house in my name. With my job and income, I felt sure I would be approved by the bank to allow me to keep my equity line of credit. That would be my source of money when I didn't have enough. I was going to do my best so the kids could stay in their school with their friends.

Chapter 46

Although we were divorced now, my life was still in turmoil. I knew he wasn't coming home. I didn't know what was going on between them. I did know that if my kids were ever around her one time, it would be the last time they would see their dad. I was determined about that. He could live his life, however, wherever, but he had better not cross that line.

Here it was, the first of February, and Reid's birthday was around the corner. The kids' birthdays had always been so important, and we celebrated them in a big way. Last year, for his birthday, we rented the Hermitage skating rink just for a party. It was a party for him and Rachel. Their birthdays were only ten days apart. We told them they could each invite twenty friends. We hired a clown to do magic tricks and ordered a huge cake. Of course, plenty of pizza. They had a blast.

How would this year be for him? I knew I would do my best. But if his dad didn't call him and tell him, Happy Birthday, what little I could do for him wouldn't be enough. I had to find a way to make it special. I had to find a way to make it so special that Reid wouldn't even notice if his dad didn't call.

The next few days at the car lot where I was working, I talked to Hal about it. Even though he was ten years younger, he seemed to have an insight into kids and their feelings. He would make a good dad someday. He asked me a few questions about Reid and what he liked to do. I told him about his birthday last year and that Reid loved football.

The next day, Hal came into work and said, "Ramona, I have an idea I want to talk to you about." "About what?" I asked him. "Your son's birthday." "Okay, what are you thinking?"

He started telling me about his plan. "Ramona, you get the cake. I will get the ice cream and the football team. Tell Reid to invite any friends he wants to invite. It will be a fun night full of surprises for him, football stories, and a celebration for Reid." "Seriously? Hal, you will do that for him?" "Absolutely, I talked to some members of the team last night. They are already making plans for gifts and celebrations. It's a plan if you are okay with it?"

"Okay, with it? It is absolutely the best idea; Reid isn't going to believe this." I hugged him and thanked him for the best plan ever for Reid's birthday. I knew Reid would be so excited and have something to look forward to. Even Rachel, at almost fifteen, would have something to look forward to. When I tell her she can invite some of her friends too when these university guys are here. What young teenage girl wouldn't be excited?

When I got home, I called Reid into the kitchen. "Reid," I said, "Your birthday is about a week away. I have been thinking about how to celebrate." He said, "Oh Mom, it is okay, I know you don't feel like doing anything. You don't have any extra money for a birthday party. It is okay. Besides, Mom, I had a big party last year." These kids are more thoughtful and understanding than their adult dad. They are so amazing.

Reid was my child who didn't like conflict. He never wanted anyone to raise their voice. He was the only child of mine that had a teacher that yelled. He was in the first grade; Reid would stay so upset every day. He would come home and tell me his teacher was yelling at him. I tried to explain she was yelling at the students misbehaving, not him. None of that conversation mattered. He just didn't want to go to school if she was going to be his teacher. I went and talked to the principal and got him moved to a different class. He was happy and went on to have a happy first grade.

Things aren't any different now. He doesn't want me to go to any trouble for him for his birthday. I asked him, "Reid, what if I could plan a great birthday party for you? You could invite anyone you wanted, and the only thing I would have to do would be to get the cake. I will be getting you a cake anyway, so I will not have any extra expenses at all."

Mom, "How could that happen?" I told him, "I work with a guy that just graduated from a local university. He was on the football team. He and the football team want to come over and celebrate with you and your friends. They want to come over and tell you guys some true football stories that they have experienced, and they are bringing ice cream too."

His eyes and his mouth were so wide, "Mom, that would be the best. How many can I invite?" I told him anyone he wanted to invite. It didn't matter to me how many. The more, the merrier. Suddenly, he jumped up, hugged me, and took off running to his room and wrote a birthday list of who he wanted to invite. Before I knew it, he was back downstairs, on the phone, calling and asking his friends to come to his party, telling each one about the University football players coming. There was so much excitement. I knew at that point. He would never notice if his dad didn't call him on his birthday. He would be so preoccupied it would be all about him, just like it should be.

It was Reid's big day. I had made him a huge chocolate fudge cake. The house was decorated with streamers, and Reid was ready to celebrate. One by one, the doorbell rang, and the boys started arriving. By now, there were probably fifteen of his friends, and a couple of Rachel's friends had come over too.

They were sitting in Reid's room, looking out the window, waiting for the football guys. It was so wonderful that I didn't have to wonder if they would show up like I did when their dad was supposed to come. I didn't have to wonder if Reid would get disappointed as he had with his dad so many times. I knew Hal would not disappoint Reid. I trusted what Hal had told me. I wished I could still trust their dad, but that ship had sailed.

The kids were upstairs when I heard what sounded like cattle running down the stairs. The boys had seen a car pull up in front of the house, then another car, then another car. They knew who it was. They came flying down the stairs. By the time Hal and his teammates got to the front porch, they could barely get into the house. The kids had them encircled.

They finally made their way inside, and I introduced Reid to Hal, and Hal introduced his teammates. Immediately, Hal said, "Reid, let's go into the living room. We have something for you." Hal handed me 3 gallons of ice cream. I put them in the freezer and went into the living room to see what Hal was talking about.

Each player had brought Reid a gift. One guy brought him a signed football poster. One guy brought him a signed football, and one brought wristbands. Each time they gave him a gift, it wouldn't be just them giving it to him. They would present it to him and say, "Reid, because you are such a good son for your mom, we wanted to give you this. Reid, because you are doing so good in school, we wanted to give you this. Reid, because you are such a great football player, we wanted to give this to you." They would say things Reid really needed to hear from someone other than his mom. He needed his confidence boosted, and they were just the guys to get it done.

After the gifts, it was a warm night, especially for mid-February. We went out back on the deck for cake and ice cream. After the boys ate, the guys started telling them about football games. Reid said, "Mom, turn the outside lights off." I did. The boys just sat there mesmerized by these guys and their stories.

It was getting time for their parents to come pick them up. The boys were still outside, listening to all the stories. The kids were so quiet on the deck you could hear a pin drop. The only noise was a guy talking about football. The parents arrived at the front door. They asked, "Isn't the party here?" "Yes, it is." "Where are the kids?" "I will show you." I took them to the den door to see what looked like a miracle. There were about fifteen, twelve-year-old boys just sitting as still as mice. They were listening intently to every word the guys were saying.

We finally had to interrupt and tell the boys their parents were here to pick them up. We took some great pictures. Even Rachel got her pictures with her, Hal, and the guys. Then some of her friends got in the pictures too. During this time, Ryder was upstairs playing a game with Gary, his best friend who lived behind us.

Did his dad call? Yes, he did. I was surprised. I answered and called Reid to the phone. I heard Reid say, "Okay, Dad, thanks." Reid then went back to his party activities. I bet his dad wondered why this conversation was so short. I didn't care. I was so happy that Reid was happy and was having a great time.

Reid felt like a million bucks by the time the party was over. The guys had told him how special he was, and that was all true; he is special. He is all the things they said he was. Add to that, his friends thought he was a superstar for having a party like this. This had never been done for them or any of their friends. It was the talk around school for weeks.

The following Sunday, Ronald came to pick up the kids. He did come inside this time for some reason. I quit trying to figure out why he would do things. It changed day by day and was always a mystery. Reid met him at the door when he came in and said, "Dad, I had the best birthday party." He began telling his dad all about it. Ronald looked so shocked. He asked, "Reid, how in the world did that happen?" Reid said, "Mom planned it." I thought, yes, your mom planned it. Your mom will always be here for you, your brother, and your sister. I thought, yes, I will do everything in my power to make this divorce as easy for y'all as possible. I thought, yes, your mom will do everything to keep y'all's confidence up, to always let y'all know how smart you are, and that y'all can be and do anything you want to. I had a long road ahead, but I would push through every day. I tried never to let them down.

I was so grateful to Hal and his friends. It has been such a blessing these last few months to have friends and neighbors rally around us throughout this.

Chapter 47

I felt like Ronald wanted me to fail. Fail at everything. He kept telling the children, there is no way your mom will be able to keep this house. No way she can pay for it and pay the bills. She will have to sell it. The more he was determined I would fail, the more determined I was to succeed. All he was doing was upsetting the kids more by making them afraid they would have to move and give up the neighborhood that they loved. Why would he do that? Just to probably get me upset. It worked every time.

I think he sat at home thinking about how he could destroy me. I was working at the car lot, the divorce was granted, and he could live wherever with whoever he wanted. He didn't have to hide his mistress from me or a legal system for fear she might have to get on the witness stand. Now, she could be with him wherever he was.

I had no idea, though; it would be where I worked. I was outside talking to a customer one afternoon. As I walked back into the building with my customer, I saw Ronald, and Barbara was with him. What are they doing here? I had business to take care of, and I had to keep doing exactly what I was doing: selling a car. After I completed the deal, they were gone. But what were they even doing here?

I saw Phillip sitting in his office. I go into his office and ask, "Phillip, did you see Ronald here with his girlfriend, Barbara?" Phillip said, "I did, Ramona." "What was he doing here?" "Ramona, I am sorry to say you need to get used to it. Ronald has apparently decided to go into the wholesale car business. He will be coming here at least once a week."

I said, "Phillip, I am working here! I can't be harassed by them coming here every week." All he would say is, "Ramona, I am sorry, but he is working, and I can't do anything about him coming here." There I was, trying to work, and now Ronald was going to be around to rub her in my face. I can't do this for long. I will have to wait until I can get myself a car. Their company car is all that I have. I didn't tell Phillip. But as soon as I could find another job and a car, I would give my 2-week notice. Ronald was not going to keep making me so upset and keep my nerves at wit's end. It wasn't going to happen. I had a choice, and I had a decision to make. I am in charge of my life and my choices. I was going to leave and do something different. I was not going to subject myself to this week after week.

Nothing changed in the next few months. I worked. I took care of the kids, and Ronald kept coming by the dealership where I was working. When he showed up, I would go into the back office to avoid him and Barbara. She made me literally sick to my stomach.

One night, I was talking to my neighbor, Anita, who worked for the airline. She was telling me how great her job was. The hours were flexible, the pay was good, and her travel was free. She said, "You should come to the airline and apply; we are hiring." That was the best news I had had in months. I asked her, "Where do I go to get an application?" She told me, "I will bring one to you tomorrow."

The next day, she brought the application to me. I filled it out and waited to see if I would hear anything. The wait seemed forever. Then, one day, they called and wanted me to come for an interview. They set the appointment for the next week. I was so excited. I knew, though, that if they hired me, I would have to buy a car. When I went to work at the car lot the next day, I looked around at the used cars to see their price. I had to get a used one, and I had to find someone to finance it.

I was going to make this work for me. The thought of getting away from Ronald. The thought of free travel. If I got the job, the kids and I could travel like we used to when their dad was here. We could maybe even travel more. I could give them a fun-filled life if I could get this all worked out. I was going to try.

The day finally came for my interview. I would put my best foot forward. I knew that, obviously, I must interview well. I had had so many other jobs earlier. The hospital had even hired me back. I had to walk in there for the interview with confidence. I did! I got there and held my head high like Brother Adams had told me to always do. I prayed. I had a few more papers to complete; now was time for the one-on-one.

They explained to me that this would probably be working in the evening; would my husband mind? I thought it was funny. Ronald acted like he did before, but he was only tricking me. I gladly said, "I am single, and nights would be fine." I thought that way, I would still be home to get the kids off to school. I would be available for their school functions during the day. I completed the interview, and they told me they should make their decision within the week.

I sat and waited for the phone to ring. Finally, it did, and it was a YES! Oh my, thank you, dear neighbor, for telling me about this job. Thank you, Jesus. I would be in training for four weeks and test at the end of that time. If I pass all the tests, I will get an official hire date. Okay, that would all work for me. I knew I would study hard during that time. I was determined to get this job.

Chapter 48

I had to weigh the money situation before I took it. It was a salary and not much at that, but free travel benefits. Working at the car lot was salary, commission, and a free car. When I got my bills out and saw my budget, my credit line was maxed out. I knew I had some tough decisions to make. Sell the house? Give up the country club? Take the kids out of the private school? I hated to do any of these. Should I keep the job I had?

I talked to the kids, and they didn't want to move. Rachel was ready to change schools since she hadn't made the cheer team. The boys had plenty of friends in the public schools; they were okay with changing schools. We had a pool, and we really didn't need the country club. Keeping the house was our final decision. I wanted the job, so I bought myself a car, gave two weeks' notice, and started the four weeks of training and testing.

It was vigorous training, but I passed and got hired on June 4. I couldn't wait to take the kids somewhere. They had never been on a plane. I checked my work schedule, and they were out of school. If seats were available, we could travel anywhere. We still didn't have any money to travel. Yes, the airfare was free, but we had to pay for everything else. I knew we could take some day trips, that it would be cost efficient.

Our first trip was to Denver, Colorado. It was a great flight. We landed and got off the plane. We walked around the airport, got some ice cream, and took the next plane to come home. The kids loved it. They were ready to go somewhere again. It wasn't much, but I was excited I could do this for them. It gave them a little excitement that they had not had before. Plus, at that time, they served food on the flights. I was saving money by flying somewhere for the day.

Ryder loved to fish; I could take him to Myrtle Beach to fish off the pier. We would fly to Myrtle Beach airport. I would call the hotel limousine to pick us up. When we got to the hotel, we changed clothes in the public restroom and went to the beach. We stayed until it was time to come home that night. The limousine would take us back to the airport. He had his little fishing box with a fishing pole and tackle stuff. He loved it.

Reid loved football; I took him to the Football Hall of Fame in Ohio for the day. These were trips none of their friends did. Not the day trips, anyway. When Reid would tell his friends where he had gone, they didn't believe him. He decided when I took him somewhere, he wouldn't tell his friends or talk about it. He felt that was easier for him.

Rachel loved ice skating and shopping. Her favorite trip would be to New York City. There, she could ice skate and shop. She loved it.

These trips seemed to boost the kid's confidence too. It also seemed to confuse their dad as to how they were doing these things. I was so glad I could do this for them. To do the things he wouldn't do for them. They were still able to enjoy things, although he had walked off.

Chapter 49

I really enjoyed my job, especially the perks. It was so great seeing the children enjoying the travel that we were blessed to be able to do now. There were a lot of people that worked there. I made a lot of new friends. It was really a blessing to be around people and enjoy life again.

As I was sitting at work one afternoon, Rilla Manor, a friend I had met there, wanted to talk. She was upset with some girl coming into her husband's office and flirting around with him. He was the owner of a health studio. She told me the daughter of one of the ladies who worked for him had been trying to get him to take her out. We talked about it for a few minutes, and then she mentioned a name, Juanita.

I thought for a minute and thought, surely not the same Juanita I had talked to last year. Juanita was working at a health studio the day I called her. There is no way this could be the same person. If it is, it sure is a very small world. With curiosity at a max, I asked Rilla, "What is Juanita's daughter's name?" She said, "Barbara." Unbelievable! This had to be the same Barbara living with Ronald. What are the odds of there being a daughter named Barbara, whose mother's name is Juanita, who is working at a health studio in Nashville, TN? Here, Barbara was still living with Ronald and flirting with Bill. Ronald should have known that would happen; look at the girl's character, drugs, and robbing a drugstore with a loaded gun. What else could he expect?

I felt so sorry for Rilla and explained to her what I had just gone through with Barbara. Rilla told me, "Barbara better not try any stunts with my husband." Rilla was a tough cookie; Barbara might have met her match with this girl.

It wasn't long until Ronald told the kids that he and Barbara had broken up. I would not have believed it to be the truth. Except for the fact Rilla had told me about Barbara's flirting. Possibly, Ronald found out and kicked her out. Barbara had drained Ronald financially, just like Aunt Sadie said she would. I guess Barbara decided she had to go and find herself another rich man. Of course, Ronald wasn't rich; she just thought he was.

Chapter 50

Is Barbara out of the picture? I didn't know, and I really didn't care. I just never want her around my children. We are divorced now, and I am trying to start a new life without him. But he keeps popping up. When it was time for the monthly child support, he would stop by my work. He would have another excuse for only paying a small amount of money that he owed. First, he told me he had cancer like his mother and couldn't work right now. That went on for months until I found out that it was a lie. Then, when I found out that was a lie, he said he had had a heart attack. This time, I questioned him. I asked him, "What hospital did you go to?" He screwed up and named the same hospital where I was still working. I told him, "I am still working there." Then he backed up and told another story. He said, "Oh, I have a friend that works there, and I didn't have to register." I knew that was a lie for sure.

His supposed money problems and his lies continued. But despite it all, I really wanted to believe him. I still wanted to believe he could tell me the truth. I wanted to believe that somewhere in that body was the guy I had married 16 years ago. Was he in there at all? Had he ever been there?

A few weeks passed, and now he was calling and telling me the creditors were hounding him. He said, "If I don't get the creditors paid, I will need to leave the country to escape going to jail." Then, he asked if he could get an equity loan against the house. The house that is now in my name. He knew I still loved him, and he knew I didn't want him to go out of the country. If that happened, the kids would never see their dad again. I had already maxed out my equity line. He would have to go to a bank and see if there was enough equity to get another loan against it.

I told him, "I don't care if you do. I just don't know if the bank will lend it." He was going to go and talk to Roy Barger, a banker we knew. Roy's children went to the same private school that our children had been attending. I said, "Okay."

Two days later, I got a call from Roy. Roy explained that Ronald was there and wanted to borrow money from the house. He asked me, "Did you know Ronald was coming here?" I said, "Yes, it is okay. He said he would pay the loan back." "Ramona," he said very firmly, "He will not pay it. He will leave you with a loan to pay." I still wanted to believe Ronald wouldn't do that. Roy told me, "I will have him complete a credit application. If his credit is good, I will let him borrow the money. If not, I will not let him. I can tell you right now he will not have good credit." Once again, God put someone there to protect me and the kids.

Chapter 51

I have tried to live my life right and raise my children to do right. Among other good things, I tried to teach my children that two wrongs don't make a right, to trust God with all your heart and to give thanks in all things. I wanted the children to respect their dad, even though he sure was presenting lots of challenges for them to respect him. My former brother-in-law had married Lynn. I talked to Lynn about Ronald and how he was treating the children. She could relate; she had been divorced too. Her daughter's name was Michelle. She told me what she had told Michelle when they were having similar issues with Michelle's dad.

She said, "Your dad is the only dad you will ever have. Please try your best to keep a good relationship with him. He will probably die before you do. When he dies, I do not want you to have any guilt. I don't want you to wonder if you could have done more to have kept a good relationship with him. Do all you can now; do this for you, Michelle!"

I thought Lynn had given her daughter some great advice. I shared the same advice with my children. I told them just as Lynn told Michelle, "This is for you, not for your dad." My goal was to do my best. I wanted my children to be happy and confident. I wanted to be sure to provide all their needs. I tried to be sure they didn't do without any of their major wants. I wanted to instill confidence, strength, and power so they knew they could do anything they wanted. I wanted my kids to always feel just as good as the next kid. Just as powerful. Just as tough. Just as confident.

It seemed their dad wanted us to lose our home, and we didn't. He seemed shocked that we were traveling. He probably thought I could never get the children back in the private school, but I did! He probably thought the children would never go to college. With the kids' determination, they all completed college. It appeared he thought we would fall on our faces, and we didn't. We stood tall! We stood confidently! We proved trusting in God and working hard; we would rise above this hardship.

Seeing my children today, I completed my goal. It was only done with God in my life. I give him ALL the glory. In all things, give thanks! My children are now grown. They all are married with children of their own. They are Christians and love the Lord. They are happy. They are successful in their marriages and in their careers. They are all great parents. Their dad can have nothing but praise and admiration for them for the life they created for themselves.

As for me, I am happy now with a wonderful man. He loves me. He loves, as he says, "our children." He loves, as he says, "our grandchildren." He is active in everything they do. Once again, God was a step in front of me. God always cleared the path for me and protected me and my children. God led me to this wonderful man. I am so very grateful!

What did I always want from Ronald? The truth! An Apology! I knew I would never get it. The best way for closure was to write this letter to me from me.

Dear Ramona,

This has been an extremely long time coming, but here it is. I am extremely sorry I left you. What happened to me? I am not sure. I had it all. I guess the adventure seemed like a challenge. You were begging me to come home, and I knew you would always be there for me. Like an idiot, instead of realizing how special that was to have my wife always there for me, I used and abused that love. I am sorry!

Sorry, will never be enough. I know I hurt you even more than I can imagine. I could never make it up to you. You were a wonderful wife. You loved me as I had never been loved, and I didn't deserve it. I wrote you a poem once, and I meant every word. You depended on me for trust, honesty, and love, and I let you down.

You struggled alone raising the children, you struggled financially, you struggled physically, and I was not there for you. I was traveling and enjoying my life while you were left with responsibility and stress. You gave our children stability, love, and a successful life. You did without for yourself to give to them. I could never thank you enough for the sacrifices you made.

You never got vengeful or angry with me. You maintained your love and faith in me. I was a fool. Ramona, that says it all. I was just a fool. All I could ask for is your forgiveness, although I don't deserve forgiveness. Please accept my sincere apology for the life I gave you and my sincere gratitude for the way you raised our children. They are all happy and successful. That is all because of your love and devotion to them. Thank you!

With all my sincere love and apology,

Ronald

"In All Things, Give Thanks for This IS The Will of The Lord"

1 Thessalonian 5:18

Made in the USA
Monee, IL
04 August 2024